Sita Brahmachari

Artichoke Hearts

MACMILLAN CHILDREN'S BOOKS

First published 2011 by Macmillan Children's Books
a division of Macmillan Publishers Limited
20 New Wharf Road, London N1 9RR
Basingstoke and Oxford
Associated companies throughout the world
www.panmacmillan.com

ISBN 978-1-4472-0797-9

Copyright © Sita Brahmachari 2011

The right of Sita Brahmachari to be identified as the
author of this work has been asserted by her in accordance with the
Copyright, Designs and Patents Act 1988.

1

A CIP catalogue record for this book is available from
the British Library.

Printed and bound in the UK by CPI Mackays, Chatham ME5 8TD

For Maya, Keshin and Esha-Lily,
in memory of their extraordinary
grandmother, Rosie Harrison

When I was still eleven . . .

I have an ache in the pit of my belly, and a metal taste in my mouth, the kind that comes up just before you puke.

Out of my bedroom window I see Millie stride around the corner. I close my eyes and start counting . . . making my deal with Notsurewho Notsurewhat. If she's here on the count of zero, I'll go to school; if not, I'm taking a sickie. Ten, nine, eight, seven, six, five, four, three, two, one, zer—

Millie's determined hand clanks our letterbox right on the 'o'.

Now, the usual scuffle as we try to find the keys.

'Who *is* that at this time of the morning? It's only seven thirty, for God's sake,' shouts Dad from the top of the stairs.

'What if there was a fire? We'd all be locked in,' yells Mum from the kitchen.

As if prompted, the smoke alarm sirens its high-pitched squeal.

'Krish, you've burnt the toast again,' moans Mum, as she confiscates his football, mid-flight.

'But I like it burnt.'

It's true, he does.

I'm always the first to find the keys.

'It's only Millie,' I yell back.

'Does your bell *still* not work?' groans Millie, peering round me at the spectacle of Mum dementedly wafting a tea towel at the smoke alarm.

When its screech is finally silenced, Mum lets out a world-weary sigh. Then she spots Millie standing in front of her.

'Ah, Millie! You're the early bird this morning,' she chirps, as if keeping the lid on a ready-to-blow pan of popcorn. By the look on Millie's face, she knows my mum has totally lost the plot.

'Muuuuum, Laila's lobbed porridge at me again. It's splatted all over me,' shrieks Krish as Mum spins on her heels, tea towel whirling. Millie, who only has one very sensible older sister, stares at the massacre of our breakfast table. Now Laila turns her widest gurgly grin on Millie, as if she's done something to be truly proud of.

'Don't make a fuss, Krish . . . just run upstairs and get changed now,' Mum pleads.

'Laila, you're SUCH a pain. That was my best Spurs top,' moans Krish, throwing his spoon across the room, slamming the door and stomping back upstairs.

'What's all the noise about?' shouts Dad, appearing at the top of the staircase in a towel, his face smeared in shaving foam.

'Oh! Millie, it's you.' Dad grimaces, backing away from the banisters.

Millie grabs the door handle, ready for a quick escape.

'We've got to be in early for Literature Club,' she announces.

Mum looks blank.

'To work with the writer . . . you know, the "Spring into Writing" project,' Millie explains to Mum, whose vacant expression doesn't change. 'Didn't you get a letter?'

She didn't because I didn't give it to her. If I show Mum or Dad anything like that, they're always so interested, so enthusiastic, they would just go on and on about how important it is to be able to 'express' yourself, so I just don't tell them.

Mum shakes her head, turning to me accusingly. 'You didn't mention it, Mira.'

'I forgot. Sorry.'

Only four of us turn up. I think Miss Poplar, our 'there for us' Year Seven tutor, is a bit embarrassed, because she's the one who's set up this whole thing. She keeps fussing on about how well she's advertised the group, but the writer just smiles sweetly and says that we're a 'jewel-sized cluster'.

The writer woman is called Miss Print.

'Don't laugh – I've heard all the gags before,' she says.

Nobody laughs.

Miss Print tells us that as well as being a writer, she reviews children's books for newspapers. She's doing these workshops as part of her research to understand 'the reading habits' of ten- to thirteen-year-olds. It makes us sound like a rare species off *Animal Planet*.

'Who knows, maybe some of you will write a book for me to review.'

That seems like a bit of a long shot to me. I suppose, out of all of us, maybe Millie could write a book . . . one day.

Miss Print starts by asking us our names. She says you have to watch out for writers because they won't think twice about stealing your name if it's a good one. She says if you're going to make up characters in books names are important. Miss Print wants us to call her 'Pat', but she doesn't like her name – it makes her think of a footprint in a cowpat . . . Pat Print . . . now she's said it, I can see what she means. Apparently, in the village where she grew up, there was a fashion to call girls by boys' names. She thinks it's because they were farmers and really they only wanted boys to work the farms, so if you were born a girl they just gave you a name that could be made into a boy's name anyway.

Miss Print, I mean Pat, does look a bit like a man. She's got a bony face and short brown wiry hair, cut over the ears and right into the nape of her neck. It's the kind of sensible cut my dad hates when he's just come back from the barber's. You can tell she's a woman though, because of her delicate swan neck . . . and her gentle watery eyes; they're grey-blue, the colour of slate. They actually look younger than the rest of her. Pat Print is one of those people whose age it's very difficult to guess. She's tall and strong-looking. On her feet she's wearing walking boots with dried mud caked to the bottom. It's hard to make out the exact shape of her body because it's covered by a baggy navy blue cardigan, cashmere I think, with holey elbows. She's not wearing any jewellery, not even a ring. Miss Print, I mean Pat, is obviously very posh. My nana says there's no such thing as 'posh', but there is – Pat Print is posh.

She starts by asking us our names, but the way she does it isn't like a register at all. It just feels like she really wants to know who we are. Even so, it's me who's sitting next to her dreading the sound of my own shrill voice slicing into the silence.

'Mira Levenson,' I whisper.

5

There, it's over.

'Millie Lockhart.'

Her voice is steady, low and confident.

Ben Gbemi booms his name around the classroom as if he's calling across a playing field. And finally, Jidé Jackson speaks. The strange thing about Jidé is how gentle he looks compared to how he acts. The two just don't add up.

'It's Jidé with an accent – not Jeed like speed – you say the "e" in Jidé like the "e" in Pelé . . . you get me?'

'Acutely!' grins Pat Print. 'Now we've got that straight I think we can conclude that some of our parents clearly enjoy alliteration. Anyone know what alliteration is?'

Millie shoots her hand up.

'No need to be so formal,' says Pat Print, smiling kindly at Millie, taking her hand and lowering it back down. 'That's the beauty of a small group. There's something about people putting their hands up that makes me nervous. It's healthy to be interrupted . . . stops people getting too comfortable with the sound of their own voice.'

That's a laugh because Pat Print is the sort of person you would never interrupt. Something about her really reminds me of my Nana Josie, like when she says the opposite of what you would expect most adults to say or think. I don't think Pat 'gives a toss', as Nana would say, what we think of her. To answer her question about alliteration, we all speak together, so you can't actually hear what anyone says.

'That's right,' she shouts over us, as if she's heard each and every one of us. 'Alliteration is Pat Print, Jidé Jackson and Ben Gbemi, with a silent "G". As for Millie Lockhart, although you don't alliterate, your name is straight out of a romance novel.'

Millie giggles, and just when I think she's forgotten me altogether, she adds, 'And Mira Levenson is obviously a dual history name.' I don't say anything so she carries on talking, making another attempt to cue me in to her conversation. 'Taking a guess, I would say that one of your parents has Indian heritage . . . I think Mira's an Indian name, am I right?' I nod. 'And Levenson. Is that Jewish? "Lever" to rise, and "son" . . . could be "baker's son"? I'm taking a wild guess here, but it's one of my pet interests . . . discovering the derivation of names.'

The way she speaks you can really tell how much she loves words, as if she's tasting them on her tongue. She pauses for a minute, waiting for a reply, but I blush up my usual attractive colour of crimson. I have no idea if that's what my surname means, but she's right about the Indian Jewish thing, so I just nod, because I can't think of a single thing to say.

'And I suppose Jidé Jackson isn't a "dual history name"?' Jidé mocks.

I haven't thought about it before, but I suppose it must be.

'I imagine so, *and* you alliterate,' smiles Pat Print, unfazed. Jidé just scowls back at her, as if to say, 'It's none of your business.' Jidé never wants to talk about himself but Pat Print won't let this one drop. For next week's class she asks us to research our name. We have to find out why our parents gave us our first names and 'the derivations' of our surnames.

'Names hold histories, so get digging,' Pat Print orders, rummaging in her beaten-up old satchel and handing out a passage of writing to each of us.

We have to say what we think of the piece we've been given. What I notice first is the tense it's written in. When I read something in the present tense, I can disappear into it, like I do when I'm painting. It's as if I don't exist any more; I just get lost somewhere in there among the characters . . .

It's hard to say exactly what it is that makes me hate school so much. It starts the moment I wake up and realize that I have to step into my bottle-green uniform. That's when it seeps away, what little confidence I have. On with the shirt . . . I'm slipping away . . . the pinafore to keep me in my place . . . and now the tie . . . to knot tight the hard lump of swallowed words swelling my throat. The day drags on . . . hour after hour until 3.30 p.m.

What is it about me they can detect, even through the armour of this uniform? I've never been able to get a comb through my hair, more frizz than curls – that probably

8

doesn't help. Girls are supposed to have silken locks, aren't they? All I want to do is work on the farm, feed the pigs, climb trees or just stand on the open moorland catching the force of the weather and never wear this stupid skirt, never ever again. Instead, I'm trapped neatly in my row of wooden desks, with the golden-locked Jacky sticking the tip of her freshly sharpened pencil deep into my right thigh.

Pat comes over and asks how I'm getting on. I nod. I tell her I understand this passage . . . it draws me in. I try to explain the tense thing but somehow it doesn't come out right.

'I'm glad you like that one because it's one of mine. It's a memoir of "the happiest days of my life" . . . Ha ha!'

I nod. I want to tell her that I know exactly how she felt, but as usual the words won't come.

'The tense thing is a really complex idea,' she agrees, nudging me for a response.

I just stand in front of her nodding and looking stupid. I can feel everyone's eyes fixing on me, but luckily so can she, so she stands up and taps on the desk, shifting the spotlight.

'Pick out one line from the passage you've been reading, something that really grabs you, just a line or a phrase . . . something you would like to have written yourself. It's an exercise I call "Stealing Lines".'

I know without even looking again the exact words I'll choose.

'Now, swap them round, so you each read some-one else's favourite line,' orders Pat. 'Come on then, who's going to kick off?'

'*I am Rajvathan Rathour, ruler of the Ancient Palaces of Patiala,*' booms Ben Gbemi.

Jidé grins as he hears his own favourite line blasted around the room.

'What did you like about that line?' Pat Print asks.

'The character's like a superhero?' Ben shouts. He always shouts, no matter how small the room.

'Anything to add, Jidé?'

'He's a noble character, mythical . . . from an ancient land,' shrugs Jidé, knowing he's got exactly the right answer, but pretending he doesn't care that much. Jidé tries too hard to hide the fact that he is the braini-est boy in our class . . . probably in the whole of Year Seven. It's because his mum's Head of History that he's so keen not to look like a creep, so if he's here you know it's because he really wants to be. Probably, he persuaded Ben to tag along with him, just like Millie persuaded me. He catches me watching him and I feel the blood start to snake its way up my neck so that the whole world can track the hot path of my embarrass-ment up my throat and over my face, and all because I think, just maybe, Jidé Jackson might have smiled at me. I can't even be sure of that though, because I now have my head stuck deep into Pat Print's writing, in a pathetic attempt at covering up my blush.

'Exactly, and what was Ben's favourite line?' Pat Print asks Jidé.

I can't even remember what we were talking about now.

'I didn't have one,' interrupts Ben.

'OK, next time,' says Pat Print, not even glancing up at Ben.

'Now, Millie. Let's hear what you've got.'

'. . . the tie . . . to knot tight the hard lump of swallowed words swelling my throat,' Millie reads.

I keep my eyes trained on Pat Print's beaten-up old satchel. Was that her school bag? I wonder.

'I think it's about someone who finds it hard to speak or say how they're feeling,' Millie answers.

'That was me, at school. Now, you can't shut me up!' Pat Print smiles. It's weird because the way she smiles at me makes me feel as if she already knows who I am.

'What about Millie's chosen line, Mira?'

Somehow it's not so bad reading out Millie's line . . . I suppose it's because I'm not responsible for what it's saying.

'At the Tate, the modern sun shines through a long winter,' I read.

'What do you think?' Pat looks to me for an answer. Millie jumps in, like she always does, to save me the embarrassment.

'I like the "modern sun", because the sun is so old, but in a way it's always new. Every day there's a sunset and a sunrise . . . Every day you wake up, it's new. I saw that exhibition at the Tate Modern.'

'Wonderful, wasn't it?' Pat agrees, and then catches sight of a bored-looking Ben sprawled over his desk doodling graffiti.

'I can see I'll have to find something more interesting for you, Ben. We don't want to bore you senseless. What are you into?'

'Skateboarding!' he booms.

Pat Print is amused. 'Not one of my specialist subjects but I'll do some research.'

Then she springs this on us.

'Now you can do something for ME! Your ongoing project is to write a diary. We'll call it "The May Day Diary" – I like that.' Pat Print grins, pleased with herself for coming up with the title.

'Only it's still April,' Ben grunts.

'No need to be pedantic, Ben. It's called "artistic licence" . . . a tool of the trade . . . comes in handy, I can tell you.'

Ben and Jidé shoot each other a sideways glance as if to say, 'What have we got ourselves into?'

'Writing is about writing. You can't learn to write if you don't write. If you never keep a diary in your life again, at least you'll have captured a month of your lives to look back on.'

'Why would we want to look back?' mumbles Jidé under his breath.

'One day, you won't need to ask that question.'

'One day when?'

'What's the point of doing it for just one month?' moans Ben, tagging on behind Jidé.

'A lot can happen in a month, Ben.' Pat sighs, as if she's remembering something important.

'Not for me. All my days are the same,' grumbles Ben.

Pat completely ignores him, picks up her bag and starts to pack her things away. That's it! Ben's been dismissed.

'Mira, would you help me gather up these papers?'

Actually there's hardly anything to clear up, but teachers always do that when they want a private word with you.

Everyone leaves. They know the score.

'I thought what you said about the present tense was fascinating. That passage you read . . . first time round I wrote the whole thing as a memory . . . I got to the end and it just didn't work. It took me ages to find out what was wrong, but it wouldn't come alive until I rewrote it in the present tense.'

'I find it easier to paint than write,' I tell her.

'Mira, we can't all be talkers. Think of writing this diary as painting a portrait in words. Make a start in the present tense, if it's easier for you, but you can

13

be sure that before long the past will creep its way in there somewhere. Even at your age, there's plenty of past. Right then! See you next week.' She waves me off without looking up.

As she walks out of school, she leaves a trail of dry mud behind her.

My May Day Diary
Saturday 30 April

It's a weird thing, a diary, isn't it? I mean who do you talk to? Yourself? I suppose . . . but that just doesn't feel right. The only way I can think of to do this diary thing is to imagine that I'm talking to someone else. But what kind of someone could I let in to the mixed-up mind-maze that is me, Mira Levenson? I'll have to imagine that I'm writing to a friend, a best friend like Millie. The strange thing is though that I used to be able to tell her anything, but recently – I don't really know why – I've started to keep some things to myself . . . secrets. Perhaps the thing is not to think too much about anything, but just start writing and see where it takes me.

OK, here goes. Facts are the easiest . . . start with the facts. I'm twelve years old today. Twelve years and four hours old. I was born at seven o'clock in the morning. So, to be exact, twelve years, four hours and twenty-two minutes old. My twelve-year-old self is neither tall nor small, neither skinny nor 'plumpy', as

Krish calls Laila. My twelve-year-old self has long, dead-straight black hair, and dark brown eyes that my dad says sometimes turn black with emotion. My skin's brown, but not dark enough to hide my blushes. Looking in the mirror, which I do quite a lot recently, I would say I don't love myself (my teeth have come down a bit wonky), but I don't really mind how I look. My nana calls me a 'beauty', but she would, wouldn't she?

Like I said, facts are easiest, but none of this really says very much, does it? Maybe words just aren't my thing. Give me a paintbrush any day. My school reports always say stuff like 'Mira now needs to work on building her confidence and contributing to class discussions'. Now that *is* something I really hate to do. The main thing about me is whenever I go to say anything in class I blush up bright red so that before I've even opened my mouth, everyone knows how embarrassed I am, and after that I just clam up and lose the will to live. The mad thing is I actually can't stop thinking. I wake up in the middle of the night worrying about things like . . . how I'm going to get through a lunch hour if Millie's not around . . . and, well, I suppose I can say it here, can't I? Since Pat Print's writing class I have mostly been waking up thinking about Jidé Jackson's smile.

I'm a doodler and a daydreamer and a night dreamer.

The last few weeks it's been nightmares mostly, really bizarre stuff that freaks me out. Actually, I've been feeling a bit strange lately – it's hard to say exactly how, but it feels like I'm walking a tightrope. I'm not sure what it is I'm going to fall off, but it definitely feels like I'm about to find out.

I am sitting in my Nana Josie's flat with the rest of my family gathered for the usual birthday tea. I would rather not be here. Mum and Dad have given me a mobile phone, a watch and a diary. The mobile is a sea-green pebble, and it fits perfectly in the palm of my hand. The watch has a black leather strap, glass face, silver edging and a number for each hour. It's definitely my first grown-up watch and that somehow seems like a sign. I'm into signs, omens, super-stitions . . . whatever you want to call them . . . mostly *I* call them 'Notsurewho Notsurewhat'. This watch makes me think that something is about to happen to time. Today feels like the end of something, and the countdown to the beginning, of this, my red leather diary with golden edging at the corners of each page.

'Where are the dates?' I ask Mum as I flick through the pages of the diary.

'I thought you'd prefer to fill them in yourself. That way you can write as much or as little as you want and, knowing you, I expect you'll want to add the odd art-work. When I used to keep a diary, some days I had nothing much to write about and other days I'd write pages. It's more of a journal really . . . for your writing class.'

So I start writing, just like I would for any other piece of homework, because Pat Print's told us to, only now I've found something to keep all my secrets wrapped up in I can't stop, because no matter what's happened to me before today, or what's going to happen in the future, something is happening to me right now. Present tense.

Nana is inspecting my new mobile phone.

'It's *quite* pretty, I suppose, but I just don't understand the point of having a mobile phone at your age . . . and I'm sure I read somewhere that the rays can cause tumours. Uma, have you checked that out?' Nana calls out to Mum, who's in the next room. I don't think Mum even hears. She's too busy trying to get Laila to stay still while she changes her cacky nappy.

'I mean who are you going to call? You're always with your mum and dad or me anyway.'

Jidé Jackson . . . he's the person I would most like to call, but I'll never have the guts to actually do it.

'Well?' nudges Nana.

'You, Mum and Dad, Millie, Aunty Abi, Nana Kath and Grandad Bimal,' I list.

'That's five numbers. I rest my case.'

Nana Josie is quite hard to argue against, even if you really disagree with her, which I do, about the phone, but of course I don't say anything. She has her feet up, resting on my knees. I smooth my hands over the skin of her cracked brown leather soles. On the sides of each foot, she has hard bony knobbly bits, bulging, where mine are smooth. Her feet are icy cold, like she's just stepped out of the North Sea, but it isn't cold. In fact, it's a sunny day, the cherry blossom trees are out in the garden, like they are every year on my birthday . . . but Nana feels cold, because she's so thin. She feels cold all the time these days.

Nana lies on her schlumfy old sofa, with her bright purple shawl wrapped round her shoulders, holding her present for me in her hands.

'Come on, Mira, aren't you going to open it?'

What I love about Nana is how she's always so excited when she gives you a present. Even though she's this ill, she's still gone to the bother of wrapping it up in pale green tissue paper and covering it with sparkly butterfly stickers. I always open her presents so carefully, because it's like the wrapping is part of the gift, and you don't want to do it too quickly, or it would seem clumsy.

It's a skirt, folded between sheets of tissue paper. It's bright pink (why can't people notice when you've moved on from pink, like, years ago?) and sea green, with sequins and butterflies sewn all over it . . . and there's something else . . . a tiny Indian purse, with a button for a clasp. It's one of Nana's; I've seen it before.

'Open it then,' she orders.

As soon as I see her bare wrist, I know what's inside.

For as long as I can remember Nana has always worn this silver bracelet. It's a delicate silver chain with just one charm on it, in the shape of what I always thought was a flower, but now I look closer I see that it's actually some kind of vegetable.

'What is it?' I ask Nana, inspecting it closer.

'An artichoke. Uma! Haven't you ever cooked up an artichoke for them?' Nana calls out to Mum.

'Probably not!' Mum calls back wearily.

The artichoke charm is the size of the nail on my little finger. It has layers and layers of silver leaves, painted at their tips with green enamel. Each leaf gets smaller and more delicate until it reaches the centre . . . a tiny blood-red heart. I look down at Nana's bare wrist, where this charm bracelet has always lain against her skin, until today that is.

'This hand is past adornment,' she sighs, lifting her bony wrist up to the light and staring at it as if she doesn't recognize it as her own.

I walk into the bathroom to get changed and I lean hard against the door so Krish doesn't barge in. There is no lock; Nana doesn't believe in them. There are lots of things my nana believes in or doesn't believe in.

I look in the mirror. The skirt is too pretty but it'll be all right with jeans underneath and some Converse, I suppose. I fumble to close the catch on Nana's bracelet, but it's tricky to hold it together and seal the clasp at the same time.

'I can't do up the bracelet,' I tell Nana, coming out of the bathroom.

'Ah! You're a vision,' she whispers, swirling me around.

I hold my wrist out for her to fasten the clasp.

'No, no, no, no!'

At first I don't understand why she's got herself worked up into such a state, but then she holds the two pieces of broken chain apart, one in each hand, as the artichoke heart rolls on to the floor.

'Isn't that typical? I've worn this bracelet forever, and it has to go and break, today of all days.'

The charm rolls towards Laila. Her beady eyes are following its path across the wooden floor as her crab-like fingers reach out to grab it, but I get there first so, of course, she sends up one of her blood-curdling screams.

'Never mind, you can always replace the chain,' Nana sighs, sliding the charm back into the little purse. 'It's the heart that matters.'

She's upset. I can tell she's upset and trying to hide

it. It matters to her that the chain is broken, and it matters to me, and you can tell by the way no one knows what to do or say next that somehow all this means more than it should. Birthdays are like that, aren't they? Too much pressure.

Aunty Abi draws the curtains. We're in the half dark now. It's a bit embarrassing but I have to admit the flickering candles still make me breathless with excitement. Everyone sings 'Happy Birthday'. It's one of those 'Happy Birthdays' where people start off slightly after each other and in a different pitch. Krish sings 'crushed tomatoes and poo', as usual, but the rest of them plough on, willing a harmony that never quite happens in our family . . . it's a relief when they get to the final 'you'.

Aunty Abi, who is brilliant at baking, has made me a heart-shaped cake with pink icing (of course!) and white marshmallows on the top. Mum can't bake because she doesn't use weighing scales and she's not precise enough. But Aunty Abi's cakes always look so pretty – prettier than you could buy in a posh cake shop – and they taste even better.

Before I have the chance to get a closer look, Laila dives at the marshmallows, burning her podgy fingers on the candles and sending up an outrageous screech as Mum pulls her clenched fist away. There is no way she's going to let go of those marshmallows. Now that the spongy sweet goo is safely stored in her hamster cheeks, she scrunches her eyes closed tight and wills it to melt on her tongue.

I blow out my candles in one go. I like to get it over and done with as soon as possible. Krish loves all the attention on his birthday, not me.

'Make a wish,' says Mum as I slice into the cake.

I close my eyes and start out wishing that this wasn't my birthday . . . that it could all be over, but then I end up wishing . . . well, thinking about Jidé. The truth is I can't get his smile out of my head. Wishes are like that, aren't they? Sometimes you don't know what to wish for and then something or, in this case, someone just springs into your mind . . .

'Be careful what you wish for.' Nana breaks the spell and I open my eyes. 'It might just come true.'

I hope so.

We all take a slice of cake, except for Nana, who promises she'll have some later, but I know she won't. Inside the pink icing, the cake is chocolate goo, not just spongy, but thick puddingy chocolate. There's a moment's silence while we pay our respects to Abi's cake. I watch Nana bobbing Laila up and down on her knee and stroking her little plump wrists – 'fat bracelets', Nana calls them.

The bell rings, making us all jump. Dad goes to answer, with Piper yapping and hurtling up the garden path after him. Dad walks slowly back down the path and whispers to Nana, very gently.

'Well, go on then, show him in,' orders Nana, setting Laila down on the floor and slowly pulling herself up off the sofa. She's quite out of breath, but you can see how keen she is to greet this visitor. She's expecting . . . him.

A ridiculously tall man strides down the path, chased by Piper leaping up into the air, all four paws off the ground at the same time, but even his highest jump only brings him to the man's knee.

'A Norfolk terrier,' he says fondly, bending down and scooping Piper up into his arms.

'That's right,' Nana laughs. 'My faithful guard dog!'

I can see Nana instantly likes this crane-like man who has to stoop to get through her door.

'I'm Josie. You must be Moses.' Nana smiles and shakes his hand as her words come tumbling out. 'Thank you so much. I wasn't expecting express delivery, but I'm delighted because I've got to crack on with this thing now. You see I want to paint it myself, but I'm afraid if I don't do it soon I'll run out of energy, or time, or both.'

'It is my privilege.' The man called Moses bows and flashes Nana, Mum and Aunty Abi, especially Aunty Abi, a smile full of white teeth. He turns to Dad and nods. I know exactly what Dad's thinking: You can't trust anyone with teeth that good.

Dad always says that.

'This is my son, Sam,' says Nana, gesturing to Dad.

Moses holds out his hand for Dad to shake, but he doesn't exactly shake it, not properly, like he's taught Krish and me to do. He doesn't look Moses in the eye either. Instead his attention is caught by the state of Moses' feet. Moses has sawdust stuck to the bottom of his floppy pink shoes. They're handmade, like the ones Nana wears.

Moses looks as if he thinks Dad's being a bit rude staring at his feet.

Nana coughs.

'And this is my daughter, Abi . . . and Uma.' Nana points to Abi, then Mum.

'We spoke, on the phone,' Abi reminds Moses.

'Of course, I remember your voice.'

'It's her profession, her memorable voice,' chips in Nana proudly.

'You are a singer?'

'Actress,' Abi mumbles, shooting Nana her 'Mum, did you have to bring that up?' look.

But it's true. Aunty Abi does have a beautiful low velvety voice.

'And these are my grandchildren, Mira and Krish.'

I nod. Krish says 'Hi!' and Laila makes a high-pitched screechy noise, throwing both her arms into space, demanding to be picked up.

'Oh! And not forgetting Laila, of course.' Nana laughs at the spectacle of Laila's desperate out-stretched arms.

'Pleased to meet you all.'

Moses talks slowly and just a bit too quietly, so you have to lean forward to hear him.

'Where are you from?' asks Nana.

'Denmark.'

'I knew it,' Nana laughs, patting Moses on the shoulder. 'It's a hobby of mine, accent spotting.'

'Usually people think that I am from Germany,' Moses says, flicking his long fringe away from his eyes.

Moses has a thick mane of blond hair flowing right down to his shoulders. He's a definite hippy. From the back he looks like a girl, with his green linen shirt and white baggy trousers, and his collection of woven friendship bracelets and rings. Round his neck he's wearing a white stone with a hole in the middle on a leather strap. Moses is the sort of hippy you always meet round Nana's.

'Ah! A fellow lover of holey stones.' Nana claps her hands together in excitement. 'I have quite a collection of those at my cottage in Suffolk.'

'This is certainly a coincidence,' Moses smiles, holding up his holey stone. 'That is the exact place I found it, on a beach in Surf-folk.' That's how he pronounces it, with an 'L' in folk. 'The ladies in the museum told me they call them "hag stones". If you hang them in the doorway they keep those evil spirits from your door.'

'Nonsense! I don't believe in all that. I collect them

because I figure, if they've got a hole in them, they've already had a long and interesting life. I often wonder how many human lifetimes it takes to make a hole in a stone,' Nana babbles on.

You can always tell when Nana's nervous, because usually she chooses her words quite carefully.

Dad raises his eyes to the sky and smiles at Mum, but I agree with Moses: it is a real coincidence about the holey stones, because they are one of the things that Nana's obsessed with. We've got our collection in Suffolk, and she always carries one in her pocket and she's given me one of her favourites, which I never take off, even at school (well, it's not strictly speaking 'jewellery', is it?). Nana says a holey stone can tell a better story than a whole one. She talks like that, my nana. You're never quite sure you've understood exactly what she means.

Moses is still grinning from ear to ear. He casts his eyes around the flat at all Nana's objects and paintings. He especially likes the half-finished painting on Nana's easel, the one with the baby Indian elephant standing on a giant pink lotus leaf.

'These are your paintings?' Moses asks, walking over to take a closer look.

'A spattering of them,' Nana says, following Moses' eyes around the room.

He smiles and bows to her admiringly. Then he turns to Dad.

'I'll need some help carrying it in from the car.'

'Of course,' mutters Dad, looking as if he'd rather not.

Dad and Moses walk out into the garden together.

'This garden is beautiful,' Moses declares.

I hear Dad telling him that we used to live here but that, since we left, Nana has transformed the garden. It's true – when we lived here, it was a real mess.

This is the flat we were born in, me and Krish. You walk in through a wooden gate in a tall brick wall, which in summer is covered in roses, like you're in a secret picture-book garden. Once you're inside, you step on to the sloping brick path – the 'herringbone path', Mum calls it. When we lived here, the garden was all overgrown with trees, and the grass was mud because we used to wheel our bikes all over it, but Nana has made the garden grow. These days, as soon as you walk in you get blasted by the smell of cherry blossom, hyacinths and the sweet scent of straggly old honeysuckle, which Nana says just goes to prove that beauty is more than skin deep. I wish we still lived here.

Nana follows Dad and Moses up the path. Mum whisks Laila off the floor and we parade up the herringbone path together, through the tall wooden gate in the wall and out on to the street. Moses has double-parked his car, although he doesn't seem to be in a particular hurry. He has one of those long blue Volvos that can fit everything in the back – children, dogs and luggage – except this car doesn't have any of those things in it.

A queue of traffic is building up behind the car. A woman in a brand-new shiny black Jeep throws her hands up in the air, beeps her horn and starts shouting at Moses, who walks slowly round to her window.

'I am so sorry to make you wait. I won't be so very much longer,' he says in a polite and patient voice.

Now she looks even more annoyed, and the other cars start beeping too, as if to echo how angry she is.

'Take your time!' she yells back at Moses. He ignores her.

'Why don't you just bog off!' Dad spits at her under his breath.

'Sam!' Mum always tells Dad off for swearing, even though, like Nana, he's got a whole repertoire of made-up not-quite swear words.

Then Charlotte, Lizzie's mum from across the road, appears on the front steps of her house.

'This is turning into a bit of a spectacle,' Nana laughs.

'Everything all right?' Charlotte asks Mum, looking worried.

'Well, we're trying to get *this* –' Mum points into Moses' car – 'into the flat. Ideally we could do with a parking place.'

Charlotte peers into the car. I watch the blood

slowly drain from her face as it finally dawns on her what's inside.

'I see,' she nods, staring back at Nana, her eyes filling up with tears, before she pulls herself together and springs into action. 'Of course. I'll move my car. They'll all just have to back up.'

Charlotte is redirecting the traffic, running into her house for car keys, reversing, forcing all the other drivers to back up so that Moses can park his car right where she was parked, outside Nana's flat. It's like one of those puzzles where you have to move the pieces around in the right order to make the pattern work.

By this time Jeep Woman's face has turned purple, there are car horns blasting off all down the street and Nana Josie, Krish and me have got the giggles.

'I'm glad you find this so funny! Some of us are in a hurry,' Jeep Woman screams out of her window.

Nana is suddenly seriously not amused. She can do that, Nana . . . just suddenly turn from sunny to steely in a few seconds. Now she's walking over to Jeep Woman and sounding out every word as if she might not quite understand English.

'That is my coffin, in the car in front. And if you don't calm down you'll be getting straight out of your big fat Jeep and into one of those yourself. Now concentrate on your breathing and calm yourself down. We share the same air, you know . . . if only you weren't set on poisoning us all.'

Then Nana turns on her heel with her nose in the air and walks as slowly as I've ever seen her back to the pavement. Normally Nana's a bit of a strider. Dad, who is laughing now, puts his arm round Nana's shoulders and kisses her on the cheek.

'Ooooooh! Go, girl, go, girl,' chants Krish. Moses' head is bobbing backwards and forwards, rocking with laughter. Jeep Woman looks at Nana like she's the devil and quickly clicks her 'window closing' button as if Nana's about to attack her.

'You'd think *we* were the ones in the armoured vehicle,' Nana yells after her. 'Big fat Jeep! Is it really necessary, in the middle of London? Does nobody care about global warming? Her children will fry.'

Nana's on a roll.

Now that Charlotte has sorted the parking situation, she's offering to take us 'kids' off Mum's hands. I watch Moses and Dad ease the casket, which is basically a freshly painted white box, out of the car and carry it through the gate in the wall. Nana goes to follow them in, but stops short. Mum seems like she doesn't quite know what to do for the best. She looks at us, as if she's asking *us* to decide. Then suddenly Nana takes Krish and me by the shoulders and turns to Charlotte.

'The thing is it's Mira's birthday today, so we're having a bit of a party, but thanks for the offer.'

Charlotte casts me a 'poor you' look but wishes

me a happy birthday anyway.

'Thank you,' I mumble.

Dad and Moses are carrying the casket into the front room. It's quite hard for them to balance it, because Moses is much taller than my dad. Moses is walking forward and Dad backwards, so it seems to dip downhill, forcing its way into his body.

'Just plonk it in the middle,' orders Nana, steering them through the room like a traffic controller. It's not something you can really 'plonk' though, is it . . . a coffin? Nana stands and looks at it for a few minutes as if she's inspecting a newly delivered piece of furniture.

'Good,' she nods. 'Just what I wanted . . . a blank canvas.'

Moses asks if we can send him a photo when it's painted, so he can use it in his Eco-Endings catalogue, but, by the looks on their faces, I don't think Dad or Aunty Abi are very keen on that idea.

'I'm sure it could be arranged,' smiles Nana helpfully.

Moses folds his legs in half, bending his body as low as he can, which is not very low at all. Suddenly his arms are round Nana's shoulders and he's hugging her! Nana looks a bit surprised, but she lets him hold her.

Then he looks her straight in the eye and says in a very serious voice, 'So, Josie, I wish you a happy ending.'

Nana laughs. 'That reminds me of something –'

she's scanning her brain for the exact words – 'Frida Kahlo said something like that on her deathbed . . .'

Nana loves Frida Kahlo. She's one of her favourite artists. She goes on and on about her. She wants to take me to her exhibition in June.

'Now how did Frida put it?' Nana asks, as if 'Frida' is one of Nana's very best friends, rather than a dead artist. 'I think it was something like: "I wish for a joyful exit, and never to return." I share her sentiments exactly.'

Moses laughs nervously, like he doesn't know exactly what to say. So he just says goodbye, very slowly shuffling backwards, bowing himself out of the room.

After Moses has left, we all sit around, looking at the coffin.

'So that's what the grim reaper looks like!' Dad mumbles.

'Who's the grim reaper?' Krish asks.

'Moses,' moans Dad.

'Don't talk such nonsense, Sam! I liked him,' says Nana.

'You would! Danish hippy dude. Just your type!' teases Dad.

'A bit too young and intense for me.' Nana giggles like a little girl.

*

Nana's coffin sits right in the middle of her front room and stops the conversation.

Nana always used to say 'casket' when she was talking about it, but now it's here, she calls it a 'coffin'. Somehow a 'casket' seems quite light and friendly, like you could put a picnic in it, or dressing-up clothes . . . but a coffin is just plain grim. I ask Nana why she's suddenly started calling it a coffin.

'May as well call a spade a spade, Mira.' She shrugs.

For a few minutes nobody goes near; nobody touches it.

Then suddenly Krish has lifted the lid and is jumping up and down inside. He moves like that, my brother, like a gecko – now you see him, now you don't. You can never quite know where he's going to pop up next.

'Krish, what do you think you're doing? Get out of there!' Mum spits out the words as if Krish has really done something terrible.

'I'd rather this, Uma, than the silence.' Nana sighs, touching Mum on the arm to calm her.

Krish bobs up and down, in and out of the coffin, making jack-in-the-box faces at Laila. She giggles. Each time he peeps over the edge, Laila giggles a bit louder. Usually when Laila laughs it sets everyone off, but not today.

'You're a good boy for entertaining your sister. Our little jack-in-the-box,' Nana says, tousling his

34

long sandy hair. 'Don't let anyone cut this hair – it's your crowning glory,' Nana tells Krish, kissing him on the forehead. Krish grins at Mum. She doesn't say anything, but I can tell she's annoyed. She's spent the whole week trying to persuade Krish to get a haircut!

I was here the day Aunty Abi had to do the research to find the coffin company. It's called Eco-Endings because they do 'ecologically friendly' funerals. That means they don't use hard woods that destroy the rainforests. Some people have wicker baskets or grow a tree where they're buried, that sort of thing. I remember when Aunty Abi called them they asked her lots of questions on the phone and she told them that Nana was very ill and that she's an artist and wanted to paint her own coffin. Aunty Abi said the man on the phone, who was Moses, thought that was fantastic. He said he would quickly knock together a hardboard casket, paint it white and drive it to London himself. Aunty Abi went quiet on the phone after that, and told him that she'd call back later. Nana was so excited. She wanted to know how long it would take to get here.

'I haven't ordered it yet. They need your exact measurements.' Aunty Abi looked suddenly sad when she said this, as if she had only just realized that it was Nana who had to fit inside the coffin.

Nana ordered me to go and hunt around for her

tape measure. When I'd found it, she got up off the sofa and lay on the floor. Aunty Abi and me just stood and stared. Without saying another word, Aunty Abi measured Nana from her head to her toes.

'Write this down . . . five foot,' said Abi.

'Five foot what?' Nana asked.

'Five foot nothing, Mum,' whispered Abi, which made Nana laugh, but there was no sign of a smile on Abi's face.

Next we had to measure across the widest part of Nana's body, but the truth is, it was quite difficult to find a widest part. Abi told me to write down 'under one foot' and that included quite a bit of extra space.

'Only *you* could make your daughter and your granddaughter measure you up for your own coffin,' groaned Abi.

'Well, someone's got to do it. Come on, I need to get this thing painted while I've still got life left in me. Get on the phone and tell him my vital statistics!' Nana bossed Abi along.

So Aunty Abi called Eco-Endings back and asked for Moses. Nana was drinking some water at the time, but when she heard the name 'Moses' she burst out laughing, splattering her water halfway across the room.

'Ask him if that's his real name!'

That set Aunty Abi off laughing, but her laugh was the kind that could just as easily turn to tears at any moment. Nana was still choking on her water when Abi finally calmed down and gave Moses Nana's measurements.

'Five foot . . . No, I'm sorry, you'll have to convert it yourself. We're very retro here – we only do feet.' As Abi listens her eyes fill with tears 'He wants to know if we're sure. Apparently that would be the smallest adult coffin that they've ever made. Moses says we should make it a bit bigger, otherwise it might look like a child's coffin.'

Nana just shrugged. 'Suits me.'

And I remember the chill that that thought sent through me . . . a child's coffin . . . how wrong is that?

Just like Pat Print predicted, the past does come creeping its way in. Ordering that coffin was in the past, but now it's sitting right here in front of me, in the present. Not much of a present, is it? There's nothing funny about it; not even Krish can make us laugh now.

In the silence I can hear the tinny ticking of my new watch as if someone's turned up the volume . . . tick . . . tick . . . tick . . . it's as if the coffin is waiting for Nana to die.

'Mira, you're supposed to eat your cake, not sit in it!' teases Krish, pointing to a brown stain on the back of my new skirt.

I can't stand any more of this, so I run into the bathroom and lean hard against the door, swivelling my skirt around to inspect the damage. I take it off and rinse it under the tap, but it doesn't come out. What does it matter? Everything's ruined anyway. I slump down on the toilet seat. Then I see it, on my jeans, the same dark stain. I pull down my jeans and there it is again, not birthday cake, but a brown-coloured bloodstain.

'Mira!' calls Nana, knocking on the door. I quickly pull up my jeans, keeping one foot against the door until I've done up my zip and button. Then I let her in.

She holds my hand and places her tiny artichoke charm in my palm, closing my fingers around it.

'I'm sorry this all had to happen on your birthday, but I want to explain something to you. I've given you this, Mira, because you're so special to me . . . how can I explain? Most people, by the time they get old, have grown themselves tough little shells around their hearts. Babies, like little Laila, start off with tender, loving, trusting hearts, but gradually, gradually, they learn to protect themselves and, as the years go by, grow tougher and tougher layers. Look at this! The outside layers of an artichoke are so tough they're not even worth eating, but they get more and more tender as you come closer to the heart. These tough outer layers stop you feeling so much, so people walk around with hard little hearts that no one can touch. Of course, there are some people who don't have a choice – they just never learn to protect themselves . . . now that can be a blessing and a burden.'

All I want is for Nana to stop going on about the charm and let me sort myself out. All I want is for Nana not to notice the bloodstain.

'What kinds of people don't have a choice?' I ask her to try and distract her from my skirt.

'People who need charms!' she smiles, kissing my hair. 'You'll know them when you meet them. Mira, darling, I am sorry the coffin arrived today – that was bad timing, I'm afraid – but . . . I wanted to ask you . . . will you help me to paint it?'

I nod.

'I knew you would,' she whispers as she lowers my head on to her shoulder.

As soon as I get home I search the bathroom cupboard for the pads I've seen Mum store in there. I peel off the strip and stick one into my knickers. Even though it's supposed to make me feel grown up, having a period, this actually reminds me of one of Laila's nappies. It doesn't hurt, just like Mum told me it wouldn't, except for the ache in my belly and the strange rusty taste in my mouth. I suppose I *should* tell Mum, but she'd just make a big fuss of me and try to celebrate or something. I don't think I can take any more celebrations, even if it does mean I can get my ears pierced. That's when Mum said I could (when my periods start), but, just for now, this is one birthday present I'm going to keep to myself.

We are reflected in the bathroom mirror, Nana and me. I am wearing my birthday skirt. My lace is undone, so I bend down for a moment to fasten it, but right next to my shoe there is a tiny circle of blood, about the size of a one-pound coin.

'What's this?' I ask Nana, but when I stand up again she's not there. I run into the front room to look for her, but the room is empty; all the furniture has gone – everything except the coffin.

Nana's coffin is painted with bright blue waves, leaping dolphins, butterflies and birds; birds everywhere. Right in the corner, peeping out at me, is a little dog that looks like Piper. When I peer closer, I can see that the dog has his leg cocked over the corner of the coffin, sprinkling yellow pee across the sea. I laugh. Then I see her . . . Nana Josie, lying in her watery coffin . . . floating . . . her face half covered. I reach for her hand through the icy cold. 'Nana, wake up, wake up,' I whisper, but she doesn't open her eyes. I try to lift her body, but she slips back under. Then I see something moving under her blouse, and I think she is alive after all – that must be her heart beating – so I lift up her top, and thousands of tiny birds fly out. I look down at Nana. The coffin is empty, plain wood, no water. A dog yaps wildly, and the painting of Piper jumps off the coffin and runs out into the garden. Leaves rustle and tiny birds

40

swoop round and round the room.

Now the waves begin to roll on a rough sea. Dolphins surf on the wind, diving down into the deep water. The birds panic, battering their wings against the windowpanes, desperate to be freed. I fling the window wide open and let them escape into the garden. They gather and sway on currents of air, separating and coming together, migrating birds, agreeing their moment to leave. They are so high now . . . faraway dots in the clouds. I stand and watch until the sky is empty.

I go back into the flat and find Piper's bright red lead. Out on the Heath I try to walk fast, but people stop me and ask, 'How is Josie?' and I say, 'I think Josie has flown away,' but people keep on following me. More and more of them, people with dogs, asking where my nana is, over and over again. I try to get away from them, but they follow me up Parliament Hill, hundreds of people with dogs. Big dogs, little dogs, all kinds of dogs. 'Where has she gone?' they ask over and over. I start to run.

I climb to the top and look behind me, but the people have all disappeared. There are hundreds of dogs running free all over the Heath, all except for one huge black dog, like a bear, plodding slowly up the hill – Nana's old New-foundland, Claude. Beside him is my Nana Josie, in her cherry-red crocheted hat and long trailing scarf. She smiles at me. Piper starts to bark, pulling the lead as hard as he can to get to her. She waves to me, and climbs up on to Claude's back. He breaks into a trot. Now he pounds towards us with his great big bear paws. Just at the moment when I reach

41

for Nana's hand, Claude's front paws leave the ground . . . one last kick with his back legs and he is flying. Nana's hat slips off her head and her long black hair streams behind her like the tail of a kite. Piper yaps like crazy and leaps off the ground to catch her.

Now I am running with Piper, flapping my arms, hard, so I can fly after her. I'm hurtling down Parliament Hill, flapping, pushing off with my feet, but no matter how hard I try I can't kick the ground away, and that's the moment when I see him: Jidé Jackson walking closer and closer up the hill, with his arms outstretched towards me.

'You were thrashing around a bit,' Mum explains. She is lying next to me in my bed.

'I was trying to fly. Me and Piper were trying to catch up with Nana,' I tell her, still out of breath.

'Where was Nana?' Mum asks.

'Flying away on Claude's back.'

'Just a dream,' Mum says, like in *The Wizard of Oz*, when Dorothy wakes up and the whole story is make-believe, even the nightmare bits. I wish it was – just a dream – except for the end. I wish I could click my red shiny heels together and make it all go away . . . the blood, the coffin . . . make it all go away . . . except for Jidé Jackson.

*

11.59 p.m. I wait for the last minute of my twelfth birthday to tick away before I take off my new watch.

Maybe if I don't wear it time will slow down and things will go back to normal. Since I strapped it to my wrist this morning something strange has happened to time. I can hear it beating, all day long, under the surface of everything.

Sunday 1 May

'What's that?' asks Nana, pointing to a spot on my cheek that's mushroomed like magic overnight. It's just as I thought . . . this oozy red spot is doing its best to blow my cover.

'Oh! Darling Mira. Such a shame . . . and you've always had such perfectly peachy skin,' Nana exclaims, poking the head of my painful pustule and making me flinch away from her.

My mum is shooting Nana a 'Do you have to?' look, not that Nana notices.

'It all starts to change from now on. It'll be boyfriends and periods next. You know it might not be long, Uma,' Nana announces, giving me the once-over, before turning to Mum. 'They're starting earlier and earlier these days, you know. It's something to do with their weight. How old were you?'

Great! Now she's talking about my weight as if I'm not even in the room. I know every detail about periods. There is nothing that my mum hasn't told me about why you have periods, how they can make you feel and, yes, I know when Mum started her period – she was twelve, like me, and Nana Josie was fourteen. Aunty Abi was thirteen. And this is probably the moment I should tell them, right now, except that Nana would probably get dressed up and do some ancient ceremonial dance around the room, or light a candle or something to celebrate me becoming a *woman*. So I don't tell because that's what a diary's for, isn't it?

'It's hard to believe I've been buying art materials from Dusty for half a century,' sighs Nana, as we munch on leftover birthday cake. Even Nana's tucking in today.

'Let's see how the old boy's getting on.'

Nana stands up and shakes the crumbs off her lap. She's determined to make this trip.

Half of a hundred. I can't even imagine fifty years. Actually, I can't imagine anything in numbers. I'm rubbish at maths. If someone asks me one of those questions like, 'If your Nana was born in 1931 and she lived till 2005, how old would she be when she died?' (which of course they wouldn't) I'd know how to work it out, but it would take me so much longer than everyone else. Krish would jump in with an answer way before me. I'd spend ages just staring at the numbers, and when I look at numbers my mind goes blank.

Nana is seventy-four years old. That sounds really old to me, but she doesn't feel like an old lady. My

Maths teacher is always nagging me to learn my 'number facts'. The problem is I don't really believe in number facts because Nana is seventy-four years old, but, to me, she's younger than most of the mums and teachers at school. I don't mean how they look, I mean . . . they're just not as young or as fun as she is: they don't get excited about things like painting or music or wrapping presents, not like Nana Josie does. Maybe, if you stop getting excited about things, that's what makes you old. Then, when I think about it, it's the exact opposite with Laila, because she's so new, only ten months old, but it seems like she's been in our family forever. So I don't think how old you are is really a number fact at all. Nana says she has never felt older than sixteen, but time took no notice of how she felt – it just kept on ticking.

We park right next to Dusty Bird's art shop. Nana leans on my arm as Mum and I walk her inside. She wants acrylic water-based paints. Nana says it's very important to choose the exact colours she has in her mind. I can't believe how many shades of the same colour you can buy. First we go down the white row. When you really look, most of the paints aren't white at all. Nana reads my thoughts.

'It's a good lesson in relativity, isn't it? Something that looks white next to red can look mauve next to another shade of white. Does that make any sense?' she asks.

I nod. It sort of does.

'It's not all white, innit!' That's Nana's terrible East End accent.

'Look at this.' She picks up Opaque Titanium White, which is actually bright white, then she pulls out a paint called Lilac Pearl, that makes Titanium White look lilac.

'See what I mean?' Nana lifts the bottle up to the light.

I do.

Next, we walk along the rows of yellows; Nana knows the exact colour she's looking for.

'Ah! Yellow Ochre. You'll get a lot of use out of this one.'

Nana talks to me as if I'm already an artist, like she knows something about me that I don't really know myself yet. Dad says it's natural for grandparents to want their grandchildren to follow in their footsteps. I can understand that, but when Nana Josie talks about art it's not about what I'm going to be in the future. It's about what I am now. Sometimes Nana really embarrasses me when she introduces me to her friends, saying things like . . .

'This is my granddaughter, Mira, a fellow artist.'

We are walking down a corridor of golden colours. The precious golden paint is on the very highest shelf, but Nana's so small she can't reach. Dusty Bird, who is as short as Nana, comes over with a ladder. As he climbs

47

up, I can hear his knees creak on every rung. Dusty Bird looks older than Nana, or maybe it's just that I don't think of her as being old, because I know her.

'What kind of gold are you after, Josie?'

'Nothing yellowy, nothing sharp or brassy, more of a deep burnt gold, Dusty.'

'You always were a class act.' Dusty Bird peers under his glasses down the ladder at Nana, and winks.

'Thanks, Dusty,' Nana giggles, running her fingers through her spiky silvery hair, as if remembering how long and silky it once was.

I love the way Nana talks about colours, like she thinks each one has a personality. Dusty brings down a few bottles for her to inspect. In the end she chooses Dark Gold.

We are moving through Dusty Bird's corridors of colours, passing through a rainbow . . . red (just the sight of it brings up that tin-metal taste in my mouth) and yellow and pink and . . .

'This is the one: Golden Green Lake.' Nana reads the label fondly, as if she's just bumped into an old friend.

Dusty Bird follows us around with his ladder, offering to help as Nana scans her memory for the names of the colours she's used before. Purple and orange and . . .

'We're painting the sea . . . ultramarine, I think, Dusty.'

'Ultramarine Blue Light?' he guesses.

'That's it, Dusty.' Nana grins and claps her hands together.

It's a new game, where Dusty has to match the description to the paint.

'Turquoise?' Nana asks, testing him.

There are about ten different shades, but he picks out Deep Turquoise Blue.

'That's your usual, Josie.'

Nana nods and drops the bottle into the basketful of paints that Mum's carrying for her while attempting to distract Laila from pulling every paint pot in her reach off the shelves.

'Just the grey, I remember,' groans Nana. 'Payne's Grey. Well-named, that one, Dusty, because if pain has a colour it's definitely grey.'

Dusty Bird peers at Nana with a question in his eyes, but he doesn't ask her anything. When we finally get to the checkout, Dusty offers Nana a seat.

'What are you up to these days, Josie?'

'I'm working on dying at the moment.' Nana smiles at Dusty as if she hasn't said anything out of the ordinary. 'It's my swansong, this coffin. It's all going up in smoke, Dusty – that's why it can't be oil based, you see,' Nana explains, smiling at him.

Dusty Bird smiles back.

'You're an original, Josie. Damien Hirst's got nothing on you.'

Laila starts gurgling and Dusty Bird crosses over to our side of the counter to coo at her.

'This your latest?'

Nana nods. It sounds funny, as if Laila is Nana Josie's baby. He doesn't seem to notice my mum.

'Pretty little thing, isn't she?' Then he looks from me to Laila. 'Another beauty, just like her nana.' Dusty Bird winks at Nana again. She pushes him away, as if to say 'stop talking such nonsense', but she's pleased with the compliment, all the same.

Dusty takes Nana's hand and walks her to the car. They're like toddlers supporting each other . . . a delicate grey-haired girl and a tubby bald boy. By the time Nana finally gets into the car, all the colour has drained from her skin. She can't seem to catch her breath; it's as if she's been running. Dusty scurries back into the shop, returning with a glass of water. Nana takes tiny sips, but it's a huge effort for her to swallow.

'This blasted pain,' Nana gasps.

She carries on sipping, swallowing deep breaths of air, and eventually her breathing slows. Dusty Bird leans into the car. They look straight into each other's eyes, for what seems like ages, but it's probably just seconds ticking slowly. Then he holds Nana's face in his hands and kisses her right on the lips . . . the kind of kiss that means something.

When someone is dying, everything you say and do

means more than it normally does. When someone is dying, you notice things . . . everything really. The whole of life is in slow motion. Dusty Bird's eyes fill up with tears. My nana holds his hand for a moment and then he quickly closes the car door and gives the roof a tap. His rooftop tapping says, 'Go on, get out of here. I can't bear to say goodbye.'

He stands in the doorway of his shop and waves us off. Mum waits for a gap in the traffic. I turn round to look at Dusty Bird as he walks inside. The last thing I see is him 'man crying' (that's what Mum calls that sort of choked-up cry). His back, round like a tortoiseshell, heaves up to his ears, and then drops down again. He rubs his eyes with his fists in a rough way, like he's angry with himself, but his tortoiseshell back carries on heaving up and down, up and down.

At last there is a space in the traffic and we turn out on to the road.

By the time we pass The Forum, where a line of people, all with the same quiffy hairstyle, like Elvis Presley, are queuing up for tickets for a gig, Nana has finally got her breath back, enough to laugh at the 'characters', as she calls them, in the queue. Nana thinks, compared to the 60s, we live in a dull ironed-out world where everyone pretty much looks the same.

'Dusty Bird's always had a bit of a soft spot for me. We used to show paintings together on the

Embankment. Dusty would flirt outrageously with me and then he and Kit would start their usual banter . . . "What's your secret, old man?" he'd ask Kit, and your grandad would always answer the same way . . . "Charm, Dusty. If you've got to ask, you haven't got it." " Then make sure you don't lose it," Dusty would tease . . . '

Nana stares out of the window. I don't even know if she's talking to us, or herself. It's like her memories are kaleidoscoping her back in time.

'He wasn't bad-looking in his day. He had this long mane of curly black hair and green eyes, a bit of a gypsy look, a real beatnik.'

'What's a beatnik, Nana?' I ask.

'Arty types, writers, us lot, in the fifties and sixties . . . rebels, protesters. We couldn't stand being told what to think or how to behave. We had a lot of battles to fight,' she sighs. 'We were young! You'll do the same one day, hopefully.'

For some weird reason, when Nana talks about having battles to fight, I can't help thinking of Jidé Jackson, but then again it seems like I can't help thinking about him, whatever anyone says.

'I thought you were a hippy?' I say.

'We evolved,' laughs Nana.

It's impossible to think of Dusty Bird as a beatnik or a hippy, or whatever. He's bald and quite fat and old. But when he looked at Nana I think he could see

52

her as she was when she was young, and she could see him too. Sometimes you just think of people as old and you don't think about who they are, or what they've done in their lives.

It's easier for me to imagine Nana when she was young because I've got photos of her, and she was more beautiful than most people I've ever seen, even in magazines and films. She had long, thick black hair with a short fringe, and huge dark brown eyes. She was small and slim . . . as small as me. She looked a lot like that actress in the old films Nana likes to watch – I think her name is Vivien Leigh.

It's not just the photos that make it easier to imagine her being young. Nana still wears clothes from the 60s. Aunty Abi calls it 'vintage gear', but Nana says it's just her original Biba wardrobe that she's never grown out of. She says she's been waiting for a new fashion that would make her ditch her old look, but she hasn't been convinced by anything else yet, and now, apparently, 'the wheel of fashion has turned full circle'.

Nana Josie has got to be the most stylish person I know. She always wears beads and jewellery and something – a scarf, a ring, a handbag, anything really – that nobody else has, because you wouldn't know where to buy the things she wears. I can see why Dusty Bird wanted to go out with Nana and I can understand why he cried man tears for her and kissed her on the lips, even though he is bald, and old, and fat, and Nana Josie is seventy-four years old, and dying of cancer.

When we get back to the flat, we walk Nana to her bedroom. She's trying to slow her breathing. Mum eases Nana's shoes off and helps her on to the bed. Then she opens a pot of lavender cream, and starts to massage her feet. Since we were babies Mum has always massaged our feet, so I kind of know how to do it. I take Nana's other foot and massage the cream into her hard skin. Nana sighs the air out of her lungs, as if to say, 'Thank you.' Her foot is getting heavier and heavier in my hand. You can hardly hear her breathing now and I can tell, by the weight of her foot, that she's fallen asleep. We cover her with the duvet, then Piper jumps up on to the bed and lies on top of her feet. I think he likes the smell of lavender. Usually I like it too, but right now it's making me feel quite sick.

I try to keep Laila entertained by reading her books, but she can't keep still for very long; she's always crawling into trouble. She's drinking the water out of Piper's bowl now, but when I bring her a cup of her own she screeches in that high-pitched way that makes you give her anything she wants.

Mum's in the kitchen making Nana some soup. After about an hour I can smell it all around the flat. It makes my tummy rumble and I don't even like lentils. I hear Nana get out of bed and sniff her way into the living room . . .

'Something smells good.'

We sit down at Nana's long table where I always check out what new bit of food, jewellery or art stuff has fallen down the cracks. Probably every person who has ever sat at this table has a bit of the food they ate stuck down the gaps between the wooden slats. Laila swallows a few mouthfuls, then discovers how to blow soup bubbles, spraying orange-brown mush all over the table so that it dribbles down the cracks to mulch with all the other spilt food. We try hard to ignore her, but Nana has to turn her face away so Laila doesn't see her laughing. Now I really do feel like puking.

As I follow the path of the soup along the wooden grooves, I feel . . . I feel something change. I wander through to Nana's bathroom, trying to make everything look as normal as possible. I thought so . . . the brown stain has turned to . . . what would it be called on one of Dusty Bird's labels? Blood Red.

Monday 2 May
– May Day holiday

Mum has spent all morning turning Nana's front room into an artist's studio. There are white plastic paint pots, mixing sticks, all sizes of brushes and sponges, and a palette. Now Mum clears the table and covers it in newspaper and when she's done I help her lift the coffin on to the table. It's quite heavy for me, but I just about manage to lug one corner up on to the tabletop, sliding the rest over by tugging at the cloth beneath. It reminds me of a magician's trick; if only I could make this coffin disappear.

Mum says she'll be gone for a couple of hours, but not to worry because, if we need her, she can be with us in five minutes. Our flat, I mean Nana's, is only one road away from Hampstead Heath where Krish does his running.

'In case you need me,' Mum whispers, handing me her mobile number.

'I've got it saved in my phone book, Mum.'

'Ah! Yes, the mobile. Have you used it yet?' chips in

Nana. 'You can always use the landline if you need to call your mum.'

'But she wouldn't be able to call *me* if I didn't have my mobile,' Mum explains.

'Which is my point. *You* need the mobile, not Mira.'

Mum winks at me, as if to say 'don't worry about it'. Nana's like that – once she gets hold of an idea, she won't let go, which can seem a bit mean because the phone was Mum's present to me.

For a moment I let myself think of the reasons why I might need to call Mum. If Nana gets breathless, I will help her to lie down. If . . .

I look at Nana and she seems to know what I'm thinking, as she so often does.

'I'm having a good day today, Mira. I'm on a mission and nothing is going to get in my way, except maybe Laila!' she jokes, taking hold of my hand.

Mum's having to wrestle Laila into her pram. She's arching her body, making her back as stiff as a rod. Mum tries everything to distract her, but in the end she has to press Laila's tummy hard until she's forced to fold, like a rag doll. Quickly, Mum straps her in, before the next wave of protest begins.

Laila's in a rage and the whole street knows about it. I feel sorry for her, because she doesn't really have a choice about what she wants to do. I'm helping Nana, and Krish is already out there doing his warm-up, but Laila just gets dragged about. She thinks she should be able to choose what she's going to do too. Mum says when I was little she had a lot more time for me. I think Laila's decided that she would prefer to help Nana and me with the painting, but there is no way that's going to happen! I do feel sorry for her, but not *that* sorry.

The flat is filled with Laila's wailing. You can hear her screaming all the way up the path.

'An excellent protester,' jokes Nana, covering her ears with her hands.

We sit at the table staring at the white coffin, listening to Laila's high-pitched wail fade into the distance.

'Any ideas for painting?' asks Nana.

I tell her about my dream – not all of it, not about the drowning. I don't want to upset her because that's the thing Nana's most afraid of . . . drowning. I tell her how the coffin looked in my dream, about the doves, the silver butterflies, the leaping dolphins and the little dog peeing into the sea. She laughs when I tell her about the dog.

She puts on a CD. It's Italian and I like the tune, but I can't understand the words. The woman's voice sounds like it's skipping through the music: 'diddli di diddli di diddli di, di di, di di di'. Nana mixes paint and dips a sponge into the colours, dabbing shades of blue, white and green all over the coffin. As she paints, she tells me what the woman's singing about . . . It's a house, but the house she's describing is really the whole world. Nana listens and translates.

I want a house . . . with bright colours to . . . delight the
eyes.
　I want a house, where you can hear . . . birdsong.
　I want a house full of laughter and . . . light . . . and . . .
love.
　I want a house where no one is . . . hungry . . . or lonely . . .
or sad.
　I want a house,
　I want a happy house, diddli di diddli di diddli di di di,
di di di.

'I can translate the diddli di bit,' I tell Nana, which
makes her laugh.

'You'll make sure they play this at my funeral, won't
you, Mira?'

I nod, though I'm not sure it's going to be up to
me to decide. What if no one else agreed with me? I'd
be left with Nana's voice ringing in my ears. This is
the sort of thing that wakes me up at night worrying.
Anyway, I don't want to think about Nana's funeral,
because right now she feels so alive.

Nana hands me another sponge so I can start on
the lid. Next, she takes her brush and dips it into
the Lilac Pearl paint, swirling waves on to the sea . . .
waves and gentle ripples. I watch how she works in the
colours. Underneath, the paint is wet so the colours

run into each other: blues, greens and ochres flowing into the sea. Nana hands me her brush to finish the waves on the other side of the coffin. Then she takes another brush and starts to paint her first dolphin, leaping out of the waves.

My nana can transform a hardboard coffin with her imagination. She can make it dance . . . *diddli di diddli di diddli di di di, di di di*. Another brush dipped in white paint, this time Titanium White, makes a dove rise out of the spray. Nana doesn't stop for a second. She's in the waves, leaping with the dolphins, flying with the doves. Last of all she paints the little dog with his leg cocked over the coffin corner. It's a Piper dog with a wiry brown coat.

'Here, Mira, dip your brush in the Yellow Ochre – Piper needs a pee!' she orders, handing me the pot.

I take hold of the thickest brush and get ready to splatter the pee across the sea. The yellow spray hits the coffin sides, splatting back into Nana's face.

'You've peed in my face,' she laughs.

Then she dips her brush into the blue paint and, with her thumb, flicks the end of the brush at me! This time the spray covers my face.

'You look like Shiva,' she says admiringly.

When we get our breath back from giggling, Nana dips her hand into the blue paint and presses her palm against mine, like a high five. She holds my wrist and presses my right hand, hard and flat against the

60

side of the coffin. Then she places her left hand next to mine to make her own handprint, as if we were one person with a left and right hand of the same size. Two bright blue handprints, one left, one right, one mine, one Nana's. Only when you look at the lines on the palms of our hands, can you tell they belong to different people.

The doorbell rings. I hear Krish's voice before I open the gate. He pushes past me, practically knocking me over as Mum parks Laila under the porch in her pram.

'Guess where I came?' Krish shouts.

'Shhhh,' hushes Mum, pointing to sleeping Laila.

'Nana, Nana, guess where I came?'

'Now what was it? The under-tens?'

'Yep!'

'How far was it?'

'Five K, and the start was up Parli Hill. That was a killer!'

'How many runners?'

'About a hundred.'

'Considering everything . . . I would say you came . . . in the first twenty.'

Nana plays with Krish, like a cat with a mouse.

'Nope.'

'I don't know, Krish . . . tenth?'

'Try again.'

'Fifth? Fourth? Third? Second?'

Nana knows he's come first, because Krish wouldn't be making a fuss if he came second or third or anything, in fact, except first.

'Nope!'

'First place!' yells Nana, clapping her hands in excitement and reaching out to give Krish a hug. 'It takes such stamina to do what you do. I used to try and race when I was your age, but I just couldn't keep going.'

Nor me, I think.

We first found out that Krish could run when he was six. We were staying with Nana Kath and Grandad Bimal in the Lake District, and we went to this country fair, where they had all sorts of sports including fell running, which basically means you have to run up a mountain and down again. Why would anyone want to do that? Mum said the people entering the race would have trained a lot so it might not be a very good idea, but Krish just walked straight up to the starting tent and signed himself in. Then the man stuck his official race number on his T-shirt. Number fifty-two.

We watched him running up that fell, above Lake Grasmere, scrambling up and up for miles in the pouring rain and finally disappearing into the cloud. I didn't like that feeling of not being able to see him; neither did Mum. She paced up and down biting her lip, her eyes scanning backwards and forwards across the fell for a glimpse of Krish's bright blue shirt. Then

I saw him, my brother, skidding and sliding down towards the bottom of that mountain, smeared in mud from head to foot, so you could just make out his eyes peering through the dirt as if he'd fallen into a bog. When Krish appeared through the rain-mist, Nana Kath jumped up and down, like she was on springs. She announced to everyone around us that number fifty-two was her grandson and that her own Grandad Billy, my great-great-grandad, had been a famous fell runner.

It looked as if Krish was going to come in third place. Then suddenly, right at the end, he made his arms and legs pump faster, and pelted straight past the other two boys.

'Aye, there's no doubting, the lad's got it in his blood,' croaked the old man in the green tweed cap, standing next to Nana Kath.

Krish had this look of complete determination on his face, like he just *had* to win. Nana Kath, Mum, Dad and me, and the old man with the cap were all cheering him on, and I saw Grandad Bimal, who was sitting in the car, punch the air as Krish ran for the finish line.

After the race, Krish had to stand in the middle of this podium, on the first place stand, which is the highest bit, and two other boys, who came in second and third place, stood on either side, in the pouring rain. The loudspeaker played 'God Save the Queen', like it was the Olympics or something. Dad said that was a bit over the top, but I thought Krish was lucky to be standing on a podium in the middle of those mountains . . . Even in the pouring rain, it's one of the most beautiful places I have ever seen. It's like he belonged. Watching Krish standing there did feel like a historic occasion in our family, even though they announced the winner to be someone else . . . 'Chris Levenson'.

It was then that I saw Grandad Bimal hoist himself out of the car, and walk very slowly over to the caravan, where the man was chattering away on the loudspeaker. The next thing I heard was Loudspeaker Man's voice.

'I have an apology to make. I am standing here with—'

'Dr Bimal Chatterjee,' Grandad interrupted him.

'Quite, and the doctor lives locally, married to a Cumbrian lass . . .' That made Nana Kath smile, to be called a 'lass'. 'It's his grandson who has just won the Junior Guides Race. He's the youngest ever child to win this race, and my apologies because I mispronounced his name. It's not Chris Levenson . . .'

Then I heard Grandad's voice again with the proper pronunciation of Krishan's name, which actually sounds quite different from how we all say it.

'It's Kri-shan Levenson.' Grandad's bass-drum voice echoed through those mountains and for a moment people stopped to listen, as if they were trying to identify strange birdsong. It felt as if the mountains were listening too, to the news that there's another fell runner in the family. Maybe the old man was right . . . it's in the blood.

Since I started my period, every time I think of anything, there's blood involved somewhere. Krish will never have to feel like I do now; he can just run free, not worrying about what's happening inside his body. Suddenly Krish and me are living in separate universes, because of the blood. I don't even think I could run today and I have never in my life felt further away from flying.

We've always been different, even in primary school, Krish and me. The things I like to do aren't really about winning. Even Art at school is not the same as it is with Nana. I know I can do it, but I hate the kind of project where you have to look at an artist's work, like Van Gogh's *Sunflowers*, and learn about the techniques he used, and then paint your own vase of sunflowers. You just get everybody trying to do the same thing, and nowhere near as well as Van Gogh, which, to me, is not really the point of art. With art like that, you don't get a chance to work out of your own imagination, except for once in primary school when there was a competition and we could do anything we wanted. I made this collage with photographs and food and flowers. I used the inside plastic tray from a biscuit tin and painted each compartment a different colour, depending on what I was putting in it . . . the one that had a picture of me swimming in the sea I painted pale silvery grey and stuck a tiny holey stone inside. Then I painted another with a photo of my dad and Krish before they went to a Tottenham match, deep blue . . . that sort of thing. I put an old golden frame of Nana's round it, and stuck it together with superglue. When it was finished, I was secretly quite proud of it, but even at the time I knew other people would think it was weird so I tried to smuggle it into school under a towel but, of course, on my way in I had to bump into Demi.

'What's the big secret?' she asked me, peering under the towel.

'Nothing,' I lied, pulling away from her, but before I could do anything about it, she'd snatched away the towel so I was left standing in the middle of the playground holding this enormous frame. I felt as if I was standing there naked.

'*What* is *that* supposed to be?' she shrieked at the top of her voice, which, like a magnet, drew her crew towards her. She might as well have stood there with a sign advertising an opportunity to rag Mira Levenson . . . and of course her friends came running.

The worst bit is I actually won that competition.

'A most original entry,' Mr Needham announced,

as he examined the frame with a puzzled expression. I had to walk up the aisle to the accompaniment of sniggering behind my back. Whenever I think about it, it still makes me cringe. I could just imagine what they were thinking (for 'original' replace with 'weird'). That's nothing like the glory of winning a race, is it?

'What happened to you two?' Mum jolts me back into the room, staring from Nana to me. 'Have you had a paint fight or something?'

'We've been having a wild time,' Nana laughs. 'What do you think, Uma?' Nana stands aside so Mum can see the coffin, which we have, more or less, finished.

Krish walks round it, his eyes filling up.

'You've made it look like a painting.'

'It *is* a painting, der!' I say.

'No it's not, it's a coffin,' shouts Krish, the tears stinging his eyes.

'It's a painted coffin,' explains Nana, wrapping her arms around Krish.

'I don't get it. What's the point of painting it if it's just going to be burned?'

'What's the point of running in a race?' argues Nana.

'Because I love running.'

'Well, I love painting. This coffin will probably be my most valuable work of art.'

'I don't get it, Nana,' Krish sulks.

'Because the dolphins, and the doves, and the waves, will stay in people's memories . . . just like you, winning that race today. I bet your mum will never forget that,' Nana says, turning to Mum, who nods and smiles but says nothing because she's on the verge of crying too.

Krish collapses on to Nana's sofa, his stick-thin legs folding under him.

'You look all washed up,' says Nana, slumping down by his side.

'So do you,' Krish lobs back.

Nana tips Krish's chin upwards, planting a kiss on his cheek. Krish squirms out of Nana's grasp as he attempts to rub her blue handprint off his face.

'I suppose we may as well all be blue together,' sighs Nana.

Tuesday 3 May

I pack my school bag.

Mobile

Books

Pencil case

Gym kit

Packed lunch

and . . .

Pads and panty liners, sanitary towels . . . even some tampons . . . some of each . . . just in case. Even the names are a nightmare. I mean 'sanitary towels' – could they think of a worse name for them? But then I imagine myself getting a job in advertising and having to invent a name for all this period stuff, and guess what I come up with? A big fat blank. The advert I find the funniest is the one where the pads have wings and they have little pictures of birds flying around, because the last thing you would ever feel like doing when you've got your period is flying. I mean, as if, with that pad stuck inside your pants and the ache in your belly.

In my mind, it wasn't supposed to happen like this. Millie was going to be first, just like when we started wearing bras. Up until now Millie has always gone first with everything. This is how I imagined it. Millie would start her periods and I would follow maybe a couple of months after. I wouldn't have wanted it to be too long after, just enough time for Millie to have become a specialist in all things periody. We would have had one of our mad sessions round at hers when no one else was in, like we did the time when we were trying to work out what bra size we were. It turned out there wasn't a size small enough (!), but we still tried on her mum's silky bras while Millie started up a commentary about how the 'fashion note' of the season was to wear your oversized bra on the *outside* of your clothes.

'Prada is so last year! Proudbra is this season's must-have item.'

Then, as we heard Millie's mum coming in, we practically died of laughing trying to undo the catch on the bra I was wearing, and stuff all the underwear back in her drawer before we got caught.

So, in my head, Millie and me would have had a laugh about the whole period nightmare and, by the time I got to the stage of packing my bag, I would definitely know what I should be using (and how to use it), because Millie would have told me. Instead I just feel a bit sick worrying about the whole thing.

'Are you ready, Mira?' Mum shouts up the stairs. 'It's nearly half past eight. What *are* you doing up there?'

What I am now doing is dabbing some of Mum's foundation on to my enormous spot, but the make-up just makes it a million times more obvious, so I end up washing it off.

Just one last thing I say to myself as I stare at my volcano-sized pustule in the mirror . . . I close my eyes and beg Notsurewho Notsurewhat to please please please make Jidé Jackson be off school today so he doesn't see me like this. For a moment I think about trying it on for another sickie, but then the letterbox clanks and Millie makes my mind up for me.

'All right?' asks Millie, her owl eyes zoning right in on my zit.

Millie is far too polite to comment. I should tell her right now. This is the moment I should tell her, and then, when *she* starts her period, it would just be like the bra thing all over again, but the other way round, with me helping her. Except it won't be like that. This is so unfair of me, but in a way I feel a bit annoyed with her for not being able to help me out. It's not her fault that I've started first, but in a way I feel as if she's let me down.

'All right,' I say.

There is a Notsurewho Notsurewhat after all! At morning registration Miss Poplar announces that Jidé and Ben are out at some sporting event. At least that's one less thing to worry about. Maybe the pustule will have shrunk by tomorrow.

Each time I go to the loo, I am convinced that some-one will hear me unzipping my bag and unwrapping the towels. I swear suddenly the acoustics in the girls' loos are of a concert-hall standard. Just undoing the stupid pads, each wrapped in its own 'discreet enve-lope' cover, makes so much noise I have to pull the chain at the exact same time as I open the packet and tear off the sticky strip. It works, if you get the timing right.

At lunchtime registration Miss Poplar calls me over. Just my luck that it's my day for her to inspect the teacher's notes in my planner.

'Mira, is there any particular reason why you've

been late for just about every lesson this morning?'

As she's supposed to be the specialist Year Seven tutor you'd think she might have guessed.

'Sorry, miss,' I mumble.

Maybe I should tell her, because every few minutes I shift around on my seat and look behind me, to make sure I haven't leaked.

'Mira Levenson, what's got into you today?' asks Miss Poplar. 'Have you got ants in your pants?'

At the mention of 'pants' I feel like I'm going to die. Of course, I blush bright red and Orla, Demi and Bo fall about laughing.

All afternoon I duck into a loo every time I pass one . . . just in case.

'Are you sure you're feeling all right?' asks Millie.

'Dodgy stomach,' I lie.

'See you later, zit face!' Bo calls out as she pushes past me through the school gates, which is odd, because Bo's forehead and just about her whole face is covered in acne.

'How was your day?' Mum asks when I get back from school.

'Good.'

And it has been a good day, because Jidé wasn't in and nobody found out.

Wednesday 4 May

It's swimming today but I'm missing it, because we're going on this 'adventure', as Nana calls it. To be honest I wouldn't have minded going swimming today because my period is over. I thought it would go on for longer than this, but when I looked it up in this book called *Questions You Might Not Want To Ask Your Parents* that Mum 'just happens' to have had lying around the bathroom for ages, it said that it was quite common for your first period to be really light. It hasn't actually been that bad, except for the appearance of the period pustule, and even that has shrunk to half its size overnight. You could almost call it a normal-sized spot today. So, if it wasn't for going away with Nana Josie, I would have gone swimming today. I like swimming in a pool, but I love swimming in the sea best, when the waves come crashing over you!

We started swimming lessons in Year Six and I remember thinking that it seemed a bit late because the chances are, if any of us were going to drown, we probably would have done it before we were ten, so I always just assumed that everyone could swim anyway . . . but then there was Orla, who had never once in all her life been taken to a swimming pool. It's not *that* unusual according to the not very subtle swimming teacher who shouted across the pool to her: 'Don't worry, dear. There's usually at least one "non-swimmer" in every class.' I think she was trying to make Orla feel better.

Now we're in Year Seven, while the rest of us mess around in the big pool, Orla is still in what she calls the 'Pee Pool' with the mums and babies and the beginners. Mostly, though, she pretends she's 'got stomach ache'. The last time we went swimming one of the teachers said, 'You can't have tummy ache *every* week,' and Orla looked at the woman and said in a really loud voice, 'Actually, I've got my *period*, miss!'

As if you would actually say that!

So, for all the swimming humiliations that Orla has suffered she has come up with a strategy for revenge. Orla and her 'glamorous assistants', as she calls Demi and Bo, have devised a competition about who's got the best (and worst) body. It works like this. There are three judges, Orla, Demi and Bo. They hand out marks out of ten for each bit of your body. When it comes to judging, Orla is definitely the most scathing. She will literally dissect you, limb from limb. You could have a score of six for your legs and four for your tummy and three for your arms. If you've got boobs growing, you get a low mark from Orla, because that's just embarrassing. She grades the boys too. Ben Gbemi always gets ten out of ten because he's been working on getting a 'six-pack'. Jidé usually comes in second place. If you asked me anything, I would switch it the other way round.

Orla never gives any of the girls a ten, because she thinks *she's* got the best body. Orla is definitely the thinnest girl in our class. You can see her hip bones and ribs sticking through her swimming costume. If you've got any fat on you at all, you get a low grade in Orla's scoring system. I only get four out of ten because I'm a bit rounded. Millie gets a really good body score except that Demi always makes a point of saying something horrible like 'shame about the four eyes'. But Millie doesn't care what they say; neither do I.

Nana has a brilliant rant about what a load of rubbish it all is, people worrying so much about how thin they can get. 'Haven't they got anything better to worry about? What a bore to be so weight-obsessed!' The other day when I was sitting with her and she saw me looking at how thin she is now, she said, 'To think, some people actually aspire to being a size nought.' She kept stroking my cheek over and over.

'Don't you ever get into all that dieting crap. It's the quality of your skin, its plumpness, that makes me want to paint you over and over. You're a beauty, Mira Levenson.'

I get really embarrassed when Nana talks like that, but I know she really means it, and the truth is that most of the time I don't think too much about what I look like and I would hate to be bony like Orla. I just am how I am.

Yesterday, Mum had a word with Miss Poplar and she's given permission for me to take the next couple of days off as 'compassionate leave'. Nana Josie wants us all to go to her cottage in Suffolk. I think she sees it as a kind of a family pilgrimage. I actually woke up early this morning and I couldn't get back to sleep, thinking about Jidé and Pat Print's writing group.

Clank, clank, clank. Last night I got my keys ready so I wouldn't be so hassled.

'We're late. It's already quarter to eight,' Millie says, peering through the letterbox and snapping it closed as I unlock the door.

'I'm ready, Millie.'

'I'd be ready too, if I were you, only coming in for the best bit of the day!'

She runs, flat out, to school. I trail way behind her, because when I got up this morning I made one of my 'don't ask me why I do it' pacts with Notsurewho Notsurewhat, that if I trod on a single crack in the pavement, along the walkway to school, our car would break down on the way to Suffolk. Which is not a great pact to make when the probability is pretty high that our car will break down, as it's so decrepit. Why did I do that? If it does break down with Nana in it, it'll be really awful, and now, for no reason at all, except for having the stupid thought, I'm going to feel like *I* made it happen. Not only that, but it also means I look like a lunatic weaving around all over the place, when I could be walking in a straight line.

'For God's sake, Mira, what on earth are you doing?' Millie shouts as I pick my way, like someone demented, between the cracks in the pavement.

By the time we get into the 'safe haven' of our Year Seven block that Miss Poplar has tried to make all cosy so as not to shock us because our new secondary is one of the biggest schools in London, Ben and Jidé are already talking to Pat Print and fussing over her sheepdog. But when Millie and I come in the dog spirals round, practically knocking us over with its frantically wagging tail.

'Moses, behave yourself, my boy. You're so excitable anyone would think you're still a puppy,' she laughs, dragging him by the collar back to her side. Pat Print either doesn't care, like Nana, or she just doesn't know that dogs aren't allowed in school. I love the way she talks to him, as if he can understand exactly what she's saying.

'Why did you call him Moses?' I ask, and as soon as

78

I speak Ben elbows Jidé in the side. Jidé elbows him back as if to shut him up. Of course, I can't look him in the eye but what I do notice is that Jidé has gelled up his hair at the front, he's not wearing his tie and his shirt is all hanging out. I blush again, even though there is no way on earth that Jidé Jackson can know how much I've been thinking about him, even dreaming about him . . . One day someone will make a fortune inventing an anti-blushing device. Whenever you feel one coming on you could just press a button and stop it in its tracks.

'You'll have to read my book if you want to find that out. I collect strays!' Pat says, smiling at me.

It's weird how that happens. Before last week I had never heard of anyone actually being called Moses, apart from Moses in the Bible, and now within one week I've met Eco-Endings Moses and sheepdog Moses.

'So what have you all found out about your names?' Pat asks. That's when I remember what we were supposed to do. She looks around the room, letting her eyes rest on Jidé.

'My full name is BabaJidé. It's an African name . . . it means "father has returned", that's what Jai, my dad, told me anyway. He said Grace liked the "Baba" bit when I was a baby, but when I started to grow up they dropped "Baba" and just called me Jidé and Mum says it goes well with Dad's name . . . Jai.'

I think it sounds really weird calling your mum and

79

dad by their first names, especially when your mum's a teacher at school . . . she's Ms Jackson to everyone else.

'Interesting, isn't it, how some names are better for babies and others feel too grown up to call an infant,' Pat Print comments.

Jidé doesn't reply. He seems lost in his own thoughts so Pat Print turns her attention on Ben. He's funny because he just launches into things; he often makes me jump. I peer over his shoulder at his notebook. Ben always does as little work as he can get away with. He's got about three notes written down, that's all, but he tells Pat Print this whole epic story of his name, hardly even glancing at his book. He seems to have no nerves at all.

'Well, my mum and dad couldn't decide what to call me. They couldn't even agree on any names they both liked before I was born. My mum's Irish and my dad's Nigerian . . . that's where my surname "Gbemi" comes from . . . Nigeria. Dad told me that "Gbemi" means "favoured one". A long time ago the name used to be "Fagbemi", which means something like "favoured by the Oracle", but somewhere along the line we dropped the "Fa" bit. My mum thought I should have an Irish first name but Dad wanted a Nigerian one, and even after I was born they still couldn't agree. So Mum says she just lay in the hospital bed thinking about what to call me. Then one day she looked up at Big Ben, because Mum was in the hospital just opposite, and she thought, That's it. The answer had been staring her in the face and blasting her ears, all that time. That's why she called me Ben, and Dad said it sounded good with Gbemi. So that's it, that's why I'm called Ben Gbemi.'

Ben definitely speaks as though he's projecting his voice across London. He's tall too, probably the tallest boy in Year Seven.

Pat has been smiling all the way through Ben's explanation.

'Big Ben! I'm predicting a bold career in broadcasting for you!'

'What's broadcasting?' asks Ben.

'I'm thinking . . . you could be a presenter, no, maybe more daring . . . a journalist reporting while battling against the elements, earthquakes or storms, or even in a war zone . . . surviving against all odds and still bringing us the news.' Pat Print is obviously enjoying herself making up a story for Ben's life.

Jidé laughs and slaps Ben across the back.

You can't help but smile, because you can just see Ben Gbemi in a job like that.

'Which comes first – the name or the personality?' asks Pat Print. It's one of those questions she's not expecting us to answer.

Ben looks down at his feet and tries hard not to show he's smiling underneath his copper glinting curls.

'Now who's next?' Pat's sharp eyes settle on me. 'Mira?'

'I'm sorry, Miss Print, I didn't do the name bit. I wrote the diary though.' There it is again, that thin little voice of mine.

'OK! I'll hear that later. Call me Pat, please. Now Millie, what have you got for me?'

Millie needs no encouragement.

'My ancestors are Scottish and, further back, originally from France, dating right back to 1066. Dad's told me all about it, but it's a bit complicated. Apparently, one of my ancestors had Robert the Crusader or Marauder's heart locked up in a box.'

'Which was it? A crusader or a marauder?' Pat Print asks, looking amused.

'What's the difference?' asks Ben.

'Good question.' Pat laughs. 'Sorry, Millie, I interrupted your flow.'

'Well, my ancestor's job was to keep Robert the Something's heart locked up in a box. That's why I'm called "Lockhart".'

'Why would he have to keep the heart locked up?' butts in Jidé, forgetting again his own rule that he's not supposed to be this interested.

Millie sighs, fed up with being interrupted.

'Fascinating, Millie.' Pat smiles. 'It's a great name, "Lockhart" – beautifully iconic. The heart is the subject of so many wonderful stories. I bet if I asked you,

you could all write a different story about love. Now you've given me an idea.'

Ben and Jidé groan at the same time . . . back to their double act again.

'Write down as many words as come to mind when I say the word "heart". Just make a list. I'm giving you fifteen seconds so don't think about it too hard, just scribble down whatever springs to mind . . . starting NOW! The word is "*heart*".'

artichoke
blood
love
layers
break
pig
blood
black pudding
brave
stop beating

That's all I write in fifteen seconds.

'Now STOP! Exchange papers and have a read of each other's,' orders Pat.

I was going to swap with Millie, like I always do, but before I can, Jidé Jackson has swapped papers with me. In fact, he's sitting shoulder to shoulder with me, and just that closeness makes me turn my most impressive crimson colour. At least I can keep my head down while I read his list.

love
hate
murder
blood
machete
lost
scar
mother
father
sister
cloth
empty
river

'Now see what words you have in common and choose one word from the list that you would like to ask your partner about,' Pat instructs us.

I look sideways at Jidé and for a second I do what I can never usually do . . . look him in the eye. Jidé makes a tiny movement with his head that tells me not to ask him anything about his words, so we talk about black pudding and pig's blood and how my Nana Kath's friend tricked me into eating it by telling me it was a vegetable.

'And you believed her!' Jidé laughs.

Then he asks me about the artichoke, so I tell him about Nana Josie's artichoke-heart charm and what she told me about it, and all the time I'm talking I'm thinking of what *his* story might be behind those words.

'Let's have a couple of examples then,' calls out Pat Print as Jidé and I go back to avoiding eye contact with each other and her. For a moment I forgot we were even in class. Now that I've actually looked into them, I realize that Jidé's eyes have a hazel light in them.

It takes me a while to get my head back into the room, and by the time I do Millie's reading out the word 'transplant', from Ben's list, because what he didn't tell us earlier is that he was one of the youngest babies in Britain ever to have a heart transplant. It's hard to believe that Ben Gbemi could have ever been small and weak.

'I've got the newspaper clippings. I can bring them in to show you, if you want,' Ben booms.

I can't help thinking of Big Ben's tiny baby heart.

'You see,' smiles Pat Print. 'You were only just born and you'd already hit the news.'

Then Ben reads out Millie's word: loyalty.

'We talked about Millie's ancestor, guarding the heart,' Ben says. 'He must have really cared about the person whose heart he was protecting, to stay loyal to them for all that time, even though they were dead.'

85

Ben's dad left home a few years ago. I bet that's what he's thinking about, but he's not the type to say anything.

Pat nods. 'The heart is probably the most powerful symbol in life and literature. My guess is that Millie's ancestor could have either been protecting the heart, because it was such a precious symbol, or preventing it from being returned to its people, like a scalp or a macabre trophy. You might have to dig a bit deeper to find out,' Pat Print tells Millie. 'So what do you think? If Millie did the research, would you want to read that story?'

'I would, for definite . . . that's what I go for . . . adventure, mystery, that sort of thing,' perks up Ben.

'Indeed. You've got an epic historical novel on your hands there, Millie Lockhart. If anyone can handle it, you can. Why don't you write the opening paragraph for next week? Let's see if we can help you out a bit. Jidé, if you were reading that book, what would make it a page-turner for you?'

Jidé doesn't even need to think before he answers.

'She'll have to make a link between herself and that story, like an adventure through time.'

Millie nods.

'I think I'll just give up my day job,' jokes Pat Print. 'With a writer's note like that, I may as well pack up and go home.'

A noise that never escapes my mouth in school

fills up the room. It's strange and low and loud and it shocks everyone, my laugh, because I don't think, except for Millie, the others have ever heard it before. It's so embarrassing. I don't even know why I'm laughing.

'Now, that's a first!' Jidé Jackson nudges me on the arm, playfully.

My face is as hot and red as if I've been running a very high temperature. How did that slip out? And now my laugh and Jidé's nudge have made my temperature shoot up to boiling point and left behind a stupid grin that I can't wipe off my face. I can't even look up. Pat Print must realize that I am paralysed with embarrassment because she switches to Jidé instead.

'Jidé. What about your surname? Did you find out anything more?'

Jidé shakes his head, Suddenly Jidé the joker looks miserable. It's like we've swapped roles.

'That's a shame,' sighs Pat.

'"We don't have that information." That's what Grace said when I asked her if we could ever trace my original surname. I wasn't always a Jackson.'

I've never heard Jidé talk so quietly.

'I don't know what my birth name is. I had a sister, she was about three when she died, they think, older than me anyway . . . but she wouldn't speak, not even to tell them her name or mine. Grace said she was too traumatized to talk. Grace and Jai, they

87

gave me the name "BabaJidé" when they found me. I told you, didn't I, it means "father has returned," and even though Jai met so many children out there he had a feeling, as soon as he saw me, that he should be my father. I was about a year old, they're not sure. I have a made-up birthday. And . . . my birth parents, who knows? You probably watched them on the news, floating down the river.'

The words from Jidé's list echo around my mind.

A blueberry-coloured rash starts to spread up Pat Print's neck and over her face. I didn't have her down as a blusher.

'Rwanda . . . is that right?'

Jidé nods.

'What did Grace and Jai do out there?' she asks gently.

'Aid workers in one of the refugee camps, the one my sister walked into with me. I suppose I could re-search what happened to people *like* my birth parents, but I could never find out my proper name,' explains Jidé. 'Anyway, I'm lucky to be alive, aren't I? If it wasn't for Grace and Jai . . .' Jidé trails off.

He suddenly looks exhausted. I don't think he talks about his past to many people. I haven't really understood this before, about Jidé, how much he doesn't say. The layers of his heart are well protected. Even the way he tells us all this is said in a matter-of-fact sort of voice, but he can't disguise the fact that he's angry. Now I think I understand why there are all these different edges to him. 'Jidé the joker', 'Jidé with attitude', 'Jidé trying his best to hide how clever he is', although at least in Pat Print's class he seems to be giving up on that one. Nana thinks I'm lucky because I haven't had a reason to grow protective layers. Jidé has, and suddenly this all makes me feel like I live in a very cosy little world. A minute ago we were discussing names. Now, suddenly, we're in Rwanda. I don't even know where Rwanda is.

I've been trying to work out what's different about this class. I don't know what it is about Pat Print, but she's definitely got this way of letting people say what they want to say. Once she gets us all talking it's as if she's almost not here at all; she sort of disappears from the room while the conversation's flowing and only really steps back in to start it up again, like keeping one of Laila's spinning tops whirling. Maybe that's why Jidé Jackson has talked about himself for the first time ever. I don't think anyone in this room knew that, about Jidé, and I've been at school with him since primary. By the look on Ben's face, he didn't know either.

Pat Print sighs deeply. That's the other thing about her. She's not scared of long silences like some teachers are. It's weird, but you don't get embarrassed in the silence in her class and it doesn't feel like a punishment either. It's actually a relief to have the time to feel whatever it is you're feeling, and after what Jidé's told us I think she's right . . . we need a bit of time to let it all sink in.

'Now, how did you get on with your diaries?' Pat asks, breaking the quiet.

'Nothing happened to me this week,' booms Ben.

'Nothing never happens,' replies Pat, smiling.

'It does to me,' sulks Ben.

'I did it,' perks up Millie enthusiastically, 'but I'd rather not read it out aloud.'

'You're just trying to get us interested,' jokes Ben.

'Did it work?' laughs Millie.

I think Millie and Ben are flirting with each other!

'Fair enough,' says Pat. 'Jidé?'

He shakes his head.

'Now you said you've got something for me, Mira. Will you read it out to us?'

I take out my red leather diary. I have already decided which bits I don't mind them hearing about – obviously there are some things I wouldn't want any of them to know, not even Millie and especially not Jidé!

'I got this diary last week. It starts on my birthday, but I'll read last Sunday. That's the day me and Nana went to buy paint,' I explain.

We park right next to Dusty Bird's art shop. Nana leans on my arm as Mum and I walk her inside. She wants acrylic water-based paints. Nana says it's very important to choose the exact colours she has in her mind . . .

All the way through reading this I feel Jidé watching me and properly listening, and all I can feel is guilty, because I'm talking about my nana dying . . . and in a way she's had her life, and such a good life, and a rich life. I just wish that Jidé's family were alive. I wish that his little sister hadn't died so young and that he knew her name. Because I can't stop thinking about Jidé, I've forgotten how much I hate reading aloud. Anyway, reading out your work isn't so bad because at least you can lean on the words you've already written. I don't manage to get to the end because the bell rings for the start of school. Usually everyone jumps up and starts packing their things away, but today, nobody moves till I get to the end of my sentence.

When someone is dying, everything you say and do means more than it normally does. When someone is dying, you notice things . . . everything really. The whole of life is in slow motion.

There's that silence again . . . the one where you can hear people's thoughts echoing around the room. Jidé nods and smiles at me sadly. Somehow, since he told us what he told us, he seems less tough.

'Everything OK?' chirps Miss Poplar, peering round the door and spotting Moses. She raises her right eyebrow. That means something's happening that shouldn't be happening . . . Miss Poplar never raises her voice, just her right eyebrow. In this case that right eyebrow is managing to say two things at the same time – 'Dogs aren't allowed in school,' and, 'Why aren't you wearing your uniforms correctly?' but she doesn't say anything to Pat Print, not in front of us anyway.

'I wish you could have heard what I just heard. Mira read us a diary entry about her grandmother,' Pat Print tells Miss Poplar.

Sometimes, because I don't talk very much, some adults might assume I don't think much either. Maybe Pat Print thought that about me.

'When I agreed to take this job, I anticipated it would be a nice little bit of research, nothing too stretching, but I feel absolutely wrung out by the talent and the bravery of your students,' Pat says, looking from Miss Poplar to Jidé. 'Jidé, could you just stay on for a minute.' It's Jidé's turn for a private word.

I wonder what she could possibly say to him, to make it better.

'Excuse me, I've got to go now,' I say, standing up and packing up my diary.

I feel Jidé's eyes on my back as I leave the room.

Millie and Ben follow me out into the corridor.

'Where is Rwanda anyway?' Ben asks Millie.

'Africa,' Millie answers without hesitation.

'How do you get to know so much about everything?' asks Ben.

'Try reading!' smiles Millie.

Ben sticks his tongue out at her and wanders off laughing and occasionally glancing back at her.

'Did you bring your mobile in today?' asks Millie.

I get my pebble out of my pocket to show her.

'You're so lucky. My mum would never let me bring mine into school.'

'Mine wouldn't either!'

'Aren't you the rebel! What's your number?'

I have it stuck to the back of the phone until I remember it, which will probably be never because I'm rubbish at memorizing numbers. Millie repeats it over a few times out loud.

'OK, got that. I'll call you. I wish I could come with you. Remember the last time we went?'

It was only last summer that Millie and me were together in Suffolk, jumping off the dunes and making a den down on the marsh. I can't imagine us doing that now. It feels like a whole lifetime away.

Still, the thought of Millie being the first person to call me on my mobile cheers me up as I walk along the corridor following the faint mud trail of Pat Print's journey into school.

As we drive past the school, on our way to pick up Nana, Pat Print and Miss Poplar are standing at the end of the walkway to school that leads out on to the road. Miss Poplar waves and says something to Pat, who peers into our car. She glances from Mum to Dad, past my brother and sister till she finally sees me. Then she waves, smiles and blows me a kiss.

'Who's that with Miss Poplar?' asks Mum.

'That's Pat Print, the writer woman I told you about.'

'Why did she blow you a kiss?' asks Krish, pulling his grossed-out face.

I shrug. 'I think she likes my writing.'

'It's a bit weird though. It's not as if she knows you or anything.'

'Miss Poplar's probably told her why we're going to Suffolk. Maybe she feels sorry for us.'

'Why do you call her by her first name anyway?'

I can't be bothered to answer Krish.

'Guess what her dog's called?' I say, attempting to change the subject.

'Shep,' tries Dad. 'Or Lassie? Or—'

'Do you want to know or not?' I say, cutting him off and wishing I'd never asked in the first place.

'Want to know what?' asks Dad.

'Her dog's name,' I sigh, almost giving up completely.

'Go on then,' encourages Mum.

'Moses!'

'Jesus, not him again,' groans Dad.

'Not Jesus, Moses,' jokes Krish.

This is how conversations go in our house. What *is* the point?

*

We are making this trip to Suffolk because Nana needs to see the big Suffolk sky just once more. There is a lot of sky in Suffolk – that's why people from London like it, because of the wide-open sky and sea, with nothing on the horizon.

Nana has a little wooden cottage, like a doll's house; everything in it is small and delicate. It's got a white porch, like a summerhouse, looking on to the garden. There are pots and hanging things on little hooks all over the porch . . . pottery birds, horseshoes, a rusty green wind chime that's lost its chime, a Jeremy Fisher frog sitting on a lily pad, a rusty Indian metal heart with bells threaded through it and Nana's long string of holey stones, stretching from one end of the porch to the other. I learned to count on those holey stones.

High up, on a whitewashed shelf, always in exactly the same place, sits the flycatcher's pot. Every summer a family of flycatchers make their journey over the Sahara desert from Africa to the same little white pot that sits on Nana Josie's porch. They've been coming here for as long as Nana can remember. Those little birds could have sat on a branch near Jidé's mum and dad and flown thousands and thousands of kilometres over land and sea, just to be in Nana's garden. She says she feels privileged to have what she calls her 'feathered guests', and that when she's gone we must be very quiet, at the time of the flycatchers, so they will know they're still welcome. But we can't really be quiet enough. Nana used to stand for hours painting at her easel in the garden, hardly moving at all, but Krish is always kicking a football or playing cricket or swing ball, and as for Laila, well, you can't make her be quiet unless she's asleep or ill. Even I can't be as quiet as Nana. Anyway, it's too early for the flycatchers.

Nana and Laila have both slept all the way from London. They look so peaceful when they're asleep, like, when they wake up, nothing in the world could bother them. We finally turn off on to the bumpety lane leading to the cottage. We wait in the car while Mum and Dad get out and unlock the flaky blue door that Dad and me painted Duck-egg Blue. As Krish races out of the car, slamming the door behind him, Nana wakes up. She sits and stares at her cottage as if she's seeing it for the very first time. Then she turns to sleeping Laila and touches her rosy cheek with the back of her hand. I think she might not even know that I'm still sitting next to her until she slips her hand into mine.

'Muuuuum, Miiiiiiira, what are you doing?' Dad calls to us from the open doorway of the cottage.

'Remembering,' Nana whispers.

'I've lit the fire, just to air the place out a bit,' Dad says, as he opens the car door and gently eases Nana out of her seat. Then he wraps his arm round Nana's shoulder and walks her slowly inside.

We sit together, Nana and me, watching the flames dance while Mum and Dad are busy unpacking and making the beds up for tonight. Laila's still asleep in her car seat, and Krish is out playing swing ball in the back garden.

The walls of the sitting room are covered in Nana's paintings. I follow her eyes around the room at all that she has created. There are paintings of me and Krish and one of Laila too.

It's like this between Nana and me – we've always been happy just to sit together. We don't even need to talk. When I was eleven, we used to play her game, A Penny For Them, where we would try to read each other's thoughts, and Nana was nearly always right about what I was thinking . . . but not today, because my silence is full of Jidé Jackson who she doesn't even know exists. I get out my mobile and the manual I haven't read yet, and start to mess around with the functions, finding out all the things it can do. I check for messages, but there are none. I turn to the texting page of the manual to work out how to text. I like the idea that you can send messages without anyone over-hearing what you're saying.

'That's what I hate about those things. They stop people from living in the moment. Have you had *any-one* call you on it yet?' Nana asks, jolting me back to her.

97

I shake my head and slip my mobile back in my pocket.

'It's far too hot in here. Come on, let's have a look at the garden,' Nana says, standing up and walking towards the back door and out through the porch.

Nana's garden is for birds, butterflies, frogs, dogs and humans. 'In that order,' she jokes. All through the winter she hangs fat balls from the trees for the birds to eat. If she hasn't been for a while, she'll make a special trip just to replace them, so the birds don't go hungry.

In the middle of the garden there's a pond, which used to have fish in it, but a heron moved in last year and ate them all. There are grasses at the corner of the pond, and a few newts, which Nana calls 'the ancients of the garden', swimming in the murky water. There are always frogs hopping around, or bathing just underneath the slimy green leaves, at the water's edge. By the side of the pond is Nana's spring garden, which is just about still flowering, though Nana says it's past its best. There are primroses, bluebells, bright pink tulips and snake-head flowers with veiny, plum-coloured leaves . . . delicate as Nana's hands.

The stone man we bought Nana for her birthday a few years ago – and which she calls 'my man in Suffolk' – stands in the middle of the spring garden in his artist's smock, enjoying the flowers and the birds.

Behind the stone man you can just see the disused

old railway wagon through the thicket of brambles, the wagon that my dad and Aunty Abi used to camp in when they brought their school friends to Suffolk. When Millie was here, we had this big plan that we would renovate it, but we couldn't even get to it through the thicket of brambles.

I sit next to Nana on her rusty old bench.

'What are you looking at, Nana?'

She places her hand in mine. 'The past. Do you want to see?'

I nod.

'Over there is your daddy, my little Sam, six years old, taking his white rabbit for a walk on a lead . . . Pipkin, his name was. Sam's pulling him away from the pond – he's worried he might hop in. And there on the porch is my beautiful Abi, with her long curly locks, pacing up and down, practising her lines for *A Midsummer Night's Dream.*'

As she speaks, Nana points, as if each person from the past is appearing in front of her eyes.

'Out of sight is the railway wagon, covered in brambles. There I am with your mum and dad painting sunflowers and butterflies, red admirals and cabbage whites on the railway wagon. They keep disappearing round the back to have a snog. They think I don't notice.'

I groan at the thought of Mum and Dad snogging, but Nana doesn't seem to hear. She takes a deep,

deep breath, as if she would like to breathe in all these memories as she holds my hand and we walk around the garden together.

'And there you are, my darling Mira, standing next to me, under my parasol . . . just four years old . . . and little Krish tottering around trying to catch goldfish in the pond with the stick-and-string rod I made him.'

Nana paints the picture of the past so clearly that it almost feels like part of my own memory. She has a way of drawing you in like that . . . making you feel like you're the only one that matters in the world.

'Lunchtime,' Mum calls, opening the door on to the garden and releasing a delicious smell.

Jill, one of Nana's Suffolk friends, left a soup simmering on the stove so that Nana would have something to eat as soon as we arrived. We sit round Nana's rickety table, slurping. You have to be very careful not to lean too hard on this table, or it will collapse.

Nana keeps looking from one of us to the other, giving us the loveliest of smiles, like she's completely happy now that we've brought her here. Then suddenly Dad starts to cry. He's trying his hardest not to, but his body is shaking with man tears. He leans close to his bowl to cover it up, but he just ends up crying into it.

'It doesn't need salt!' Nana jokes, holding Dad's hand. 'I wish you weren't in so much pain,' she sighs, hugging him to her as if he's still a little boy.

I think this is a strange thing to say, because it's Nana who's really in pain.

Later, at night, I can't get to sleep. I listen to my family breathing. You can hear Dad's snoring and tiny noises creaking around the cottage. There are definitely birds fluttering around in the roof. But mostly I can hear people breathing. Then I feel my own breath, in and out, and the little space between the in breath and the out breath, just like Nana's taught me. After a while I start to feel quite sleepy. Then I hear Nana's sandals padding on the wooden floor and I listen to her trying desperately to catch her breath. She walks slowly to the sink and fills a glass with cold water so she can swallow her pills. Nana has to take so many pills now.

Her body is silhouetted against my bedroom doorway. I watch her leaning against the sink taking little sips of water. Suddenly, she drops the cup, as if it's burned her. Now she's clutching on to her shoulder like she's being attacked by a wild animal. For a moment I think she's going to fall over, but she just leans against the sink, holding herself up and making this horrible groaning noise.

I hear Dad call out, 'Mum, what's the matter? What's going on?'

Nana looks up in this helpless way as Dad walks

towards her. 'Take the pain away, Sam, just take it away,' she pleads.

'We'll do our best for you, Mum.'

Dad puts his arm round Nana and leads her into the front room. I just lie here, staring at the empty doorway. This is not a nightmare. I am wide awake.

Thursday 5 May

Outside everything is grey, Payne's Grey. There's not even a cloud to watch, scudding across. This whole sky is one great low fog pressing down on me. Even the air is a misty damp swamp you don't feel like breathing in. On days like this there is too much sky in Suffolk.

I take Dad's laptop off to Nana's little pink bedroom and plug in the Internet stick. I type in 'Ruwanda', and it asks, 'Do you mean <u>Rwanda</u>?' I click on that, and a whole list of choices comes up for me to read about Rwanda . . . genocide . . . mass killing . . . photos of hundreds of skulls of children on school desks and altars in churches. I can't take in the nightmare of what I'm reading. More than a million people killed . . . with machetes, knives and guns . . . Civil war, tribes fighting each other, neighbours ordered to kill neighbours, or be killed themselves . . . priests preaching killing . . . How many people exactly? No one counted, but the reason for all the killing? To wipe out a whole tribe of people.

Just like Hitler tried to destroy Jewish people, but in Rwanda no one did anything to stop it. Not the British, not the Americans. What did Jidé say? 'You probably saw them on the news.'

Here I am sitting in my Nana's pink room with roses painted on the wall reading these poisonous words with a red-hot anger starting to burn in my belly, filling my throat and mouth with a bitter acid taste that I can't get rid of. Now I think I know why Jidé Jackson doesn't want to go there, doesn't want to think about it . . . He said he'd had a sister who wouldn't even speak of what she'd been through.

It's true what Jidé said: with this sort of past, why would you want to look back? And, reading all of this, I still don't know the story of why his sister died.

Suddenly the marshmallow sweetness of Nana's pink room makes me want to break out. I run into the grey mist and keep on running down the lane and on to the marsh. I gulp in the damp air, running and running until I can't breathe any more. But I know there is nowhere to run to, because, although I've seen terrible scenes on the television of people suffering and starving, it's never really got to me before, not like today . . . because once you know this stuff happened to your friend's mum and dad, to his sister and to a million other people, you can't un-know it. Can you?

'It'll be all right, Mira, with Nana. We're going to sort

it out,' says Dad when I get back.

He wraps his arms round me. I don't tell him that my tears are not for Nana but for Jidé Jackson and his mum and dad who he never knew . . . and his sister with no name.

Nana is still lying on her white wicker sofa snuggled in her purple shawl. 'Accepting visitors, like the queen,' she says. This sofa can only be used by Nana, Krish, Laila and me, obviously not all at the same time. It would just snap if a big person sat on it. But it's perfect for Nana. She looks beautiful with all the patterned cushions around her, like a Matisse painting. I find my sketchbook and start to draw her. Nana smiles at me. She likes 'sitting' for people. Since she was very young, artists have painted Nana, and photographed her for newspapers and exhibitions. We've got a black and white photo in the hallway at home of Nana when she was about twenty years old with her bulldog 'Toro'. The writing underneath says: 'Beauty And The Beast Make An Entrance Among Embankment Artists.'

All through the day different people come to visit Nana Josie. Mum and Dad are worried that it's making her too tired, but when they suggest she has a rest she waves away their worries, telling them not to fuss, that this is what she's here for. Even so, later, when people arrive, she's sleeping. Some people can understand about dying, and others can't really deal with it at all. Some of my nana's friends are happy to hold her hand for an hour while she sleeps. When she's awake, Nana just lies there, smiling at everyone with her eyes. She lets the visitors do the talking, if they want to. Some people find it impossible to stop talking . . . to say goodbye. One friend comes back again and again. After he finally leaves, Nana sighs, 'It's bloody hard work dying well.'

That's what we're trying to help Nana to do, I think, die well. Just like people try to have a good life . . . we are trying to give Nana a good death. But Jidé Jackson's mum and dad and sister did not die well. More than a million people in Rwanda did not die well . . . I can't get the picture out of my mind of their bodies floating down a river, with no one to care for them.

When you draw someone, you see things in them that you don't notice in normal life. It's like the world slows down and grows silent so you just see the person in front of you, like peering out at a tiny speck of the world through a holey stone. Even though it's my nana I'm drawing, and I know what she looks like, it's as if I'm seeing her for the very first time . . . like how you can tell, by her mouth and her chin, what a determined person she is. But when I'm drawing her eyes I notice something new. Her expression tells me that she's trapped; she can't wait to get out of her body. These are the things I see when I'm drawing Nana Josie.

Dad's on the phone talking to someone about Nana's pain in the night. An hour later the phone rings. It's the Macmillan nurse. She's the one who's been coming to Nana's flat to look after her. When Dad's finished talking, he comes over and sits quietly with Nana, and at that very moment Laila wakes up and starts to cry. Mum picks her up to comfort her.

'Who wants a walk by the sea?' Mum rallies us, trying her best to sound enthusiastic.

Krish is climbing the walls with excitement. I don't really want to go, but I say yes because it's obvious that Dad and Nana want to be on their own.

Mum straps Laila into the baby carrier and hoists her up on to her back. Laila kicks her legs as if she would like to run to catch up with us. The wind smears my hair on to my face so I can hardly see ahead. From the crabbing bridge, me and Krish race for the dunes, like we always do. He wins, like he always does. Once over the dunes the sea stops us short. Great breaking waves roar in my face and the spray threads a foam necklace all along the beach. If you lean back, the wind almost holds you up, but you know that if it decides to it can just as easily knock you down flat. I wish we'd brought Nana with us. She could have stood on the beach and the wind would have picked her up and flown her over the sea, like a kite set free. I love the way the wind and the sea and the cold blast everything else away, so the only thing you can think about is not being blown away. When she was a little girl, Nana used to dream of flying all the time, just like I do. Now that my period's gone I feel as if I could fly over the dunes again, like I did last summer with Millie.

Krish and Mum are shouting to me, but their voices are swallowed by the sea and the wind.

'Piiiiiiper!' I call.

But Piper has found another dog to play with. They're splashing around in the foam. A woman with a green headscarf appears through the spray. She's walking up the beach towards me, waving.

'Mooooooses,' she calls over and over.

At first I think she's just calling to the dog, but as she draws closer I realize she's waving to me.

'Hello, Mira! I thought maybe there was a chance we'd bump into each other.'

I don't really know what to say. It just feels so odd seeing Pat Print here, on the beach. I look over my shoulder to see where Mum and Krish are, but they've disappeared over the dunes.

'I've got a caravan, a bit further up the beach. I keep it parked up, permanently. My secret hideaway,' she whispers, placing a finger over her lips.

I still can't think of anything to say to her. So I stare down at the sand and Pat Print's bare feet. She follows my eyes.

'Since I was a little girl, I could never see the sand without throwing my shoes off – whatever the weather

I've just got to feel the sand between my toes. Call me a free spirit.'

I hardly dare look up at her because the thought crosses my mind that maybe she isn't really here at all, but then Piper and Moses fly at us, shaking the salty water off their coats and soaking us with their spray. Pat Print laughs and clips Moses back on to his lead.

'Who's this?' asks Pat, stroking Piper.

'Piper, Nana's dog.'

'Lovely to see you, Mira. Maybe we'll walk together again one day,' Pat Print says, smiling at me.

Then she turns away and glides off down the beach. Her bare feet, the wind whipping up the beach and her disappearing into the sea-mist, coat ends flapping, makes me wonder if that actually happened.

I trail up and down the bank looking for holey stones. If (I say to Notsurewho Notsurewhat) I find a holey stone, then Pat Print is definitely a ghost, spirit, angel, or whatever. As soon as I've thought it, there it is in front of me, a perfect oval holey stone. This one's for Millie. I squeeze it safely snug inside my jeans pocket. Now Krish is sprinting back up the beach, yelling at me to hurry up as Laila's screech carries on the wind. It's too bitter for her out here.

As soon as you walk over the dunes, the sea is gone. With every step, the roar of the waves and the wind is muffled, until the world grows grey again.

'What took you so long?' shouts Krish in a voice as

109

loud as Ben Gbemi's, as if I'm miles away instead of standing right next to him. I think about telling them about Pat Print, but he probably wouldn't believe me anyway.

'I was looking for a holey stone for Millie.'

When I get back to the cottage, I show Nana the holey stone. The holey stone that means Pat Print is a ghost.

'Millie will love that, but don't forget it's *our* collection, yours and mine, so keep adding to it . . .' She wraps her arms round my shoulders protectively. There it is again, the sentence that's not finished . . . 'When I'm gone.'

'Nana, do you believe in ghosts and spirits?'

'Of course. I've seen a few of that sort of thing in my time,' she smiles.

'Did they frighten you?'

'Not really, they just give you a bit of a jolt.'

'What are you two so secretive about?' asks Mum, helping Nana up.

Nana takes off her purple shawl, folds it and places it on the back of her comfy chair.

'Just sharing ghost stories,' laughs Nana.

Mum gives Nana one of her 'Sure that's a good idea, Josie?' looks, but her repertoire of meaningful glances is wasted on Nana.

'Mira, what were you looking up about Rwanda?' asks Dad as he goes to shut down his laptop.

'Nothing. We're doing a project on Africa, that's all.'

'What sort of project?' pursues Dad.

'Oh, I dunno, can't remember now,' I say, wandering away and hoping he'll let it drop, but then he starts to read what I've read. He's shaking his head now and sighing, which draws Mum over to him. She stands behind him reading. Occasionally they both look over to me with those matching furrowed brows of theirs. When Dad finally switches off the computer, he looks up at me and says, 'We'll need to talk about this later.'

Mum nods in agreement.

Sometimes I wish I came from a family where the parents just let you get on with it. There are loads of kids in my class whose parents haven't got a clue what they get up to. Just my luck to be born into a family who have to *talk* about everything. We have this whole vocabulary given over to 'talking'. 'Chats' or 'talks' are supposed to be not that important, usually a short 'private' word with Mum or Dad about a minor worry. 'Meetings' are more serious. The whole family has to get together and have a proper 'discussion'. When a family 'conference' is called, you know something really off the scale is about to happen, like moving house or something. So, I've got to have a 'talk' with Dad later about Rwanda, though by the look on his face it might turn out to be a bit more than that.

When the cottage is nearly cleared up, Dad calls

a 'meeting', but there's something about it that's re-minding me more of our last family 'conference'.

'Come on, Krish, put that football down, just for a minute,' says Dad, patting the seat next to him to try to stop Krish from dribbling the ball around the room. When Krish is finally still, Dad explains that when we get back to London Nana is going to stay in a hospice, so that the doctors can sort out her pain. Krish asks Dad how long she will have to stay there. Dad says he doesn't know. I know.

When we pack our bags, it's as if Nana is packing that part of her life up and storing it in her head. She says that since she was a little girl she's always felt sad when she packs up to leave a place. She calls suitcases 'joyless things', that's why she always just slings her stuff into a soft cotton bag.

As we are leaving, Nana goes out to stand on her porch to take a last look at her garden. Then she closes the door, locks it with the little silver key, and places it on top of the light switch, like she always does.

We drive down the lane in silence. At the junction Nana suddenly asks Dad to turn left.

'There's just one view I have to see again,' she says.

Dad nods. Without having to ask where she wants to go, he turns left, then right and down the winding country lanes and across the sea of yellow gorse. This is Nana's very favourite view. She's brought us here loads of times before. The people at the bird sanctuary shop don't even charge her any more, because she knows Dunwich Dan, who works there, and anyway they know she only comes to sit in Bittern Hide.

When we get to the car park, Dad drives as close to the shop as possible. He steps out of the car and into the place where you buy your tickets.

'I was hoping I'd see Dan,' says Nana, as she catches sight of him through the window.

Dan pushes a wheelchair towards the car. He opens the door, swinging it back, in a grand sweep.

'Josie, how lovely to see you! Get in, I'll drive you up there myself ,' he says, as if he's her personal chauffeur.

'I just had to see it once more.' Nana smiles at Dan.

'Don't blame you, Josie.'

Working at the sanctuary shop is one of Dunwich Dan's retirement jobs. He's actually quite old, but he's one of those old men who looks really healthy and strong. He has red cheeks with deep lines in his face like he's spent all his life outdoors. Dan comes to Nana's garden once a month to tidy it up. He used to work in lots of people's gardens, but not any more. Nana says the main reason Dan keeps her garden on is to watch the flycatchers go backwards and forwards to their nest on her porch.

Dan pushes Nana down the bumpy path to Bittern Hide. I still think it's a funny thing to do . . . hide from the birds, so you can spy on them. Nana looks up through the trees as occasionally Dan stops to point out a nest, or listen to birdsong.

As Mum wheels the pram over the path to the hide, Laila's head starts to nod.

'Thank God!' Mum sighs.

Bittern Hide has quite a few steps to climb. Nana stands up out of the wheelchair to take the first step, but, before she can take another, Dan wraps one arm round her neck and slides the other under her knees, lifting her up, just like Dad holds Laila when she falls asleep in his arms.

'This is really not necessary,' giggles Nana.

'Reason not the need. I'm enjoying myself, Josie.'

'Go on then, carry me over the threshold,' chuckles Nana.

There are other birdwatchers in the hide, but when they see us lot coming up the steps, most of them leave. Only a few give us the benefit of the doubt.

As soon as you're inside the hide, you feel the weight of silence, like when you walk into an empty church. It takes us a few minutes to get settled on the long wooden benches. Dan unhooks one of the long latch windows so that Nana can see straight out on to the reed beds. Once it's quiet in the hide, your ears start to tune in to all the different bird calls. It's as if you've never heard a bird sing before.

The reed beds are green and golden and, even though the sea is just beyond, you feel as if you're floating away on a wave of gold.

We listen to the dancing grass and the sound of ruffled wings as the birds rise up over the reed beds in great sweeping arcs. In the hide, the only sound is our own breathing. People occasionally smile at me, Krish and Laila . . . sleeping Laila. I think they're really impressed that we're being so quiet. Every time they look at us, I can feel Mum swelling up with pride. Krish is lost in the rippling reeds, rocking his body silently backwards and forwards on the bench.

There is a high-pitched squawk followed by an almighty clatter and now Krish is lying flat on his back on the floor. For a second, nobody says anything. Krish bites his lip, trying hard not to make any more noise. His eyes scan the hide from left to right as his skinny legs struggle to unravel themselves. He looks surprisingly like a startled baby bird, just fallen from its nest.

Nana starts laughing first, which makes Krish giggle, and all the people in the hide laugh too. There is a loud flapping of wings as birds take flight. The tears are rolling down our cheeks and my belly is starting to ache from laughing so hard. Dad helps Krish up off the floor, and we walk down the steps of Bittern Hide together. This time Nana insists that she walks by herself. Somehow, she looks stronger than when we arrived.

This has been the longest day. I don't think Nana wants this time in Suffolk ever to be over.

'No sign of the flycatchers yet then, Josie?' asks Dan as he helps her into the car.

Nana shakes her head sadly. 'I'm afraid I've missed out there, Dan.'

'I'll call you when they arrive, should I?'

'I really would love that,' Nana sighs, squeezing Dan's hand.

Dan walks away from the car with his head bowed to the ground. His sad shoulders remind me of Dusty Bird's.

The journey back to London is peaceful because Laila stays asleep; she likes the motion of the car. I sleep too for some of the way, and so does Nana. I wake first and watch her. She's resting her head on my shoulder, but every time the car jolts Nana knocks against my collarbone so I wrap my arm round her to make a cushion for her head.

She wakes up as we arrive in Hampstead. Dad takes a longer route to the hospice so he can drive past Nana's old house. Maybe he thought she would enjoy seeing the old place again, but when he stops outside, Nana turns away and stays silent all the way to the hospice. Dad keeps glancing at her through his mirror to check that she's all right. Her eyes look straight ahead of her, but I think she's actually seeing backwards in time. No one speaks, because it feels as if you would invade her thoughts.

A strange buzzing noise vibrates around the car, getting louder and louder. It takes me a while to realize that it's coming from my back pocket. That's one of the things I was going to do this weekend – sort out the ring tone. I flip open my mobile. Nana definitely shoots me her 'Do we really need that sort of interruption?' look, but this is my first-ever call so there's no way I'm not answering.

'Hi, Mira, how are you? How's your nana?'

'Oh, OK! Millie.'

'Not *her* again. She's in love with you,' teases Krish.

'Shut up! No, not you, Millie. It's just Krish being a pain again.'

He sticks his tongue out at me.

'Are you still in Suffolk?' she asks.

'We came back . . . We're going to the hospice with Nana . . . We're in the car right now, so I can't really talk. I'll be in school tomorrow.'

'Which hospital is it?'

'It's not a hospital. I'll explain tomorrow.'

'What is it that you can't say in front of all of us?' Nana interrupts in her stern, gravelly voice.

'Mira, I've done something maybe I shouldn't have,' says Millie, sounding nervous.

'What?' I try to sound like it's just a 'couldn't care less' 'what', because now everybody in the car is tuned in to my call.

'I was hanging out with Ben and apparently he told

Jidé you had a mobile . . . and Jidé got Ben to ask me if I had your number . . . so I gave it to him . . . I hope you don't mind.'

'Millie, I've got to go now,' I say.

'Oh! All right. See you tomorrow. Please say you don't mind. Do you?'

'No, I don't mind,' I say, flipping the lid of my pebble and trying to stop myself grinning from ear to ear like the Cheshire cat.

Dad says the hospice is quite a modern building, 1960s, but it looks older to me. It's in the middle of what Nana calls 'grand old Hampstead'.

There's a lady wearing a flowery headscarf at the reception desk, which looks a bit like the foyer of a hotel. Headscarf Lady asks our names and Dad introduces us.

'We are Josie, Sam, Uma, Mira, Krish and Laila Levenson.'

'Lovely names,' she says, ticking us off in her book and calling up to the ward on her intercom. 'The Levenson family have arrived,' she announces, as if we're all moving in. Headscarf Lady has long dangly earrings, the kind Nana wears, and bits of straggly orange hennaed hair, escaping from her scarf. She has grey eyes that smile at Nana, but her mouth doesn't move when she smiles.

'Would you like a daffodil badge?' she asks me.

'Thank you.'

She offers one to Krish, but he turns his nose up, so she hands him a chocolate football instead. She smiles when she notices his filthy hands. My brother's still covered in sand and mud from the beach.

'And what can I get for you, cutie?' she asks Laila, stroking her plum cheeks.

She rummages underneath her desk and brings out a tiny teddy bear wearing a red knitted jumper with 'London Hospice' embroidered on its tummy. Laila grabs hold of it, gurgles and graces Headscarf Lady with her widest grin. My baby sister has actually got an enormous mouth. When she cries, her jaw drops and her mouth opens out into this massive gaping tunnel in the middle of her face, but when she smiles it stretches the other way, from one ear to the other, lighting up her whole face. Nana says it's a bit of a comedy mouth. It makes Headscarf Lady laugh anyway.

We pass through some security doors into a hallway. At the end, there is a cafe and to the right of the cafe a sign says CHAPEL OF REST. In the hall there is a nurse in a white uniform waiting for the lift. The nurse waves at Laila and plays peekaboo behind her hand. She has lovely soft hands, with strong creamy varnished fingernails, smoothed with a file, not too long and not too short. Laila grabs at the nurse's hands to pull her fingers away from her eyes. She's giggling her head off, and making the nurse giggle too. Now Laila's fidgeting to get off Mum's hip and closer to the nurse.

'Come on then, little darlin'. You want to come up and play with Doris?'

Doris opens her arms and Laila literally jumps on top of her.

'It don't take *you* too long to make a friend,' laughs Doris. 'What's your name?'

'La La,' answers Laila.

Krish bursts out laughing. 'She *is* La La,' he says, putting a finger to his head and tapping his brain, as if to say, 'She's nuts.'

'Her name's Laila, and she usually has to be prised away from me,' Mum tells Doris.

'Babies love Doris. It's my round smiley face – they think I'm one of them.'

Looking at Doris's face, I can see what she means. She's got this soft dark brown skin that looks as if it's covered in a layer of baby cream, big brown eyes and no wrinkles. None. It's a baby face, but she must be about the same age as my mum.

A woman walks slowly towards us from the direction of the cafe. She has patchy, thin, dyed blonde hair, pink powder blush cheeks, and bright blue shimmer smeared all over her bulging eyes. She's a bit like an ancient china doll . . . and she's thin, like Nana. She's walking a dog on a lead, something like a police dog.

'Are dogs allowed in here then?' asks Nana, stroking its head.

'Why not?' shrugs Eyeshadow Lady. 'Thank God for small mercies,' she laughs. 'Have you got a dog?'

'Piper,' nods Nana, suddenly looking more relaxed.

'Oh goody, a friend for Lad!' exclaims Eyeshadow Lady. 'I'm Crystal,' she says, shaking Nana's hand.

'Josie.'

'Which ward are you on?' asks Crystal.

'Heath Ward.'

'Me and Lad too. We'll be dorm mates then!' Crystal smiles at Nana and squeezes her hand.

The lift arrives. There's not enough room for all of us.

'Race you upstairs,' shouts Krish. I think that's probably two things you should *not* do in a hospice, shout and run, but Doris doesn't seem to mind.

'Go on then, get after him,' encourages Nana. Krish gets there first, of course. Then we wait outside the lift.

The door opens. Somewhere between the first and third floor of the hospice Nana and Crystal seem to have become great friends. I don't know what the joke is, but Crystal and Nana are doubled over laughing and Laila is gurgling and pulling at Doris's tiny plaits.

'I can see I'm going to have fun with you two!' giggles Doris, in her warm velvety voice.

Crystal and Doris show Nana into the Women's Room. There are four beds on the ward. Doris steers

Nana to her bed by the window, which looks out on to the gardens. A great oak reaches its branches towards us.

'Best view in the house! Aren't you the lucky one!' jokes Crystal. She's working hard to make Nana feel at home – maybe a bit too hard, because she suddenly slumps down on her bed, her body collapsing like the stem of a droopy tulip.

'Come now, Crystal, get some rest.' Doris gently eases her into bed. 'You'll need all your energy for walking Lad later.'

Within a few minutes Crystal is asleep. Her make-up looks even worse now, like an ancient mask.

In the bed opposite Nana, there's an old lady with a pale, veiny face. Her head's propped up on her pillow and she's pretending to read the *Sun* newspaper, but I keep seeing her peering around it to get a closer look at us.

When Doris has settled Crystal into bed, she goes over and sits next to *Sun* Lady.

'Clara, can I introduce you to Josie and her family?' asks Doris.

Clara pretends that she's only just noticed us. She folds her paper carefully in two, as if it's something precious. Nana walks across to Clara, holding out her hand, but instead of shaking it Clara enfolds Nana's hands in hers, turning them over and inspecting them.

'Let me guess . . . soft and smooth, well looked

after . . . nothing manual.' Clara touches the sleeve of Nana's purple cotton Indian shirt and studies her white trousers and tiny beads – Nana calls them 'love beads'.

'Fashion designer?' guesses Clara.

Nana smiles and shakes her head.

'Writer then, or artist?'

'You got it!' smiles Nana.

'Your turn.' Clara offers Nana her hand. Clara's hands are rough and sore and swollen, like they've had a lifetime of work.

'I wouldn't like to say,' smiles Nana.

Then she does something very strange. She walks over to her bed and opens her toilet bag. She sits back down next to Clara, opens her tube of lavender hand cream and smoothes it over Clara's skin.

'Well?' asks Clara. 'What's the story of these hands?'

'Cleaning, scrubbing, washing . . . am I right?'

'Hole in one! In service to the great and the good, and the not so good, since I was fourteen years old.' Then she holds her hands up to her face and smells them. 'Fancy someone like you, rubbing cream into my rough old hands.'

'Someone like me?' Nana laughs and scowls at the same time.

'You know,' Clara says in her sharp little voice. 'Like one of them I clean for, like Madam over there.'

She nods over to Crystal, who is gently snoring in the bed opposite.

'I've never in my life had a cleaner. I make it my business to clean up my own mess, or live in it,' says Nana, slightly offended.

'I expect you do, though it's people like you that put me out of work. I wouldn't have minded cleaning for you.' Clara smiles.

I can't believe we've just arrived and Nana's getting to know people already. I wish I could make friends as easily as Nana. Until now, I've only had Millie, and Millie's got her orchestra friends, but me . . . I really just have Millie and . . . maybe Jidé Jackson.

Nana suddenly looks more tired than I have ever seen her before.

'Enough socializing now,' Doris says.

Doris seems to have a tiredness radar. She sees it too, that all Nana's energy has drained away. So we help her into bed; Nana takes a deep breath and her little body disappears under the bright, white sheets. I wish I could go back to Suffolk and wrap her in her own purple shawl.

Now I feel like the man in Suffolk who couldn't say goodbye. Somehow it doesn't feel right to leave Nana here. I can't stand the thought of her dying in this place without any of us with her. I know she's putting on a brave face as she waves us goodbye. Trying to make us feel better for leaving her here among strangers. As I look back at her from the door of the ward, she turns away from us towards the outstretched arms of the great oak outside her window.

By the time we get to the bottom floor, we are all blubbing. There is a tall man waiting to get into the lift who has sorry brown eyes that droop, like one of those St Bernard dogs. The man has messy dark brown hair flopping over his face. We are all a bit embarrassed because we are crying so much, that kind of messy crying where your nose streams with snot, and we haven't even got a tissue between us, so we try to hurry away but, just as we are about to leave, Headscarf Lady stops us.

'Ah! Clem, this is the Levenson family I was telling you about.'

My dad can't look up, but the man rests his hand on his arm and I see Dad's back heave. Then the man touches my brother's head, smiles at Mum, Laila and me, and steps into the lift.

'We'll talk tomorrow. My name's Clem,' he says, spreading his gentle smile over us like a warm breeze. I notice that his teeth are a bit crooked. Dad will like that. Clem bows his head towards the floor while he waits for the lift to close. Headscarf Lady offers us some tissues, which we take. She tells us that the man we have just met is Nana's consultant and that he's 'the most wonderful person'.

'In fact, I have to admit to being completely in love with him. If it wasn't for the small matter of him being married with four children and thirty years younger than me, I might be in with a chance. What do you think?'

Headscarf Lady has made us smile. A few minutes ago I thought that would never happen again.

'Have you had cancer?' Krish asks her.

Mum shoots him one of those, 'How *could* you?' stares, but Headscarf Lady just nods.

'Where was your cancer?' asks Krish.

'In my breast,' she answers calmly.

'My nana's started there.'

Because she doesn't know what else to say, Headscarf Lady rummages under her desk and finds us all another chocolate.

Friday 6 May

The first thing I do when I wake up is check my mobile again for messages. Still nothing, so before breakfast I make my deal with Notsurewho Not-surewhat. If the smoke alarm doesn't go off this morning, which would be a minor miracle, Jidé Jackson won't be in school today. It doesn't go off, and now I'm sorry I even had that stupid idea. What *is* the matter with me? I don't know why I make these ridiculous deals, because actually I would really like to see him, no matter how embarrassing it is, him asking for my number and then not calling.

When I get into school the first thing I find out is that Jidé and Ben are out playing in the second round of a football tournament. I suppose I asked for that.

'So why did he want my number, Millie?'

'Why do you think?' Millie grins. 'Ben asked me if I'd go to the end-of-Year-Seven disco with him.'

'What did you say?'

'Yes. I figure I might as well go with someone who's vaguely OK.'

'Do you like him then?'

'He's all right.'

'So you think Jidé's going to ask me?'

'Probably . . . and he was going on about some sort of student committee his mum wants us to get involved with . . . to improve the Rec. Ben's planning a skateboarding bit and Jidé's into football – now she says she needs a girl's perspective. I think he wants us to go round there after school one day.'

Whatever the reason, I won't find out why Jidé asked for my number till Monday, unless Notsurewho Notsurewhat can intervene on my behalf and make him ring me over the weekend.

We arrive at the hospice at about 4.30 p.m. for a 'family conference' with Dr Clem and the nurses who are going to look after Nana Josie. The whole family is gathered, everyone except Laila, who's at her first ever play date. As we settle ourselves, Clara and Crystal sit up in their beds as if this is their business too.

The doctor – we have to call him 'Clem' – says they will need to try out different drugs to take away Nana's pain. He says it might take them a little while to adjust the medicines so Nana doesn't feel pain any more, but eventually, he can assure us, they will get it right. Dr Clem explains that Nana has an appointment this morning at the hospital to have a 'procedure' to get her lungs drained, because they are filling with liquid, like drowning.

Doris pulls the curtain around Nana's bed so she can help her into her clothes.

'That's right, Josie, nice and slow, no hurry now.'

I can see Nana's bony ankles, like a sparrow's legs, below the lime-green curtain. Then suddenly I hear her breathing change.

'I can't do this any more . . . I can't . . . I can't breathe . . .' Nana gasps.

I see the little birds from my dream, battering their wings against the glass.

I would like to rip open the curtain and hug Nana, but that soft material might as well be a sealed brick wall. She's in a private world with a strange new family now.

A man nurse approaches silently. His body is twisted as if something is weighing him down. And he has these eyes that look like he can understand exactly how you feel. I read the name on his label, 'Mark'. That's exactly what he looks like, a question mark. He's small with sandy brown hair and watery blue eyes, too big for the size of his face, but what you really notice about him is his way of looking. Most people look out of their eyes to see things, but Question Mark's eyes seem to drink in feelings. He glances down at me and smiles, holds the curtains back for Dr Clem and quietly they walk in together.

'He's special, that one,' Clara tells me, nodding in the direction of Question Mark. Looking under the curtain I can understand how Question Mark is so light-footed. He's wearing sheepskin slippers. Nana's feet have disappeared from the floor. I can hear her voice mingling with Doris's and Dr Clem's . . . liquid voices flowing into each other.

Doris opens the curtains and there she is, my Nana Josie, sitting up in bed, with a weak smile on her face.

Even though I'm not wearing my watch something strange is definitely happening to time. It's as if we've stepped out of it.

Nana has an oxygen mask over her mouth and she's leaning back on her pillow. Dr Clem and Question Mark pull chairs up to Nana's bed and ask everyone to sit down. Dr Clem sits next to Nana Josie, leaning into the bed but resting one foot, to steady himself, on the floor. That's how he sits with patients, as if to say, 'I'm on your side.'

'Josie has asked me to speak to you.' Dr Clem's warm smile spreads over us again.

Nana Josie lifts her head up and nods encouragingly to Dr Clem, as if she has given him her blessing.

'As you have probably gathered, we tried to move Josie just now, and she became very anxious. She's in a state of exhaustion, but she has managed to tell us

130

what she wants, or rather, what she doesn't want.'

Dr Clem takes a deep breath, as if he's gathering the courage to speak.

'The purpose of the procedure we were planning was to ease Josie's breathing. It would certainly give her more time, but after a short while the fluid on her lungs would only build up again.'

Like drowning.

Dr Clem speaks very slowly, as if he's rehearsing what he's saying in his head, before he actually speaks.

'Josie has decided that, now that she's here, she doesn't want to be moved out of the hospice.'

Dr Clem pauses, looking around at each member of the family, in case we want to ask him anything, but no one says a word. Nana Josie lifts her arm and pats him on the shoulder. Something has changed. Now Nana doesn't look worried any more. Even so, for the whole meeting, my dad sits with his head practically on his knees as everyone else listens to Dr Clem. Krish even puts his hand up as if he's in class and asks Nana straight out, 'Do you actually want to die now, Nana?'

She just looks at him, in a kind way, and turns to Dr Clem.

'She doesn't want any more pain, and that's what we can do for her here in the hospice, make sure she has no more pain,' explains Dr Clem, taking hold of Krish's hand.

Nana nods. She looks like she's about to cry and so does Dr Clem, but instead he takes a deep breath and carries on. He tells us that the pain relief will make Nana sleep more and that she might have very strong dreams. He says we can come to the hospice whenever we want. All the time he's talking, Dr Clem is trying to get my dad to look at him and after the meeting he takes Dad by the shoulder and leads him out of the ward. They sit in a room at the end of the corridor, talking. By the time Dad comes out he looks better, more settled.

So here we are, my dad and me, holding Nana's hands and watching her sleep. Now it's my turn to cry. Dad strokes my hair as Nana sleeps.

'I'm not sure I agree with all this,' Crystal pipes up, pointing vaguely in my direction. 'Is it really necessary to drag the children through it?'

I don't know who Crystal's talking to. Some adults do that, talk about you as if you aren't in the room. She doesn't really talk to Clara. I don't think they like each other much, so I suppose she must be talking to Dad, but he's miles away, lost in his own thoughts. To answer, Clara shoots Crystal a stony look and reaches out to me. Something about her thin veiny arms re- minds me of the oak outside the window, stretching its gnarly branches towards us.

Saturday 7 May

No sign of Notsurewho Notsurewhat.

No call from Jidé Jackson.

Crystal is still 'beautifying' herself, applying her bright blue eyeshadow and pink dolly cheeks.

'You've caught me putting on my mask!' she jokes.

'When do you *ever* take it off?' snaps Clara.

Crystal ignores her, as usual, patting the covers on the bed for me to sit down next to her. I think it might be rude not to, so I do. She whispers to me so that Clara can't hear.

'I've been looking after myself like this since I was about your age. You've got good skin too,' she says, touching my cheek.

It's a good job my spot has disappeared, as mysteriously as it arrived.

'I used to have smooth skin like yours . . . Plenty of young men will want to kiss you.' She squeezes my cheek. I feel myself turning bright red. I hate it when people do that, as if you're a pet.

'Still, my time passed long ago – there's nothing for it but to make the best of it,' she sighs, puffing white powder on top of her pink blusher.

I can't think of what to say to Crystal so I smile politely and say nothing, remembering what Mum always says: 'If you can't think of anything kind to say to someone, don't say anything at all.' I think Crystal wants me to say that she still looks good, but there is no way I could bring myself to say anything like that without blushing bright red and revealing to the whole world that I was lying.

I think Clara and Nana must have been chatting in the night, because when they sit up in bed they smile at each other like old friends, even though it might look from the outside as if they wouldn't have much in common. For a start, it's Clara's clothes – she wears this long flowery nightie that stops just above her knee. These are the sort of old ladies' clothes they sell in Blustons in Kentish Town. Whenever we used to pass that shop, Nana would say how much she loved the name, because it conjures up the image of 'blouses on bustling old ladies, squeezing on to buses'. When we walk past Blustons, Krish stares through the shop window at the models with enormous bosoms advertising their bras. Clara is definitely wearing a Blustons nightie, but it's about three sizes too big for her. I wonder whether she was once actually quite, what Nana calls, 'Blustony'. Whatever Clara used to look like, now she is thin, like Nana. Clara mutters to herself from time to time, saying things like, 'Bloody awful business this . . . Can you get me out of here?'

She asks me that when I'm passing her bed, and she makes me feel sorry I can't help her, but, as Doris keeps trying to explain: 'Nobody's keeping you here, Clara, my dear, it's just we want to make sure you're looked after.'

Clara doesn't have any visitors.

'I don't want to bother them – my boy's got his own life to get on with,' Clara tells us, then she goes back to chanting, 'Bloody awful business this . . . Can you get me out of here?'

Sometimes, when we're all crowded around Nana Josie's bed, I see this look cross Clara's face, like she wishes someone would go over and talk to her. She loves Piper, and he loves her. From time to time he jumps on to her bed and she makes 'a right old fuss of him'. You can hear her muttering. 'Piper, good sort, isn't he, Josie?'

Crystal takes this personally, as Clara doesn't seem to pay any attention at all to Lad. Sometimes Clara adds, under her breath (just to annoy Crystal, I think), 'Never been fond of big dogs.'

The only reason that Crystal, Clara and Nana Josie are together in this room is because of cancer. I sometimes dream that cancer is like a monster's shadow and I try to fight it, but it's not even solid enough to kick or punch. I walk all around it, trying to find a way to scream at it to get out of my nana, but it doesn't have a face or eyes. I don't really know how to kill it, so I just shout at it really loudly until I wake myself up. I have this dream quite a lot since Nana got ill.

There is a Therapist Lady downstairs in the hospice where you can go to draw pictures of how you feel. She asked me and Krish if we wanted to see her room. Krish didn't want to. Her room has children's pictures all over the walls, bean bags on the floor and paints and crayons everywhere. I drew her my dream of the monster's shadow in dark smudgy charcoaly shadows. She said that my dream is my way of facing my fears. I just think that cancer is very, very frightening if you're asleep or awake, but Nana says that one day, probably in my lifetime, they will find a way to kill it off.

When I tell Nana about the therapist, she explains to me that the hospice looks after people in all kinds of pain. She says that some people are in pain because their hearts are breaking and they are about to lose the people they love.

'Like us,' I whisper.

Nana nods.

'Can your heart actually break, Nana?'

'That's what we call it, Mira, but it doesn't exactly

"break". It's something more complicated than that – it's more like a sore than a break. When the wound is raw, it feels like it will never heal. I think that's why they call it a break.'

'Has that ever happened to you?' I ask Nana.

'Oh yes.'

'Can you fix it then, a broken heart?'

'No, that's what I mean. It's not as simple as that. It sort of heals over in time, but it always leaves a scar. Each time you get hurt, you put a little protective layer round the wound, like a bandage, so that the next time you can't be damaged quite so easily. Remember the artichoke leaves?'

I nod. 'What does it feel like, Nana?'

'Hard to say. There are so many different kinds of heartbreak.'

'How many?'

'Let me think . . . Ah yes! If you draw the most beautiful picture for someone and you put all your energy and love and imagination into it, and then you give it to the person and later you find it in a bin. It's called rejection, as if they've thrown a little bit of you away.'

Nana always does that – if she's describing something complicated, she gives you examples of things she knows you'll understand, but even since my birthday Nana doesn't know how much I've changed. How can she even start to guess at how much more I know

now? She's thinking about the time when a teacher told me that the poem I wrote about India was all wrong and I had to start again because it wasn't what she'd asked for. I had researched it in the library the night before, and asked Grandad Bimal to describe the place where he was born. So when Miss Fallow threw it in the bin it was a bit like she was throwing a part of me away too.

Nana could see how upset I was so she got her famous poet friend to read it, and he wrote me a note to tell me how much he liked it, and a note for Miss Fallow too. Then Nana marched into school with Piper by her side and stood outside the classroom till Miss Fallow came out.

'A poet friend of mine has made a dedication to you. Would you like to read it? It's very short,' Nana announced, without waiting for an answer.

Then she thrust the poem in front of Miss Fallow, who blushed bright red and did not look very happy. The poem said:

Dear Miss Fallow
Feel it in the marrow
Poems aren't wrong!

Miss Fallow just looked at Piper and announced, 'Dogs aren't allowed in school.'

'Neither are bullies,' Nana shot back, stomping off

down the corridor with her nose in the air. My nana doesn't do rules.

She says it's the parents' and grandparents' job to protect children's hearts.

'What if their parents are dead?' The question is out before I can think about what I'm asking.

'Your parents aren't going to die, Mira . . . not for a long time.'

Nana thinks I'm worrying about myself. Since I decided to keep my period a secret, it's easier not to tell other things too. I always used to tell Nana exactly what I was thinking about and she would always have an opinion. But Nana doesn't know everything about me any more, and something about the way she's looking at me, right at this very moment, makes me think she knows that I'm holding a little part of me back from her.

'Nana, some people at school think I shouldn't see you so much, when you're dying,' I say to avoid her piercing look.

'That's the wrong kind of protection, Mira. This is a necessary heartbreak.'

'What do you mean?'

'When you've loved someone and you have to say goodbye, there's no avoiding it, but about Miss Fallow . . . tell me, when you do something like that now, a poem or a painting, would you show it to her again?'

'I would know the kind of person to show it to. I'd let Pat Print see it . . . I would trust her. It wouldn't bother me now if Miss Fallow liked it or not.'

'Aha! You see. You've wrapped a little protective layer round your heart, like the leaves of the artichoke charm. Who's this Pat Print anyway?'

'A writer. She's doing these workshops at in my school . . .'

But Nana's not listening to me any more. Looking at her as she drifts off to sleep, I realize that she thinks I'm so much younger than I am. What she doesn't realize is that Miss Fallow and the poem . . . that is so in the past. The truth is right now I don't know if I want to see my nana slowly fading away like this. Is this . . . a necessary heartbreak?

Sunday 8 May

Still no call from Jidé Jackson.

I am starting to lose faith in Notsurewho Notsurewhat.

Just as I arrived at the hospice today, Nana's eyes were growing heavy. She told me yesterday that when she nods off it feels like she's stepping off a mountain and falling, but it's not a horrible feeling; she says it's a bit like floating. I thought of the reed beds and the swaying golden grasses as her head rocked back on to her pillow. I have been sitting here for nearly an hour just watching Nana sleep.

She's wearing my favourite orange cheesecloth top. It has sequins round the neck and little ties with bells. Her body is the size of a skinny child. Nana's arms are more like Laila's when she was a newborn, as if they need stuffing with something, to fill the loose skin. I am bigger than my nana now, taller and more solid.

Mum and Krish wander along the corridor to the

Family Room to make some tea. I don't like it in there because you always see someone crying, and when they see you they pretend they're making a cup of tea, or getting something out of the fridge, which is always empty, except for Nana's health food. But there is a television in there, which Krish loves, and some toys and books, which Laila loves, so you can sort of use it like your own living room. You can even sleep there if you want. People do.

I look at Nana and find myself wondering for the first time in my life what I will have to say to her when she wakes up. I suppose I could ask her about Rwanda and she would definitely know, and she would definitely have an opinion, and if I told her about him she would want to know everything that I know about Jidé Jackson. I walk over to the window and look out on to the street.

'What's going on in the outside world?' asks Nana, jolting me back to her. 'Be my eyes, Mira.'

'Nothing much . . . There's a woman walking her dog.'

As she gets closer, I recognize her. It's Pat Print and Moses. This is starting to freak me out.

'What's so interesting?' asks Nana, propping herself up on her pillow, to get a better view of the street.

'It's that writer woman I was telling you about, from school.'

As she walks further down the street, Nana props

herself up to get a closer look.

'That's Mo.' Nana points to Moses. 'Piper and Mo are great pals.'

'Do you know her then, Nana?'

Nana studies Pat Print's back for a while as she makes her way up the road.

'I suppose I might have seen her about the place – she looks vaguely familiar – but it's a young girl with two or three dogs who walks Mo.'

So, instead of asking Nana about Rwanda I tell her about Pat Print's writing class and seeing her in Suffolk, on the beach . . . and what Millie found out about her ancestor actually having Robert the Something's heart locked up in a box . . . and Millie's ancestor being the only one with a key.

'The guardian of the heart . . . she's a good friend to have,' smiles Nana as Pat Print disappears round the corner at the end of the road.

'It's a bit weird, don't you think, Nana? That I keep seeing her, the writer woman?'

'Perhaps she's your guardian angel. Or, more likely, me and her, we just walk the same paths!' Nana says, winking at me.

Monday 9 May

I wake up to the smell of burning toast and the screech of the smoke alarm. Feeling more tired than I did when I went to bed, I wander downstairs in my pyjamas checking my phone for . . . nothing.

'Come on, Mira, stop messing around with that now, you'll be late for school.' Mum hurries me along on her morning conveyor belt of making sandwiches, breakfasts and attempting to get us all out of the door on time. There is no room in this well-rehearsed schedule for me to arrive downstairs in my pyjamas at 8.30 a.m.

'I don't feel well, Mum.'

'Neither do I,' moans Krish.

'You're fine, Krish. You've just eaten three rounds of toast. Do you want anything to eat, Mira?'

I hold my belly as if it's hurting and shake my head, even though my stomach is rumbling loud enough for everyone to hear.

'Go on then. You'd better go back up to bed. I'll

come and take your temperature when I've got Krish off to school.'

'Why don't you take it now? Then you'll see she's faking.'

I pinch Krish hard on the arm as I pass him on the stairs.

'Awwwww!' he yelps. 'That really hurt.'

'He's just faking it, Mum,' I say, sneering at him.

'Off to bed with you then.' Mum whisks me off, tea towel flapping.

The letterbox clanks. I hear Mum telling Millie I'm not going in and the door closing behind her. Now I feel guilty. I think about getting dressed and running into school after Millie, but it's too late.

I am bored and hungry and all Mum has given me to eat is dry toast, bread sticks and water. She says that should settle my stomach. Even though Grandad Bimal's a doctor, she hates people being ill. Whenever I'm off sick I always remember, too late, that you don't get much sympathy when you're ill with Mum. It's just not worth it. Some people get to sit in front of the TV all day, being served up drinks and bits and pieces of delicious food. Not with my mum. You have to stay in your room and read or sleep. You're much better off being ill when Dad's around.

I'm lying in bed trying not to think of food and

thinking how embarrassing it's going to be seeing Jidé tomorrow, because he *still* hasn't called, and this is the exact moment that a message jumps into my inbox. Just when I'd given up on Notsurewho Notsurewhat.

Mira, sorry you're ill.
Hope you're in tomorrow.
See you.
JJ x

That's only ten words, but it takes me the rest of the afternoon of staring at his text to try to work out exactly what it means. I wonder how long it took him to write, because it takes me about three hours to write this reply . . .

Jidé, I'm much better thanks.
I'll be back tomorrow.
See you.
Mira x

I spend at least fifteen minutes adding and removing the x before I finally press the send button with the x in place.

Suddenly my belly rumbles, demanding to be fed. As soon as I hear Mum and Laila leave to pick up Krish from school, I sneak downstairs and rummage around for something to eat. Before I can hide, Mum's back in the room, heading straight for the cupboard I've still got my head stuck inside.

'Forgot a snack for Krish,' she says, removing the packet of KitKats from my hand. 'Hungry?'

I nod.

'Good, then you can go back to school tomorrow.'

And off she goes, slamming the door behind her and bumping Laila's pram down our front steps. I think Mum's got a sickness/wellness radar. I bet she knew I was faking it, all along. As soon as she's gone, I sprint upstairs at the sound of another message jumping into my inbox.

Great!
JJ xx

Just that one word and those two kisses make me want to laugh out loud. By the time Mum comes in I still haven't managed to wipe the stupid grin off my face.

'Well, *you* definitely look better,' smiles Mum.

'I knew she was faking it,' mumbles Krish, pushing past me on the stairs.

Tuesday 10 May

Run, Mira, run! Faster! I can feel my legs stretched to snapping point, but all the time they are gaining on me, the usual suspects, Demi, Bo and Orla. Around the trees in what is supposed to be our 'oh so safe world' of the Year Seven courtyard, I trip over the loose wood chippings and, as I stumble, they stampede.

Demi grabs hold of my hair and pulls me roughly to the woodland corner of the courtyard.

'You can stay right here, creep. Don't you dare move off this spot, even when the bell goes, or we'll have you,' Demi whispers in my ear, and walks away laughing.

The bell rings. If only Millie wasn't at the dentist's. If she was here, she wouldn't let them get away with this. But she's not here, so I do exactly what I've been ordered to do, like a frightened rabbit caught in the headlights, and before I know what's happening the last person in the world I would want to see me like this is standing right in front of me.

'What *are* you doing?' asks Jidé, staring at me as if I've gone completely mad. This is so *not* how it was supposed to be, between me and Jidé today.

'Demi . . . she told me if . . . well . . . she just told me I wasn't allowed to move,' I mumble.

Suddenly, I see myself through Jidé's eyes. I feel like such an idiot. What *am* I doing? All the things he knows about . . . what must have happened to his family . . . what could have happened to him . . . He must think I'm pathetic.

'What's stopping you leaving? There's no one here, nothing in your way.' Jidé strikes his hand up and down through the air.

I bet he wonders why he even bothered texting me now.

'If you stand up to them,' says Jidé, 'they'll stop.'

I have never felt so humiliated in my whole life and, by the time we get to the classroom, I'm wearing the bright red blush of shame on my face, like a beacon of embarrassment. I hang my head as Miss Poplar launches into her topic on drugs and alcohol. She says that the only drugs you should take are what the doctor gives you, if you're ill, to make you better. As I sit there listening to Miss Poplar talk about a subject that I probably know more about than anyone else in this class, because of what Nana's going through, it feels as if my blood is literally starting to boil up in me.

'They don't always make you better. My Nana Josie's got cancer and she has drugs to stop her pain, but they won't make her better.'

It's my voice I hear saying these words.

Miss Poplar is staring at me. I know it's because she never expects me to say anything at all in class and the way that came out was all wrong. I mean, I can just about talk like that in Pat Print's class, but what was I thinking of? In front of this lot. I might as well have offered them my head on a plate. Whenever I say anything in class, Demi rolls her eyes up, to make me nervous. It's always worked until today.

'You're right, Mira. This is a very complicated issue. Of course when it comes to pain relief that's different.'

Jidé's eyes are burning into me.

'She's different,' Demi whispers under her breath, rolling her eyes into the back of her head to look like a zombie . . . and that's the moment when something inside me sparks and the words flare up and spread around the room like a raging fire.

'Stop it! Just stop! I don't know what you get out of being so vile to me, but you'll have to find someone else to pick on. I hope you never have to watch someone you love dying right in front of you, because the way you carry on you'd better hope there's no such thing as bad karma . . . because you lot have got it coming!'

As soon as it's out, I cover my mouth with my hands in case anything else escapes. Where did that come from? I don't really know what happens to me when I get this angry, because I've never felt like this before. The whole class is stunned into silence and Miss Poplar is gawping at me as if I'm a total stranger.

'Who exactly are you talking about, Mira?'

'Demi, Bo and Orla,' I say in the clearest and loudest voice I can find.

I have never seen Miss Poplar look so stern.

'You three, to my office, right now. The rest of you get on with some reading. I'll be sending someone in to sit with you in a minute,' she barks at the rest of the class. 'Mira, come and see me at the end of the lesson, please,' she says in a tone you would use to comfort a wounded animal.

The tears are stinging my eyes now, so I keep my head low as they file out of the room. There is silence. The kind of silence that until now I've only ever felt at school in Pat Print's class. I hear someone get up, walk towards me and sit down in Millie's empty seat. It's Jidé. I daren't look up in case he sees me crying.

When I come out of Miss Poplar's office, I feel taller than I did when I went in. Walking between lessons, where you have to criss-cross the school with the thousand or so other giant-sized people, is usually the bit I dread most about my day. Most days when I make this journey, I concentrate as hard as I can on becoming invisible, but not today. It's as if I'm seeing this school and all the kids who come here for the very first time . . . and some are taller than me, and some are smaller, but they all have a human face. As I walk through the crowded corridor, I feel a buzz in my pocket, so I duck into the nearest loo, locking the door behind me.

That was brave.
See you later.
JJ xxx

Three kisses. I think about texting him back, but it would probably take me hours, and I'm already late for French so I close my phone, check myself out in the mirror, concentrating hard on losing my 'Jidé Jackson just texted me three kisses face', and walk into French.

'*Tu es en retard, Mira.*'

'I've got a note, miss,' I say, showing her the note from Miss Poplar explaining why I'm late.

Answering Jidé's text is just about all I can think of through what's left of French. As I leave the classroom, I catch sight of him across the language corridor as he comes out of Spanish. I blush just about the most ridiculous colour crimson that I've ever turned. He grins at me, and I, without being able to stop myself, grin back, before being mercifully swept away on a sea of bodies. I duck into the toilets again to text him this.

Thank you.
Mira xxxx

It took me all of French to pluck up the courage to send those four kisses. Well, I suppose French *is* supposed to be the language of love.

By lunchtime Millie's back, wearing her new brace. We sit on the high wall and I tell her about the shame of Jidé finding out what a coward I am, and my explosion in Miss Poplar's class.

'Sounds like I missed all the action, but I wouldn't worry . . . he probably liked playing the hero to your damsel in distress!' teases Millie.

'I don't think so.'

'So why did he want your number then?'

'I dunno, because he hasn't called.'

Strictly speaking that's not a lie. Who am I kidding? I am even lying to my best friend now. What is going on with me? Why can't I just tell Millie the truth?

'Here comes trouble,' scowls Millie, as Demi and Bo stroll towards us.

I feel my whole body tense up. In a minute I'll know if they're going to take their revenge, but they just keep on walking without even glancing up at us.

'Result!' grins Millie, shaking my hand.

'All right, Mira?' mumbles Orla as she trails along behind the others.

'All right,' I say.

Wednesday 11 May

The phone rings.

'Will *someone* please pick that up,' shouts Dad.

'I'm in the bathroom. Mira, can you pick it up or they'll ring off,' yells Mum.

I don't know why they even bother. It's always me who answers the phone anyway. Krish won't, because it makes him nervous.

'Hi! Millie . . . Poor you! Does it really hurt? . . . OK, I'll tell her . . . Yep, I'll call you later.'

'Who was that?' asks Mum, carrying Laila, all cosied up in a towel, down the stairs.

'Millie. Her teeth are hurting. It's her new brace giving her headaches. She's having the day off. Can I go and see her after school?'

'If you like, but be back by five and take your mobile,' Mum says, trying to be relaxed about everything, but then she blows it. 'Do you want me to walk you in to your writing group, if Millie's not coming?'

'No, Mum. I'm fine on my own.'

Pat Print walks ahead of me through the great metal gates. When she spots me, she stops and waits.

'How was the rest of your stay? I nearly got blown off that beach.'

'Fine.'

So she really was there. We walk along in silence for a minute or so.

'How's your nana?'

'In the hospice.'

'I see.'

'She knows Moses,' I tell Pat Print.

'Who does?'

'Nana. We saw you walking him. We could see you from her room in the hospice. She thinks Piper and Moses know each other.'

'Now I think of it, I've heard Tilly talk about a "Piper". Tilly walks Moses on weekdays, mostly. I just don't have the time. Strange I've never bumped into your nana on one of my Suffolk jaunts though . . . So she's in the Marie Curie. That's just behind my flat. She'll be well looked after there,' she says, touching me on the shoulder in her awkward, trying-to-be-comforting way.

'Millie can't come today. She's got a new brace and her teeth are aching,' I explain, changing the subject.

'Ouch! Poor Millie, but I don't see why everyone's got to have such perfect teeth these days. It's all part of this gruesome path we're all supposed to follow to physical perfection.'

Pat Print and my dad have this much in common.

'Well, you'll have to fill her in. And then there were . . . three,' Pat counts, walking into the classroom where Jidé and Ben are sprawled out over their desks as if they would rather be in bed. Ben's wearing his baseball cap today.

'Great cap,' says Pat Print, pulling the brim down over Ben's eyes and making him squirm.

She takes off her coat. It's one of those green wax things Nana wears in Suffolk – you hardly ever see anyone wearing one in London.

'Where's Moses?' asks Ben.

'I got the impression dogs aren't allowed in school. So I've left him at home today.'

'Ohhh!' groans Ben.

'Have you got any pets?' asks Pat.

'Mum won't let me. She thinks they're filthy.'

'She's got a point!'

Before I can think of what's happening I hear Nana's words escape from my mouth, 'With love comes cack.'

Now Pat Print, Jidé and Ben are all rolling around in hysterics. Pat finally calms down enough to ask, 'Who says that?'

'Nana Josie.'

I can't believe I let that out.

'I'm tempted to steal that for the title of my next book!'

Pat Print can see that I've blushed up bright red, so she tries to change the subject. 'Now . . . what have you got for me, Jidé?'

I want to talk to Jidé, I want to ask him so many questions about Rwanda, but if I ever did he would know I'd been spying on him and what would he think of me, for wanting to know?

'I've written the beginning of my book,' he says.

'Is that all?' laughs Pat, rubbing her hands together. 'Let's have it then.'

Jidé starts to read:

He could imagine the heat and the red-brown soil, but he could not remember it. When he looked in the mirror he could imagine what his mother and his father looked like. He often wondered whose eyes he had, whose nose, whose mouth, whose skin, whose voice his sounded like, but he knew that there was no way he was ever going to find out. He didn't want people to feel sorry for him, because he was one of the lucky ones. You hadn't watched his body on the nine o'clock news floating down the river of corpses. If you had known them, you might have caught sight of his parents though. But would you have recognized them as human beings, or just a mass of disconnected limbs? If your past is hell – where only by an act of good luck . . . God . . . whatever you believe in . . . only you'd survived – why would you look back? You can have too much history when you're only twelve years old.

That's why he always looked tough, joked about, or played the fool, because although he didn't know the 'derivation' of his name, at least he was alive.

Pat Print takes off her glasses and wipes her eyes. She's not a crier like my mum, but when Jidé has finished she stays quiet, looking straight at him and nodding her head as if to say 'that's right'. Her silence is full of respect. You don't often get that feeling between teachers and students.

My eyes are also brimming over with tears. I stare at the ground so that nobody notices, but I feel Jidé glance my way and I want him to know that I care, so I force myself to look up into his eyes. We hold each other there for what seems like forever until he nods, releasing me from the spell of his gaze.

'Jidé, it wouldn't surprise me if I were to read that opening in a prize-winning novel. You should write on,' she says, smiling at him.

Then she turns to Ben and me.

'I would like you both to pick a line or an idea from Jidé's writing that stood out for you . . . Ben?'

'I like the last line, where he explains why he's a joker. Before today I didn't think there was much behind that.'

Jidé shrugs.

'There's always something behind a character. Reasons people behave the way they do,' says Pat. 'How about you, Mira?'

I can feel Jidé's eyes on me, waiting for me to speak.

'The line about "You can have too much history when you're only twelve years old" . . . because it made me think . . . it made me feel . . . that you don't really know anything about anyone. I thought Jidé was born here, I didn't know anything about Rwanda, or about him, until this writing group. You think you know the people in your class, where they come from, but you just don't. It's the same with Nana; I thought I knew her, but I only know a tiny bit of her.'

'Maybe you're not supposed to know,' says Jidé, with his eyes fixed on me.

'If you don't know, how do you ever really get to understand another person?' asks Pat.

'Maybe you only see the sides of them they *want* you to see,' answers Ben, patting Jidé on the back.

'That's an astute observation. Have you written anything for me this week, Ben?' asks Pat.

'Not much,' Ben mumbles. 'Nothing serious, like Jidé's, just something about skateboarding. It's more of a poem really . . . or song lyrics.'

'Let's have it then.'

Ben fixes up his baseball cap and begins, quietly for him, as though he's embarrassed by his own writing.

On Saturdays I go up the Palace with my skateboard,
 meet my mates.
On Saturdays I wear my skate gear, like my mates.
No helmets,
caps turned back to front.
No knee pads, bloody scabs instead.
We watch the graffiti artist 'O' spray his purple tag on
 the wall where you're allowed
And the wall where you're not,
Then we go flying, zipping, twisting mid air.

On Saturdays I go flying
on my skateboard
with my mates.

Pat Print claps. 'Excellent, Ben Gbemi with a silent G. You're a performance poet.'

Ben hides his grin under the low brim of his cap.

'Now, Mira, what have you got for me?'

'Some more of my diary, if you want.'

'I most certainly do want.' Pat Print smiles.

I flick through, trying to find something I want to read. I don't feel like reading about Nana, or the hospice, so I pick out yesterday in the classroom. Just the thought of it makes me feel stronger.

'Stop it! Just stop! I don't know what you get out of being so vile to me, but you'll have to find someone else to pick on.'

I can feel Jidé's eyes on me. When I finish reading, I look up at him and smile. He should know it's because of him that I summoned the courage to face up to Demi, Bo and Orla.

'School can be a brutal place,' agrees Pat. 'I remember from my own school days; I hated it so much I was always playing truant, but you only need one or two true friends to change everything. I was thinking, as you've all been brave enough to read out your own work, I should probably read you something of mine. Mira's already had a sneak preview of this one. I can tell you, it's certainly no better than your writing.'

'What's it about?' asks Ben.

Pat Print thinks for a moment. 'I suppose it's about loyalty . . . Now, where are my specs?' She rummages in her satchel for her glasses, which hover halfway down her nose. She leafs through her book with great care, as if she's looking for a particular moment. Then she peers at me from under her glasses, smiles and begins to read.

There should be a moment when you decide enough is enough, and you can seriously have enough of being smacked on the back of the legs with a wide metal ruler because you can't remember what twelve times eight is. Can you remember? Too long. Thwack. That's how long you got. But there was no single defining moment. It was just one ordinary drizzly day of quiet torture that made me walk

through my school gates mid-morning. It was the ordinari-
ness of it all . . . the once-too-often wound that made me lift
the latch and walk free, out on to the open moorland. That
day I made a promise to myself never again to go back to
school. I don't remember how many hours I walked before I
came to the beck. That's when I saw it . . . a picnic basket
washed up on the riverbank. My first thoughts were of bull-
rushes and Sunday school but, when I opened the hamper
lid, there, lying curled up in a mole-like ball, was the small
brown form of my first dog. I called him Moses for obvious
reasons.

The bell rings and Pat Print closes her book straight
away, as if she can't wait to stop reading. I think she's
still shy! She rummages in her satchel and pulls out
three copies of her book, handing them around.

'I've called every dog I've ever had by that name . . .
just a whim.'

'Would you sign it?' I ask her.

She nods. I can tell she's pleased.

'Can I take one for Millie too?'

In mine she writes: To Mira. Schooldays are not the
best days of everyone's life! Love, Pat Print. In Millie's she
writes: To Millie, a loyal friend, with love, Pat Print.

As soon as she writes that I feel a pang of guilt.
Millie Lockhart has always been my most loyal friend.
Why can't I just be honest with her about Jidé? It's
not like there's much to tell anyway. Tonight, I think.

If she asks me about Jidé, I'll tell her about the texts.

Pat Print peers over her glasses at Jidé and Ben. They are hovering in an awkward place between not wanting to miss out, or look too keen. Eventually, Ben thrusts his book in front of Pat without saying anything at all. She smiles to herself.

In Ben's she writes: *To Ben, for whom the bell tolls, with love, Pat Print.*

'What's that supposed to mean?' asks Ben.

'It's just another great book you should read.'

Ben groans.

Last, it's Jidé's turn. Pat's pen pauses for a moment over the page before she decides what to write . . . *To Jidé, a brave and fearsome warrior, with a heart of gold, with love, Pat Print.*

No matter how hard he tries to look like he doesn't care what she's written, Jidé has a smile curling at the corner of his mouth, a smile that I can't help but wear too until it's wiped off my face by the sight of my dad, of all people, coming out of Miss Poplar's office. He thinks I haven't seen him as he makes a swift exit out of the side door. A deep well of sadness starts to swirl in the pit of my belly, but I still it with this thought . . . if Nana has died while I've been at school today, he would be taking me home right now.

'Pat, have you got a minute?' Miss Poplar calls to Pat Print down the corridor. She is not her usual cheery self.

I watch them for a moment. Pat Print looks serious, glancing nervously back to the classroom we've just been in. She nods her head at whatever Miss Poplar's talking about, but when Pat Print starts to talk Miss Poplar keeps interrupting her. Even from this distance you can tell by the way their hands dance around that the conversation is getting quite heated.

I pass Miss Poplar in the corridor before break, and she just smiles at me and walks straight past. I want to ask her why my dad was in her office, but as she hasn't said anything I think maybe I'm not supposed to know.

At break, I sit on the wall on my own. Nobody bothers me until Jidé walks over to join me.

'Want to hang with Ben and me?'

I nod and we walk over to the bench where Ben's dealing out three piles of Simpson's Top Trumps. I can't believe he's still playing this, but Jidé and Ben laugh as they exchange 'Huggability' scores. In primary school they used to play car Top Trumps so I suppose they have moved on, a bit. Any kind of Top Trumps is, as far as I can see, a completely pointless waste of time, but I am grateful, all the same, to Jidé, for asking me over because nothing makes you more likely to be picked on than being on your own.

*

After school I drop by Millie's and give her Pat Print's book.

'So what happened today?'

'Nothing much.'

'What did you talk about with Pat?'

'We read out our writing . . . Ben did something about skateboarding, I wrote about yesterday in class and Jidé talked about his birth-parents in Rwanda.'

'That took some courage. Has he called you yet?'

'No, not yet . . . How are your teeth?' I ask.

'They ache, badly,' sighs Millie, covering her mouth and opening Pat Print's book.

'*To Millie, a loyal friend, with love, Pat Print,*' she reads, smiling up at me.

'It's true,' I smile back at her. 'You are.'

'You too,' she says, closing the book.

So much for being honest with Millie.

Thursday 12 May

Millie is still off sick.

At break, Jidé comes over to sit next to me on the wall. I feel stupidly proud to be so close to him, as if he's some kind of badge of honour.

'Where's Ben?' I ask.

'Not here. No Millie?'

I shake my head.

'You'd better not sit here,' I warn him, pointing to Bo and Demi who are nodding in our direction.

'Why not?'

'They'll probably have a go at both of us now,' I say, trying hard not to look in their direction.

'Let them!' Jidé flashes his film-star smile at them. 'How's your nana?' he asks me.

'Dying.'

He just nods and we sit there in a silence stuffed full of things we would like to say to each other.

'I didn't know about your parents, about what

happened in Rwanda,' I finally pluck up the courage to say.

'It's not the sort of thing you shout about. Anyway, I was too young to remember . . . Grace and Jai are my mum and dad now.'

'What are they like?'

'Just like anyone else's parents, except worse, because, well, you know Grace, she's always telling me what to do,' shrugs Jidé.

Another silence. This time Jidé breaks it.

'What do you think of Pat Print?'

'She reminds me a bit of Nana Josie,' I tell him.

'I wish she was our teacher,' sighs Jidé.

'Why?'

'Pat Print's deep . . . She looks into you and really sees what's there.'

'I know what you mean.'

The bell rings. Demi and Bo are still eyeballing us, as if they can't believe that Jidé Jackson is actually taking the time to talk to *me*. Jidé jumps off the wall, and before I can do anything about it he has grabbed my hand to help me down. Bo and Demi just can't help sniggering, but Jidé gives them the finger and refuses to let go of my hand. Instead, he starts swinging our arms backwards and forwards in a huge 'I don't care who sees' arc through the air. I suppose this means that me and Jidé are not a secret any more.

'Jidé, let go,' I laugh.

'But I don't want to,' he laughs back.

When I walk out of school, Demi and Bo are hanging around by the gates.

'Are you and Jidé going out?' Demi shouts.

I just keep on walking, trying to wipe the smile off my face. The truth is I'm glad she shouted it out for everyone to hear. It's what I'd like to do myself.

Dad opens the door. He's hardly ever at home when I get back from school. It's turned out to be such a great day that I had almost completely forgotten about him coming out of Miss Poplar's office this morning.

'Hey, Mira. How's school?'

Always the same boring question.

'Fine.'

Always the same boring answer.

'How's Nana?' I ask.

'The same . . . I wanted to have a little chat with you. Sit down a minute, Mira.' Dad budges up on our kitchen bench. This does not feel like 'a little chat' to me – this is more like family-conference territory, even though there's only me and him at the table.

'I dropped in to see Miss Poplar this morning.'

'I know, I saw you,' I snap back at him.

'Did you?' he asks, looking a bit taken aback. 'Well, the thing is your mum and I, we were a bit troubled by that project you told us you were doing about Rwanda, and what with everything that's going on with Nana . . .'

'Oh! For God's sake, Dad.'

'The point is, Mira, Miss Poplar told me that you're not doing a project about Rwanda and she also told me about the bullying incident and . . . you know, Mira, if you're struggling with anything, we just want you to know that you can always talk to us.'

He's waiting for me to say something, but I feel that spark of red-hot anger light up in me again so I keep my mouth clamped shut.

'Maybe it's because we've all been so focused on Nana—'

'Stop treating me like a baby. I've sorted it out myself. I don't need you wading in all the time.'

'That's good. Miss Poplar told me that you faced up to it, but if you'd have told us before, we might have been able to help you.'

My jaw aches with the effort of clenching my mouth closed tight.

'OK, I understand, you want to fight your own battles, but I don't understand why you lied to us about the research into Rwanda.'

'It's not a *project*, all right! For some people it's real life, Dad,' I yell at him, storming off upstairs and slamming my bedroom door so hard that a crack appears in the wood.

Friday 13 May

Unlucky for some.

At breakfast Dad watches my every move as if I might be ill or something. When the smoke alarm goes off *again*, I feel as if my head is about to explode. I am out of that door at 8.30 on the dot to find Millie striding along the pavement towards me. I am so pleased to see her after the blow-up with Dad that I feel like hugging her. I don't, but on the walk into school I do start to tell her about Jidé and me. Not everything, not about the texting – some things you just want to keep for yourself – but I tell her that he sat in her seat the day I faced up to Demi and I tell her how he came and sat on the wall with me yesterday.

'The cheek of it. Sitting in my seat! I was only away for two days and now you're going out with Jidé Jackson!' she laughs.

'I didn't say we were going out together.'

'What else would you call it?'

Ben comes meandering towards us with his funny, trying-to-be-cool, slopy walk that he's adopted since we came to secondary school; it's the kind of walk where he looks like he's dragging an injured leg belonging to someone else behind him.

'You're back then?'

'Looks like it,' grins Millie, showing off her double row of braces with fluorescent rainbow-coloured bands that glint in the sunshine. Trust Millie to choose the brightest colours.

'I should have brought my shades!' jokes Ben, shielding his eyes from the glare.

'Where's Jidé?' Millie asks.

'Dunno. He's not in today.'

'Probably lovesick,' Millie whispers, so I elbow her in the side.

Ben looks a bit awkward, like he doesn't really know what to do with himself. I suppose Jidé is to Ben what Millie is to me . . . One is lost without the other, or that's how I used to feel anyway.

'Written your adventure story yet?' Ben asks Millie.

'Yep, it's in my bag. Want a sneak preview?'

Ben nods.

So we sit together, just the three of us, listening to Millie read her story.

'*Lock Heart* by Millie Lockhart.' Just the way she reads the title makes you know it's going to be good.

'You'll have to dig deep,' he had said. Beatty didn't even know if she believed him. Could anything really stay hidden for all this time? As she dug into the cold soil, she heard what she thought was a voice calling to her, but it was only the sound of the wind whistling over the plain. Already a mound of earth about half the size of her own body mass was growing by her side, and with each spadeful it was getting harder for her to reach into the pit to clear more soil. Just as she was considering how if she jumped into the hole she would ever get out again, her spade struck something hard. She had to find a way of levering it out slowly so as not to damage it. She tugged several times, but it kept slipping back into the soil as if it didn't want to be disturbed. Now there was no going back. So, without knowing how she would clamber out, she eased herself into the hole.

It was surprisingly cold in the earth. She leaned her back against one wall of the pit, her legs straddling the opposite side as she levered up the heavy silver box. She brushed off the mud and was just about able to decipher the remnants of a pattern on the lid. There were indents, which looked like they might once have held jewels, but now they were hollow like empty eye sockets. She tried to cleave open the box lid, but it was locked tight. She would have to wait till she got home. Her heart was beating hard with the excitement and the effort of digging.

Suddenly the pit grew dark and she found herself cast in a giant's shadow.

'I told you, Lockhart, if you dug deep enough, you'd find it. Now hand it over–'

Whenever you're getting really into something at school, the bell always interrupts.

'That's sick!' booms Ben.

'Thanks,' grins Millie.

'What happens next?' asks Ben.

'Your guess is as good as mine!' Millie laughs.

'Want to come up the skatepark after school?' Ben shouts, even though Millie's standing shoulder to shoulder with him.

She pulls a doubtful face. 'I could *try*,' she says. I have to stop myself laughing, because the thought of Millie Lockhart in a skatepark . . . well, let's just say she might not fit in. But probably that's what you do when you go out together . . . hang out, even if it's something you don't really get, like skateboarding.

At lunch break I decide to text Jidé, but there's already a message waiting for me in my inbox.

Missing you.
JJ xxxxx

Two words. Five kisses. So it's not that hard to text him back.

Missing you too.
Mira xxxxxx

Sunday 15 May

Crystal's not in her bed and the curtains are drawn around Clara. Nana is sitting propped up on her pillows. She smiles weakly at Doris as she walks out from behind Clara's curtain.

'Where is everyone?' I ask.

'Clara died early this morning,' Doris says gently. 'Your nana sat with her all night, and Crystal's been moved to a private room.'

'Did Clara's son ever come to see her?' asks Krish, staring at her drawn curtain.

'Not a soul came for Clara, except maybe your Nana Josie,' answers Doris as she eases Nana into her wheelchair and pushes her towards the Staffroom. Krish and me follow behind them.

'You don't mind if we go to the Staffroom today, Josie?' Doris goes on. 'It's all hotting up in the Family Room.'

'No dear, I could do with a change of scenery,' sighs Nana, patting Doris on the hand to reassure her.

'But do you think she ever had a son?' pursues Krish.

'I only know I never met him,' sighs Doris.

'Did she ever call him by his name?'

Doris stops pushing Nana for a second and looks down at Krish as if she's trying to remember.

'Do you know, I don't think she ever did.'

Krish nods.

When we get to the Staffroom, Doris slumps down in a chair next to Nana. It just feels right to ask them if I should make them a cup of tea. They both nod. I get the impression that we're only here because they don't want us on the ward with Clara lying there. After a while Question Mark appears at the door and nods to Doris.

'You want to stay here for a while?' Doris asks Nana.

She shakes her head and Doris wheels Nana back to the ward. Halfway down the corridor Krish takes hold of one of the handles of the wheelchair.

'You want to push, son?' asks Doris, smiling at him and moving aside.

As we approach the ward, Krish pauses in the entrance. The space where Clara's bed once was is empty. I wonder who else, except for our family and the staff here, will remember Clara. Not to be remembered must be a sad ending . . . and soon, I suppose, her place on the ward will be taken by someone new. It feels wrong to be so easily replaced.

Dad peers around the door of the ward.

'Coming, Mum?'

Nana smiles and shakes her head. 'Send them my love,' she whispers.

Music is coming from a room along the corridor. It's Mozart, Nana's favourite. She has her eyes open and she's listening as if she's hypnotized. Then her eyelids grow heavy, like the blinking eyelids of a china doll, and she's drifting away to another place. Everything about her says, 'Do not disturb.'

I follow the music and a sweet scent as it floats down the hallway from the Family Room, which has been decorated with lilies and pink and white roses. Everyone's here: Mum, Dad, Aunty Mel jiggling Laila on her hip, and Aunty Abi and Krish, standing with some of the other visitors, patients, doctors and nurses. Mum smiles at me.

Then I see the man from the bed nearest the door in the Men's Room, the one who's not old, Mum says, maybe thirty. He's standing next to the woman who visits him every day. She looks so pretty with her hair all folded up and held in place with two Chinese lacquered chopsticks. She's wearing a lime-green silk kimono top with a bright pink border, black silky trousers and dainty pink and green Chinese slippers. She has long black hair and is very tall. The man is tall too, but bald, completely bald. He wears a silk Chinese dressing gown with silvery grey and lime-green patterns on the edging. I think the woman must have really thought about what would be the most comfortable and beautiful thing for them to wear, and how they would fit together.

He's just a little bit taller than her, but so thin. His cancer makes him look like an old man. Framed in their archway of flowers, they stand very close, looking deep into each other's eyes, repeating the marriage vows after the priest, but you can tell that they are lost in their own private world. No one else can really hear what they're saying.

I've been to a few weddings, so I know the kind of thing the priest must be saying. Suddenly, I have this horrible thought that when he asks the question, 'Does anyone know any reasons why these two cannot be joined in marriage together,' at that very moment everyone in the room shouts, 'BECAUSE HE IS GOING TO DIE.'

When it gets to that moment, of course, no one says anything, but Laila does start to cry, and the bride turns round and smiles at her and I see that her eyes are brimming with tears. Aunty Mel passes Laila along the line back to Mum.

Question Mark – he must be the best man – stands next to the groom and passes him the ring. The man's hand is shaking uncontrollably, so Question Mark has to steady him and help him place the ring on the bride's finger. Then they kiss, on the lips. I mean really snog, with tongues and everything, for ages and ages, and in that kiss you can really feel so much love and sadness at the same time – like the brightest and dullest colours all merging into each other.

I look around at all the people in the room. Every single person is crying except for Krish and me. After they've been locked into their kiss for what seems like forever, my brother says, 'Oh! Gross,' in a really loud voice, breaking the spell. My mum, who is crying her eyes out, of course, gives Krish a hard nudge, but everyone else starts laughing.

After the wedding, there is champagne. Dad says I can have a sip, but I don't really like the sour taste. Krish wants some, but Mum says he can't because he said 'gross'. Dad sneaks him a sip though, and he licks his lips. I watch Dad gulp his, like he's downing a glass of fizzy water.

My mobile rings. I still haven't found a ringtone that isn't totally shameful. I rush out into the corridor to take it, thanking Notsurewho Notsurewhat that it didn't go off during the ceremony.

'Hi, Millie,' I whisper.

'It's Jidé. Why are you whispering again?'

It takes me a few seconds of my heart beating on loudspeaker for me to think of what to say, to get over the shock of him actually calling me.

'Oh! Hi, Jidé, I'm in the hospice,' is the best that I can come up with.

'Want to come to mine after school next Friday? My mum wants to talk to you about being on some student committee for the Rec.'

'All right,' I say, trying to make myself sound not that bothered.

'How's it going, anyway?'

'I've just been to a wedding at the hospice.'

'A wedding? Are they really ill then? The people who got married?'

'One of them is . . . the man.'

'She must really love him.'

'She does,' I say.

I can't believe I'm standing in the hospice at a wedding talking to Jidé Jackson about love. Then there is an awkward pause when neither of us can think of anything to say.

'Well, see you later,' says Jidé.

'See you.'

Nana was wrong about my mobile. I have got someone to call, and someone who wants to call me.

I amble along the corridor, wondering how it's possible that just one call from Jidé can make it feel like we're properly going out together. This is turning out to be the weirdest mix-up-of-emotions day of my life.

I sit down next to Nana's bed and watch her

sleeping. That's when I hear this message jump into my phone.

Forgot the

xxxxxxx

JJ

I don't want to wake Nana up with the high-pitched beep that sounds every time I press the keypad because I still can't work out how to silence it. At least it doesn't take me half the day to reply this time.

Me too.

xxxxxxxx

Mira

My thumb doesn't even hover over the button before I press send.

'I see you're using that phone of yours now,' sighs Nana wearily.

'Sorry, Nana. Did it wake you up?'

'Yes! So the very least you can do is tell me who you're so keen to talk to.' Nana's wearing her most wicked grin.

'I wasn't talking, I was texting.'

'Whatever!'

'It was no one,' I laugh, flipping the lid closed.

'Is that a no one no one, or a someone no one, or a someone someone?' she jokes.

I laugh, but don't answer her.

'A someone someone then! Good for you,' Nana smiles, squeezing my hand. 'There's nothing sweeter than first love.'

'Naaaaana!' I squirm.

'Talking of love. How was the wedding?'

'I thought it was sad.'

Nana nods and closes her eyes.

'Nana, why did they get married, when he's so ill?'

She shakes her head and sighs as if she can't answer my question. 'It's one of the many mysteries of the heart . . . They're in love.' Then she opens her eyes and smiles, like the sun breaking through a grey cloud. 'Life goes on, Mira.'

I wish I could find a chain for Nana's artichoke-heart charm. Suddenly I feel as if now is the time I should be wearing it.

Monday 16 May

'What are you up to on Friday?' I ask Millie as we walk into school together.

'Orchestra, as usual. Why?'

'No reason, I just forgot,' I lie.

If Notsurewho Notsurewhat's looking down on me right now, I'm in so much trouble.

Miss Poplar has laid out loads of magazines, books and newspapers on the tables. We're supposed to pick out somebody famous we really admire and then write down the qualities of why we admire them so much. I find it impossible to decide who to choose, because I don't know the people, so how can you really tell what they're like?

'Right, does everyone have someone?'

She asks this question at the very moment Jidé and Ben stroll in. Jidé hears it and turns to me, grinning. I concentrate hard on not laughing out loud.

'What was the score?' asks Miss Poplar.

184

'Three nil to us. I scored two; Jidé scored one.'

'Well done, boys . . . now . . . we've all picked out someone famous who we admire, so who wants to kick off?'

Ben's on form, putting his hand up, even before Millie.

'Pelé,' he shouts out. 'He was the greatest footballer of all time, and my dad used to say he was a real gentleman.'

It's not difficult to see why Ben chose Pelé.

Miss Poplar goes around the classroom. Most people just copy each other with names like Madonna, David Beckham, Alicia Keys. Miss Poplar is moving around the room closer and closer towards me, but the only person I can really think of who is kind of famous to me is Nana Josie. Jidé chooses Nelson Mandela because he's read his biography. Orla chooses the Pope because she's Catholic and he's just died and her mum says he was the best pope ever. I expected her to choose someone like Madonna, like Bo and Demi did. Perhaps there's more to Orla than I thought. I ask Notsurewho Notsurewhat to make a name spring into my mind – anyone will do.

'So, Mira? Who did you choose?'

'I couldn't think of anyone,' I say.

The truth is that I can only really think about two people at the moment. Nana and Jidé.

'Never mind,' says Miss Poplar.

This is usually the moment when Demi, Bo and Orla would move in for the kill. I glance up at them, but they're all busy flicking through their magazines.

At the end of school Jidé walks out with me.

'Are you still coming over to mine on Friday?' he asks, slipping his arm into mine, which makes me smile, because he's obviously sure that I haven't changed my mind.

After he's walked me through the Rec to the road, we stand on the pavement, not knowing how to say goodbye.

'See you then,' Jidé grins, running off across the Rec before I can answer him. I watch him as he sprints across the football pitch and leaps off the ground, tucking his legs right under him and punching the air. I was definitely supposed to see that!

Nana says people are arriving from all the different parts of her life. There's Sylvie the poet, who always brings Nana a single flower from her garden, and cheery Lucy with fire-red hair and bright glass jewels who cries when Nana's not looking. Sometimes, I just sit and listen to them talking about the old days. When you see Nana with her friends, you get a picture of what her life was like when she was younger . . . before I was born, even before my dad was born. Before Nana was dying, I never really thought about who she is, I mean, apart from her being my nana.

'She's not famous, your mum, is she?' Headscarf Lady asks Dad as we come back from taking Piper for a walk.

'She's famous around here . . . one of the local characters. Why do you ask?'

Headscarf Lady explains that there's a woman from Radio 4 in the hospice today, wanting to interview people about what it's like to have a terminal illness, but they want an ordinary person, no one famous. The programme is going to be about how what people believe in helps them when they're dying.

They have already interviewed people about the Pope dying and now they're going to talk to the couple who got married the other day, the staff and the famous person in the hospice (no one's allowed to know her name). Then they want one other, not famous person, just an interesting, ordinary person. Nana Josie is not what I'd call 'ordinary', but I keep my thoughts to myself.

When we get upstairs to the ward, Dad asks Nana what she thinks about being interviewed.

She shrugs and laughs. 'Well, I never thought I would end up on a radio programme about the Pope, but then if it's God's will!'

Nana asks Aunty Abi to help her put some make-up on before she has the interview.

'It's not for the telly, Nana.'

'Still, I want them to hear me at my best!'

The thought of the radio programme has really perked Nana up.

A young-looking woman *clip-clops* across the ward and perches on the chair next to Nana's bed. I thought she would be older. She wears smart clothes that match. The kind of thing Nana never wears. She talks to Nana in a quiet, breathy voice, a bit like some people talk to very small children. Nana keeps saying 'speak up' to Radio Woman, who I think is scared to be so close to a dying person. Lots of people are. She asks Nana, in a very sorry way, as if she's been forced to ask this question, and would rather be doing almost anything else in the world:

'What are your thoughts at this time? What gives you comfort?'

'Do you mean, how does it feel to be dying?'

Radio Woman whispers, 'Yes,' as if she would like to crawl under the bed.

'Well, you're dying too – you're just too young to know it.'

Nana can see that Radio Woman is uncomfortable so she stops joking and answers the question.

'On the whole I've been lucky enough to do the things I've wanted to in my life. I haven't been afraid to fight for what I believe in. I've seen my children grow up and my grandchildren. I've travelled all over the world, and my work is what I love . . . my painting. As a story, everything's in the right order. You have a life, a good life, you love, you are loved, you get older, you get ill . . . you die. Maybe that bit's not in the right order. I've got this illness before I feel old. That's a shame.

Then the woman, who isn't really listening, goes on to the next question on her list.

'Can you tell us about the coffin you've painted?'

'Ah! Yes, my coffin. Well, with the help of my granddaughter here, I've painted my own coffin. It's the sea and sky dancing with dolphins and doves. Oh, and not forgetting my little dog pissing into the sea.' Nana grins at me. 'It's my grand finale! The one thing that's good about a terminal illness is, if you're lucky, you get time to say goodbye. My funeral's going to be a celebration of my life, organized by me. I've always loved throwing a party! My only regret is I can't be there among all my favourite people.'

Radio Woman doesn't even smile at Nana's jokes, which I think is pretty rude. She just moves on to the next question on her list.

'When the Pope was dying, he had his faith. How do you think that changes things? How do your beliefs help you face . . .'

'Well, I couldn't possibly comment on the Pope, but, if you're asking me what I believe in, I suppose it's the human spirit. Not wasting your life and

189

fighting for what you know is right. As for an afterlife, I don't believe in a heaven or a hell, not that kind of afterlife anyway . . . It's enough for me that traces of me will live on through what I've created in my garden, my paintings, my children, my grandchildren, my friends, even little Piper, my dog. Not just the genetic line, I mean the memory of me, what I've managed to communicate to the world. That should be enough for anyone, shouldn't it?'

Radio Woman doesn't answer.

'Who's behind the glasses and the headscarf?' Nana asks, as Radio Woman packs up her recording equipment.

Radio Woman looks confused.

'If I'm the ordinary one – who's the famous one you're interviewing? I'd love to know what sort of company I'm keeping.'

'I-I'm afraid I'm not allowed to say,' she stutters.

'Go on, I'm just *dying* to know – we all are,' Nana calls after her in an over-the-top, actressy voice. Radio Woman drops her bag in the doorway, spilling the contents all over the floor. Nana gestures for me to help her pick up her papers.

When she's gone, I sit on the edge of Nana's bed.

'I think you frightened her a bit, Nana.'

'Wicked of me, wasn't it!' she laughs. 'You could say she brought out the devil in me!'

Nana slumps back on her pillow, exhausted by the

effort of the interview. We are quiet now. I don't want to move or I might wake her, so I just sit very still with her hand in mine.

The next thing I know I'm being nudged, hard, in the shoulder. Only Krish nudges me like that.

'You're always hogging Nana,' Krish complains in an angry whisper that could easily wake her up.

'You can't *hog* a person.'

'*You* can! Just budge over,' he spits, elbowing me off my seat.

Nana Josie's gravelly voice shocks us both because she talks more and more with her eyes closed, so you think she's asleep, but actually she knows exactly what's going on.

'Krish, I want you to go to the flat, with your dad, and choose something of mine for yourself and something for Laila too . . . and, Mira, you're to take my easel,' she orders, closing her eyes as if that's all settled now, but Krish is in no mood to back down. Even though he's smaller than me, he always wins these sorts of fights. He's not happy till he's pushed me right off the chair. Then he takes Nana's hand in his as if it's his right to sit with her. How can anyone make sitting with your dying nana into a competition?

Tuesday 17 May

'What time are we going to the hospice?' I ask Dad.

'We're not. Mum's going with Krish and Laila after school. We're taking the day off.'

'But—'

'No buts, we're having the day off and that's final.'

Dad has to shout over Laila's screeching – she's being a complete nightmare this morning.

'Mira, about school. I didn't want to interfere. I was just concerned about you – you know that, don't you?'

I nod, hugging Dad tight. He really does look like he could do with a break. He hasn't had a shave in days, his skin's turned a sad grey colour and the dark rings under his eyes have sunk deeper into his face.

'OK,' I nod, 'what shall we do?'

'That's completely up to you.' Dad spreads open his arms, as if anything's possible. That's when I have the idea.

'Can we see the Frida Kahlo? I was going to go with

Nana. Then we could get a pizza afterwards and walk along the river.'

Mum and Dad look at each other as if to say, 'That's not quite what we had in mind.'

'What if we can't get in? Don't you want to go swimming, or see a film or something?' suggests Dad.

'But you hate swimming.'

'True!'

'Well, I want to go to the exhibition. If Nana can't come with me, at least I can tell her about it.'

'Have you seen any of Frida Kahlo's work?' asks Mum.

I shake my head.

'It's not very cheery, some of it.'

Dad mutates his face into his misery mask. It's supposed to make me laugh.

'I don't care. I don't feel very cheery.'

'Go and get ready then, Mira,' sighs Dad.

In my room, I think about texting Jidé, but then I decide that before I go round to his place I should at least pluck up the courage to call him. So I do, but I can't help but feel relieved when it goes straight to voicemail. I am such a coward.

'Hi, Jidé. I just wanted to let you know that I'm not going to be in today.' It starts off all right. 'So, yeah! I'm not ill or anything . . . it's just that my dad needs a break so . . . and . . . anyway . . .' Now I really wish

I hadn't left this message. 'I'll see you tomorrow.' I knew I should have texted him instead. I hang up, hurling the phone to the other end of my bed, because I've made such a mess of the call.

We take the tube to Waterloo and that's when I realize I've left my mobile at home. How am I going to wait all day to see if he calls me back? I think about asking Dad if we can go back, but then the questions would start . . . so I try my hardest, for Dad's sake, not to think about it.

Waterloo is my favourite station in London because you still get the feeling of people from the past criss-crossing paths with us. Sometimes I think people from other times, like my great-great-grandparents, and even further back than that, are just in reach of us, but there is this separation called death that stops us from seeing them. Some places you go you can feel the past generations more than others. Waterloo station is one of those places. I tell Dad this, and he wrinkles up the worry lines between his eyes.

'Are you talking about ghosts?' asks Dad.

'Not really, more like you can feel the people from different generations in certain places more than others.'

Like the Tate Modern. You can really tell that it used to be a power station. When you walk through that turbine hall you can still feel the great metal wheels turning. We take the escalator but before we get to the top I know we've wasted our time because the banner above our heads reads: FRIDA KAHLO EXHIB-ITION 9 JUNE – 9 OCTOBER.

'Never mind,' says Dad as we head towards the down escalator. 'I'll bring you another time.'

I can tell he's trying to hide the relief in his voice. We meander aimlessly along the river. Dotted along the South Bank are stalls selling books, mostly. One of the stalls is covered in bright little flags dancing in the breeze. I wander towards it and a girl with long black hair and enormous brown eyes smiles at me and then at Dad as we browse at her stall. She's selling jewellery and Indian puppets, and tiny little leather purses, incense, that sort of thing. The girl, with her long black mane and her hippy-chick clothes, looks like something straight out of one of Nana's 1960s photos.

'Looking for anything in particular?' she asks my dad as he picks up a few of the bracelet chains.

It's a bit embarrassing, because Dad doesn't answer – he is literally staring at her. I elbow him in the side.

'Sorry, yes, we're looking for a bracelet chain for a charm that will fit this beautiful little wrist,' Dad says, picking up my hand. Why do parents have to be so embarrassing?

She winks at me and rummages through a box with

Indian dancers painted on its side. Nana would love that box.

'I think I've got just the thing for you . . . yes, here it is . . . This is one of my old ones. It's just missing one charm, but the catch is still in place so you could fix yours on to it.'

It's perfect . . . a tiny silver chain with two charms already attached, a butterfly and a bird. I can't wait to show it to Nana.

'It's for a charm my nana gave me.'

The girl just smiles at me and starts to wrap it in layers of orange tissue paper, which she finally sticks together with a paisley sticker, like a bindi.

'Here you are.'

'How much do I owe you?' Dad asks.

'Nothing at all,' smiles the girl.

'Are you sure? That's very kind of you,' says Dad, still holding a ten-pound note towards her.

'It'll be my good karma. I'm telling you, because of this, I'll make a fortune today,' she says, waving my dad's hand away.

'I hope so,' smiles Dad.

We don't talk about the girl or the charm as we walk along the river. Looking at the buildings on the Thames, what I notice for the first time is that they all fit in. Even buildings like the Gherkin fit exactly into the space. Buildings can do that. They can be one great big family where all the generations are alive at the same time, as long as they're looked after properly. The great-great-grandparents like Big Ben and the Houses of Parliament or St Paul's Cathedral living side by side with their distant relatives the Wibbly-wobbly Bridge, the Gherkin and the Millennium Wheel. Instead of some of them dying off before the next generation's born, they just live here getting to be a bigger and bigger family. I wish humans could do that.

Dad's embarrassing, attempting-to-be-jazzy ringtone interrupts my thoughts.

'When? Where are you?'

The colour has drained from his face.

'I'm coming, right now.'

It wouldn't be fair if Nana died today, because we've been to see her every day since she went to that hospice, except today.

'What is it?' I pant as Dad literally yanks me along the South Bank, pelts up the steps to Waterloo Bridge and leaps in front of a black cab.

He doesn't answer me. Dad never takes black cabs. We climb inside.

'Whittington Hospital.' Dad splutters the words out.

We sit in the cab, chests heaving, not able to catch our breath enough to talk.

The taxi driver stares at Dad through the mirror.

'Everything all right?'

Dad shakes his head, still breathing hard, and then

197

he says very slowly, as if he's trying to believe it himself, 'It's my baby – she's been rushed into hospital.'

'I'll get you there as fast as I can, mate. Leave it to me.'

The taxi driver rams his foot down on the accelerator and weaves in and out of traffic, ignoring the other drivers' noisy protests.

Dad calls Mum again.

'In a taxi . . . Waterloo Bridge . . . are they sure? OK, OK, I'm coming.'

I am freezing cold, shivering from head to foot. Laila in hospital? My head's all fogged up with not understanding. I look up at Dad for an explanation, but he's staring out of the window. I think he might have even forgotten that I'm here, sitting next to him. His forehead is wet with sweat.

'She was fine this morning,' I say, tugging Dad's arm. Now I think of it, she was crying a lot. 'Is it serious?'

Dad turns to me as if he really had forgotten I was with him.

'She's got a rash and a high temperature . . . suspected meningitis.'

'Is it serious?' I ask again, because although I've heard of meningitis I don't really know what it is, except there's a poster in the doctor's surgery that says you can test for it by pressing a glass against your skin, which I remember, because it seems like a weird, not-very-scientific way of testing for something serious.

Dad just squeezes my hand and looks out of the window. Then the sky opens. It's the kind of rain that stops traffic. I watch the driver's windscreen wipers working pathetically slowly against the build-up of rain. Car lights dazzle us through the haze, merging colours into a blurred brightness . . . like looking at the world through an out-of focus camera.

That's when I remember feeling sick at the thought of a child-sized coffin, and it's that memory that makes me ask myself the question . . . it just slips into my mind . . . 'If it's going to be Nana today, or Laila, who should it be?' If Laila dies before Nana, it will all be in the wrong order. But why should Laila's life be more important than Nana's? She's just a baby, and only we really love her. So many people love Nana Josie . . . so many people will miss her . . . but Laila's life hasn't even begun yet. So, as we weave through the traffic in the pouring rain I call once more on Notsurewho Notsurewhat . . . to let it be Nana.

The taxi driver takes us right up to the doors of the Whittington, where the ambulances park. Dad checks on the driver's meter and passes him a twenty-pound note.

'Put it away, mate.'

Dad doesn't argue with him – he just shakes his hand as he gets out of the taxi.

'The best of British to you,' the driver calls out of the window as he pulls away.

I'm being yanked along again up an escalator, along a corridor with children's pictures on the walls . . . Winnie the Pooh, Tigger . . . then I spot Krish standing in the hallway looking so little and lonely.

'Mum's in there.' He points through the door. 'With Laila. We're not allowed in.'

Dad strides through, leaving Krish and me in the corridor on our own.

'What's the matter with her?'

Krish shrugs. 'They don't know . . . some kind of virus, they think . . . She had a fit in her cot . . . She was boiling hot. I found her. Her eyes were rolling into the back of her head.'

Then Krish wraps his arms round my waist and clings on to me.

'She's not going to die, is she, Mimi?'

He hasn't called me that in years.

'No,' I say, stroking his hair. 'Laila's not going to die.'

The door opens and Mum and Dad walk out without Laila.

'They think she's going to be all right. They've got her on a drip and her temperature's starting to come down.' Mum sighs with relief, throwing her arms round both of us.

'Can she come home now?' asks Krish.

'She'll be in here for at least a few days . . . I'll stay with her.'

Now I want to take it back, my wish, but you can't do that just because you've got what you want. Can you? As if he knows what I'm thinking, Dad says, 'There's no need to worry Nana about all this.'

How could I ever tell Nana what I wished for?

I can hardly look at her.

'Did you bring me a catalogue then, Mira?'

'We didn't go. It doesn't actually start till the ninth of June.'

'That's a shame,' sighs Nana. 'I was looking forward to seeing the catalogue.'

'But we did find a bracelet, for your charm.'

I take it out of my pocket to show her.

'Nice wrapping!' she smiles as I carefully undo the bindi sticker and the folds of orange tissue paper. 'Your favourite colour too.'

I nod and hand the little charm bracelet over to Nana for her to inspect.

'But these are all our favourite things. Adorable little silver bird and butterfly, about the same size as the artichoke. Oh! And there's one charm missing, but the link's still there, so you can tweezer it on. Get your dad to do it. Some things are just meant to be,' announces Nana, handing it back to me. 'Well, at least it wasn't a wasted trip. I'll expect to see you wearing it next time you come in.'

'She looked a bit like you did when you were young,

the girl on the stall,' Dad tells Nana.

She smooths her short grey hair as if remembering the feel of her long black mane running through her fingers.

'Did she indeed? We once had an art stall on the Embankment, me and your Grandad Kit,' Nana tells me.

I can't think of anything to say. It's usually me who keeps the conversation going. Not today. Krish never says very much when we come to see Nana. Usually, he goes to the Family Room and watches football with the man who got married. Sometimes he tells Nana about his football, or his running, but mostly he's very quiet, for him. Today he asks her for a sheet of her best art paper. Nana points to her bedside table and Krish tears a sheet out of her book. He doesn't think he's any good at art. Whenever he gets art homework from school, he always asks me to help him. Once he got a certificate for his 'excellent artwork'. On the certificate it said *Krish Levenson, for your achievement in art*, but he crossed out his name and added mine in instead, and handed the certificate back to me. Krish is one of the most honest people I know. Actually, he is really good at art. He just forgets that I'm two years older than him, so I understand about things like perspective that he hasn't even thought about yet.

Once, in primary school, we had this Aboriginal artist come in. He said Aboriginal people believe in dream time. He took us into the playground, led us out of the school gates and marched us up the hill. He asked us, when we were walking, to listen to the land speaking to us. I couldn't really hear or feel anything, but Krish thought he felt water under the pavement. When we got back to school, we had a look on an old map outside the Head's office and it turned out there was an ancient river underneath the street, just where Krish felt it. Some of Krish's friends said he must have known that already, but he didn't.

Because of that the Aboriginal man made Krish stand up in front of the whole assembly. He said that Krish had still got the power of dreaming. Krish looked pretty embarrassed, but I could tell he was pleased with himself. The Aboriginal artist said dreaming is when you are in touch with the energy of the earth, so your footprint feels a memory of how that place was created, even if that was thousands and thousands of years ago. Krish had to stand next to the Aboriginal man while he was saying all this. Then, in front of everyone, Krish asked if that means there is always a memory in the earth, for everything, even when it's dead. The Aboriginal man nodded and did this funny greeting to Krish, which you only do when you really respect someone.

Tonight, I think Krish came to the hospice with a plan because he's brought a bucketful of felt tips in with him. It's amazing to see him sitting so still as he dots each tiny speck of colour on to the page. He's drawing hundreds and thousands of little grey, brown and black dots in a curved shape round the edge of the paper. He's been working on it for about an hour and he's only just finished one circle, but when he gets to the part where the circle should connect, he curves the dots inwards to create the beginning of the next circle. Nana asks him what he's making.

'A pattern.'

'What kind of pattern, Krish?'

'A spiral,' he says, without looking up.

Then he picks out the blue colours and starts on the next layer of dots.

'The outside colours are the sea, then the next layers are going to be the land, and the sun's in the centre,' explains Krish as he carries on and on printing the tiny dots on the page.

'Whoever would have thought . . . Krish the runner, the jack-in-the-box, would know how to meditate,' Nana smiles.

He shrugs, like he hasn't got a clue what she's talking about.

I stand there, staring out of the window, still hardly daring to meet Nana's eye, as if just by looking at me, she will know what I wished.

'How's little Laila?'

'Fine . . . she's teething though,' I lie, without turning round. I'm getting better and better at lying.

'It's a dream-time picture, Nana,' Krish chirps up, changing the subject.

Nana nods, blows Krish a kiss and closes her eyes.

When I finally get back home, I sprint up to my room to pick up Jidé's voicemail message.

'Hi, Mira, it's Jidé. Sorry! I forgot to take my mobile in to school today. I've been thinking about you all day. Hope you're in tomorrow. See you soon.'

Now that's what I call a fantastic message. I lie on my pillow and press repeat over and over, and that is how I finally drift off to sleep listening to Jidé Jackson's voice . . . *'I've been thinking about you all day . . . I've been thinking about you . . .'*

Wednesday 18 May

Clank! Clank! Clank! Clank!

'All right, I'm coming!'

'Where were you yesterday? I called by for you, but there was no one in.' Millie scans my face for signs of bad news. I can't believe I completely forgot to call her.

'I had the day off.'

'You could have called me. You don't look like you've had a day off!'

'Sorry, it was a mad day. Laila got taken into hospital, then we had to go to see Nana.'

'Little Laila! Is she OK?'

'She will be,' I say. 'She'll be out in a few days.'

'We all thought maybe your nana . . .' She trails off, not wanting to finish her sentence.

'Millie. Do you believe in God?'

'Yes. Why? Don't you?'

'I'm not sure.'

Millie frowns at me, as if to say, 'Do we *have* to have one of these big conversations, right now?' Then she shoots me her mischievous smile.

'Jidé Jackson seems very interested to talk to me about you.'

'Really,' I say, as if I'm not that bothered.

'Really,' replies Millie, grinning at me.

I think we must be the first in school, but then we pass Orla sitting on a bench outside the Year Seven block. Without her sidekicks, Demi and Bo, she looks so tiny and, well, lonely.

'Why don't you come to this writing group we're in? See if you like it. You might as well; you're always in so early,' I say.

Orla shakes her head. I can see that there's no way she's going to change her mind.

'Maybe next time,' I mumble, walking off feeling slightly stupid for asking in the first place.

'Thanks though,' Orla calls after me.

I turn and smile at her.

'What made you do that?' asks Millie, staring at me as if she hardly recognizes me.

'I don't know really . . . I just thought . . . she's been all right to me since . . .'

'You're right. We should have asked her before. I can't believe we've just walked straight past her every week, especially me, when I know how tough it is for her.'

'Why so tough?'

'I'll tell you later,' Millie sighs as I swing open the door to the Year Seven block.

In the space of a few days Orla has been transformed from one of the three-headed bullies into a human being just because I'm not too scared to talk to her any more. I look back at her and notice, more than ever, how small and thin she is.

Jidé and Ben are sprawled in their usual couldn't-care-less pose over their desks – these days they wear their boredom like an unconvincing fashion item. Strange that they're always the first to arrive! As soon as Jidé sees me, he sits up and grins. I have to stop myself bursting out laughing because he looks like one of those cute over-keen meerkats you see on nature programmes. I sit down in the seat right next to his and out of the corner of my eye catch Millie smirking.

Pat Print looks up and smiles, as if us four sitting in front of her in this room is something that she's been looking forward to all week. How does someone make you feel like that, just by the way they smile at you?

'Good to see you, girls. Let's get straight on. What we're looking at today is . . . character . . . my favourite subject. You can't be a writer unless you're interested in people, and people are characters. All writers have to start by working out why people behave the way they do, their motivations. What makes people choose their paths in life? Or maybe they don't feel as if they have a choice. Their ambitions, their drives, their fatal flaws, what makes them tick. Now that's a lot to think about, I know, but you'll be surprised how quickly a character can emerge. This is an exercise I use myself. I call it "instant writing". The most important thing is not to take your pen off the page . . . just keep writing whatever nonsense pops into your mind. Sometimes it's the unconscious mind that provides us with the best material. I want you to choose someone you know – change their names if you want to – anyone you find interesting, and write the first things that come into your head when I give you some prompt words. Don't think too much . . . let the random in! Pens and paper at the ready!'

After about five minutes of writing, trying to get everything down before Pat Print jumps on to the next word, she orders us to lay our pens down. Nobody wants to stop writing, so we all race to finish off our sentences. When I finally take my pen off the paper, I realize how hard I've been pressing, because my hand aches so badly.

'Excellent! Now who would like to read theirs out? It probably won't make exact sense, but it'll be all the better for that. How about you, Jidé?'

Jidé shakes his head.

'Fair enough, what about you, Ben?'

Ben shakes his head, echoing Jidé, as usual.

'I see it's going to be up to the girls then.'

Pat Print turns to Millie with a slightly pleading smile. Millie nods and starts to read.

Orla Banks. Aged twelve. Looks . . . thin, small, pale skin like milk, grey-blue eyes, mousy hair. Favourite colour . . . I don't know. Personality . . . shy, only confident in a gang, bullies if she's with Demi and Bo, jealous, lonely, sad, hungry. What I've noticed . . . never eats her lunch, always gives it away or throws it in the bin, or hides it . . . never seen her eating anything. What I know . . . her dad's left home, she lives with her mum, in a flat opposite me, with her brother who's about two years old. She's always looking after her little brother. Her mum drops her off at school at seven thirty in the morning every day because she's got to get to work. She's a nurse, very thin and worried-looking, just like Orla, but her baby brother is fat.

'Comments?' asks Pat.

'It made me feel sorry for her. She only lives upstairs from me. My mum and her mum are friends but I never really think about her that much,' blurts out Ben.

'That's one of the great things about literature – you can get inside even the most difficult people, and have some understanding of their situation. It's called empathy. As a character, what were the most interesting details?' asks Pat Print, sitting right on the edge of her seat as if she can't wait to hear our next response.

It's infectious, her enthusiasm, and despite himself Jidé jumps in.

'Her hunger,' answers Jidé, who has finally given up trying to look like he doesn't know the answers, 'and her thin, worried mum, her being a nurse and having to look after everyone else . . . her fat brother . . . dropping Orla off at school at seven thirty.'

'And her dad leaving,' Ben almost whispers. 'I remember that.'

'That's right, Ben . . . that would have a massive influence on a girl that age. So you can see how from an exploration of what forms a character you've got the beginning of a story,' says Pat, and then she pauses for a moment. I think she's trying to work out how to explain something to us.

'Just a word of caution to all of you. Make sure, if you're talking about people you all know, to understand that this work is done in confidence. Perhaps I should have insisted you change the names.'

'But we still might have worked out who Millie was talking about,' interrupts Ben.

'That's true,' nods Pat. 'And I'm sure you're such a sensitive group, you'll be discreet. Now, Mira, do you want to read yours out?'

'I'm not sure now, because I'm writing about my dad!'

'Dads are fair game!' says Pat, making everybody laugh.

Sam Levenson, aged forty. Dark brown hair, what's left of it. Dark eyes, almost black. Pale skin. Favourite colour, deep blue. Personality . . . kind, gentle, makes jokes, swears a lot, hides his real feelings. What I've noticed . . . he's not keen on art exhibitions, he worries a lot about me and he doesn't like anything that's too heavy or serious. He doesn't trust people with straight teeth. What I know is my dad loves all of us, me and Krish and Laila and Mum and Nana Josie, and he's going to miss Nana so much when she's gone. What I think he thinks is that I'm a bit strange for wanting to be with Nana so much when she's dying. Generally, I think he thinks I'm a bit morbid.

'Good word that, morbid. What's *your* opinion?' asks Pat.

'Nana said it's a necessary heartbreak . . . when you love someone and you have to say goodbye.'

'But what do *you* think?' Pat asks again.

'I don't know. Yesterday was the first time I didn't want to be there.'

'What's morbid?' asks Ben.

'Someone with a tendency to think of dark things . . . dwelling on death,' answers Pat Print. 'The thing is, Mira, no matter how much you love someone, sometimes facing the end . . . can all get too much.'

Pat Print has a faraway look in her eye as if she's thinking about someone in particular, but then she seems to pull herself together, tapping her pen against her notebook and springing back into action.

'There's another exercise I like to play with character . . . pens at the ready . . . think of a character, and try to imagine what animal he or she would most be like? Quick, quick . . . first thing that comes to mind.'

I write 'horse'.

'A vegetable or fruit?'

I write 'artichoke'.

'A colour.'

I write 'green'.

'A place.'

I write 'Rwanda', folding over my paper as soon as I've written the word. Of course I'll never read this out – I'll just make something else up if she asks me. Luckily she doesn't.

'OK! Boys. What did you come up with for your characters?'

Ben says just four words, 'Seal, onion, grey, psychiatrist's.'

'Intriguing character. Let's hear yours, Jidé?'

He laughs and shakes his head. 'I couldn't think of anyone.'

'That's unlike you.' Pat Print casts him a look as if to say, 'I'm not sure you're telling me the truth.'

She checks her watch. 'I can't believe time's up already. Next week, bring something in, an object, a photo, a painting that means something to you. We're going to do an exercise where you bring the object to life. It's called the "pathetic fallacy".

'What's a phallus, anyway?' sniggers Ben, trying to embarrass Pat Print. We've just done Life Education *again* so we know all the words for willies. We had to write a long list of the words we thought were OK to use. We came up with eighteen words for a willie, but only eight for a fanny, but that could have been because the boys go so wild and the girls just give up in the end. When Millie and me tried to work it out on our own, we came up with twenty names for a fanny including a few we made up ourselves!

'Pathetic fallacy. It's when you imbue an object with a human emotion.'

'Sounds pathetic,' whispers Ben to Jidé, a bit too loudly.

'Let me offer you an example, Ben . . . ah yes! The rebellious table.'

'I don't get it,' grumps Ben.

'Well, just ask yourself. Is it the table that's rebellious? Or possibly those who sit at the table . . . what innate energy within the table itself makes it rebellious?' smiles Pat, pushing a giggling Jidé and Ben out of the room.

In the corridor Jidé hangs back. As I draw level with him, he places a note in my hand and as he does so he folds his hand over mine and squeezes it, before striding off down the corridor. My heart is beating ridiculously fast as I duck into the girls' toilets to read . . .

Mira Levenson. Aged twelve. Looks, long dark shiny hair, dark brown eyes (almost black), brown skin, beautiful. Favourite colour, copper orange, I think. Personality, clever, bright, serious, shy, funny without realizing it, holds back her thoughts, mystery girl, arty. What I've noticed: she's stronger than she thinks she is; she doesn't speak much at school. What I know: she's got a loud laugh (when she lets it out). Her best friend is Millie Lockhart. She doesn't need Millie as much as she thinks she does. Her grandmother is dying and she loves her. She's started talking in Pat Print's class. I know she doesn't know how much I think of her, how much I miss her if she's not around. What I think she thinks about me is that I'm a bit of a joker, but I'm deadly serious.

Deer . . . apple . . . green . . . sea . . .
See you on Friday!
Love
Jidé

'What's taking you so long in there?' shouts Millie from the basins.

'Nothing,' I call back, folding Jidé's note carefully into my pocket and trying to wipe the grin off my face *Love Jidé*. Now I know what it means to have butterflies in your belly.

Thursday 19 May

Sometimes as I leave Nana at night I stand and look at her, trying to remember everything about her . . . in case I don't see her again. Then the next day it's like she's almost back to her normal self, sparkly and cheery and sitting up in bed. It doesn't last very long when she's like that, but it makes you think that she might be with us for a little bit longer. Other days she's so sleepy she hardly has the energy to even open her eyes.

I peer round the corner of the ward to see her sitting up in bed, eating. When she sees me, she raises her arm in the air, and I run up to her and give her a cuddle, sploshing prune juice all over her white sheets. Nana is having what she calls an 'up time'.

I think about telling her about Jidé, and his note, but somehow it doesn't seem right, so I keep it to myself. I wonder what secrets Nana has kept from me. I watch her finishing her prunes. It takes quite a long time, because her hands are very shaky now. The only thing Nana doesn't like about the hospice is the food, which she says is 'stodge', like school dinners. So, whenever we visit, we put something in the fridge, on the shelf labelled JOSIE LEVENSON. Nana's friend Jay is a potter and a cook. Every day she brings Nana some home-made food like vegetarian soups, or a fruit salad with papaya, pineapple, blueberries and mint, or a green salad with slivers of ginger and fresh corian-der . . . the kind of food that Nana loves. Sometimes when Jay visits Nana is sleeping, so she leaves the food on her shelf in the fridge. Nana calls this food 'Jay's calling card'.

I don't want to be here any more. I want to be with Laila and her little sparkly smile. I want to sit her in her high chair and feed her until her tiny wrists grow fat bracelets again. When she came home today, it felt like Christmas morning . . . to see her smiling face again.

'I haven't seen your mum or Laila for a few days. Everything all right?' asks Nana as if she's tracking my thoughts.

'Laila's got a bit of a cold.' I'm shocked how con-vincingly I can lie these days.

Nana just nods.

'Hi, Josie!' It's Simon's sing-song voice.

He peers round the door and knocks on the wall.

'Enter!' calls Nana in her queenly voice.

Simon and Nana are always joking around together,

even when they're having serious conversations about politics, which is what they nearly always do.

'You're raining on my parade!' laughs Nana as Simon drips rainwater all over her bed. 'Mira, pass Simon a towel.'

Simon wraps it round his head like a forget-me-not blue turban.

'Very fetching,' laughs Nana.

It doesn't take them long to get to talking politics . . . the war in Iraq, and the next peace march . . .

Simon's not like anyone else I have ever met. He does painting and decorating on Mondays, Wednesdays and Fridays, but only if you get him eco-paint, which doesn't have oil in it. On Tuesdays, Thursdays and Saturdays he does things like naked bike rides for Climate Change, or candlelit vigils for the people of Tibet outside the Chinese Embassy. He's been doing that for ten years. Most weeks he sits outside Downing Street, protesting about something. Nana says sometimes you can't find Simon for days on end. That's when he's doing a meditation. Simon refuses to go anywhere in a car. He either cycles or gets on a train. He's quite old, probably about sixty, but he doesn't look it. He has this long straggly blond-grey hair which he says he last got cut in 1965, so it's not that long, considering. He's fresh-faced with pink cheeks and sparkly blue eyes. Simon actually looks like an energetic elf.

After they've talked politics, Nana's eyes grow heavy, as if she's not in control of when she's asleep or awake any more. Simon stands up to go, but Nana holds his hand.

'There's something I want you to have, Simon.'

Nana tells me to open her bedside cupboard and points to a scrapbook on the second shelf. It's the kind of book with sugar paper in it that we use at school. On the front it says JOSIE'S BOOK OF PROTEST. It's the book that Nana puts all her letters from politicians in. These are the letters where they reply to her about what she's been complaining about. Mostly the letters are from the secretaries of Margaret Thatcher and Tony Blair. Nana's written a list of all the marches she's ever been on and all the banner slogans she's carried in her life. The last march she went on was against the war in Iraq. She made a placard saying NOT IN MY NAME and I saw her carrying it on the news. I'll never forget the sight of her because I remember wondering how it was possible to be so small and strong at the same time. Simon takes the book from me.

'I'll enjoy this. Good times on the march, Josie . . .'

'Did you campaign about Rwanda?' I ask. Nana and Simon both turn to look at me, as if I have just earned a place in their conversation.

'Of course we did,' Nana sighs. 'Not that it did any good whatsoever. Why do you ask?'

'You know, I've been reading about it . . . that's all.'

'My work here is done!' Nana laughs, as if *she's* responsible for me knowing anything about Rwanda.

'Dad thinks I shouldn't be interested in stuff like that,' I tell Nana.

'Well, it's hard to see your children go out into the world,' Nana sighs. 'But you'll be next. I reckon you've got a few years' campaigning left in you, Simon. Maybe you can recycle a few slogans and leave the book to Mira here when you croak. She'll be about ready for it by then!'

Simon gives Nana a long hug. I can see that she's choking back her tears.

'Fight the good fight!' she calls out to him, clenching her fist.

A silence sits between us as I watch the smile fade from Nana's face and her fist slowly unfurling. I take her limp hand, which is now hanging carelessly over the side of the bed, and squeeze it gently in mine. She nods to me and props herself up on the pillows.

'Open the curtains a bit wider,' Nana orders.

I pull them back as far as they'll go and rest beside Nana on the edge of her bed. We watch Simon jump on his bike and pedal up the road, facing into the path of the rain. He lifts his right hand in the air, like a salute, as if he knows we're watching him. As soon as he's out of sight, Nana drifts off to sleep.

I think of all the energy Nana has put into her life, the things she believes in, all the struggles she's had, and the people she's loved; all that energy is draining away in front of me. She's giving things away: first the charm, her easel, things for Krish and Laila to choose, and now the protest book . . . these things that mean so much to her.

Friday 20 May

See you after school today
Love
JJ

Since 'love' appeared it seems that we're not sending kisses any more. Maybe Jidé's holding them back for later!

Great!
Love
Mira

'Come straight back home after school . . . We'll take Laila to see Nana,' says Mum at breakfast.

That's when I remember that I haven't even told her I'm going back to Jidé's after school, and that's when it escapes from my mouth . . . my next lie.

'Didn't I tell you I'm going to Millie's after school?'

'Oh! OK, that's fine, that's good,' says Mum, looking a bit surprised, but too busy feeding Laila to think too much about it. 'Do you need picking up?'

'No, it's OK. They'll walk me back. If not, I'll call you,' I say, waving my mobile in front of Mum.

'Any calls yet?'

'Not yet. I wish everyone would *stop* asking me that. You sound like Nana!'

Why am I lying to my mum?

Then she does something she's never done before.

'Here, you'd better have these, just in case we're late back,' she says, handing me the front-door keys.

'That's not fair! Why can't I have keys?' moans Krish, jumping up and down in an attempt to grab them off me.

'That'll be because you're only nine,' I say.

Krish pinches my arm hard. I just ignore him, tucking the keys into my blazer pocket, before Mum changes her mind. As soon as I hear Millie climbing our steps I run for the front door to stop her clanking the letterbox, but I get there just one clank too late.

'Hi, Millie!' shouts Mum from the kitchen. 'Thank your mum for having Mira for tea.'

Millie looks confused, but I slam the door behind us before she can answer.

'But I came early to see Laila,' she protests.

'Sorry, it was just madness in there. I had to get out.'

'I didn't know you were coming for tea.'

'I'm not. Mum hasn't got a clue what's going on

223

these days, what with Laila and Nana.'

'Is Laila going to be OK now?'

I nod. Laila will be fine, but I, on the other hand, will probably be struck down by lightning, the amount of lying I've been doing. I don't even know why I lied about going to Millie's, except that Mum and Dad would have probably made a big deal about me going to Jidé's house . . . and Krish would definitely have teased me about it. I suppose that's why. But the problem with lying is once you start you end up having to lie again and again, over and over.

All day long I can think of nothing else except going to Jidé's. When I sit on the wall at break time, I can't even think of anything to say to Millie. Just like with Nana, now that there are secrets between us it isn't that easy to chat any more.

'What are you doing tonight?' I ask Millie.

'Orchestra, I *told* you.'

'Sorry, I forgot.'

At the end of the day, I hang around in the classroom. 'See you on Monday,' Millie shouts, hoisting her cello on to her back and lumbering off to orchestra practice. You can just see her head bobbing up and down above the top of her case.

Jidé is sitting on the other side of the room from me. There's only me, Ben and Jidé left in the classroom and Ben's on his way out.

'Playing footie?' calls Ben from the doorway.

'I can't,' sighs Jidé.

'Suit yourself,' Ben shrugs, running out into the courtyard.

'Ready?' Jidé asks, grinning at me.

'Ready,' I say, grinning back.

'I didn't tell Ben . . .'

'I didn't tell Millie . . .' I don't tell him I didn't even tell my mum and dad, which, at least, I suppose he must have done.

By the time we get out into the courtyard most people have gone home. There is no sign of Millie or Ben. So we walk out of the school gates together. Jidé throws his arm round my shoulder, which is meant to show just about the whole world that we're going out together. He lives just across the Rec in a row of modern houses split up into flats. When we reach his bright red door, the colour of a postbox, he takes his key out of his bag and lets himself into flat 22A.

'Want something to eat? Sit down,' Jidé says, pointing to the floor. That's when I realize why this room looks so enormous – there are no chairs or sofas in it. Just loads of brightly coloured cushions scattered everywhere. There are little alcoves in the walls with sculptures in them. They look like African sculptures in dark, smooth wood . . . sculptures of women with long necks. There are photos all over the place. Quite a lot of them are of Jidé, school photos, that sort of thing, but there are other photos in black and white . . . of whole families crammed into tents. Jidé's mum and dad are in a lot of these photos, looking hot and tired. This must be Rwanda. I have to pull myself away from the faces in these pictures. Downstairs is just one big room – a kitchen and living room all together. The walls are white, full of crammed bookshelves and colourful woven rugs.

'I love where you live.'

Jidé smiles and shrugs, looking around as if he's never really thought about it before. Then there's a click in the lock.

'Hi, Jidé!'

Miss Jackson, who is Jidé's mum, lugs shopping bags and a pile of school books through the door. He helps her in.

'Hi, Grace. Mira's here.'

She looks up, as if she's completely forgotten I was coming.

'Hello, Mira! Fancy pizza for tea?'

I nod and smile but don't say anything. I can feel her checking me over.

'Good. I'll call you when it's ready.'

Then she goes over to the answerphone to pick up messages. I'm grateful that she's too busy to pay me much attention. We walk up the two steps to Jidé's room. There's just a mattress on the floor with cushions all over it. Books are stacked up all around the walls. Each pile is about ten books deep.

'Have you read all these?'

Jidé nods. I can feel him watching my every move.

He has a shelf with football medals, shells, fossils, precious stones and a photo of his mum and dad standing with two children: a girl of about three or four years old, who looks like Jidé. She's holding a baby in her arms, a bit younger than Laila, wrapped in a thin piece of orange cloth with frayed edges.

'What object will you bring in for Pat Print?' I ask.

'I dunno . . . I haven't thought about it yet, maybe a photo. How about you?'

'The artichoke-heart charm my nana gave me. I'll bring that.'

'How is she, your nana?'

'Worse,' I say.

'I'm sorry.'

'I think she's going to die soon.'

'Aren't you frightened for her?' asks Jidé.

Frightened? I think it's a strange question. It has never crossed my mind to be frightened of Nana dying.

'No, I'm not. I think it's because *she's* not frightened and she's got everyone around her who loves her.'

Jidé nods.

'What does she think happens next? Does she believe in God and all that?'

'No, she's not really into religion,' I tell him.

'I don't . . . do you?' he asks me.

'I don't know. Sometimes I want to . . . How can you be so sure?'

As soon as I've asked the question, I regret it.

'If God existed, what happened to my family, to all those people . . . it just wouldn't happen if God exists. That's what I think. But then Grace and Jai, they still have faith, even after everything they've seen.'

'I made a wish when Laila was ill. I thought maybe she was going to die so I asked for Nana to die and not Laila.'

'Asked who?'

'Notsurewho Notsurewhat.'

Jidé laughs.

'That's what I call God . . . or whatever . . . because I just don't know what I believe in.'

'I think the deal with religion is you have to have faith! Your nana is dying anyway. It's just you couldn't stand the thought of your sister dying too. That's *my* sister.' He nods over to the photo on his shelf. 'Apparently she carried me into the camp where Grace and Jai were working . . . they called it a safe zone . . . I was wrapped up in that bit of cloth. They couldn't get her to speak, not even to tell them our names, but . . . you'll probably think this is a bit weird, sometimes she sings to me in my sleep.'

'It's not weird. My dreams are crazy too . . . but you

must be so sick of me talking about my nana.'

'Why? I love talking to you.' Jidé smiles his melt-your-heart gentle smile. I wonder if he knows what effect that has on me.

'How did your sister die?' I ask Jidé, staring up at the photo of her holding him in her arms.

'Cholera, in the end. She didn't survive the camp,' he says in a matter-of-fact way, as if he's talking about someone completely disconnected from him. I don't even really know what cholera is. Then I turn to see Jidé holding out a rag of orange woven cloth for me to take a closer look. It's the same piece of cloth that was wrapped around baby Jidé in the photo.

As I feel the fraying edges of Jidé's precious cloth, I think of Krish and how much he bugs me and how I would miss him if he was gone. I think of how hard I prayed for Laila to live. If only I could do something to bring Jidé's sister back, but I can do nothing. I place the folded cloth back into his hand and as I do so he folds his hand over mine so that we are both holding the cloth and each other.

'So you read my note then?' Jidé smiles at me cheekily.

'I did . . . about a hundred times. I'm thinking of framing it!' I laugh.

'For someone so quiet, Mira Levenson . . . you've got the loudest laugh.' Jidé laughs back and before I know what's happening he's holding my head in his hands and kissing me on the lips. At first, I'm so surprised I just freeze, and then my lips feel all tingly and my face is scarlet red, but I don't pull away from him, because of how it feels to be this close, to be actually kissing Jidé Jackson. When it's over, what we've done feels so weird that I can't help it – I just burst out laughing again.

'What did you think?' Jidé asks, grinning at me.

I can't stop giggling enough to answer him.

'I was deadly serious actually! Here, I'll give you something to laugh about,' he says, grabbing hold of my feet and tickling me.

'Having fun?' asks Jidé's mum, peering round the door. 'Tea's ready in five minutes.'

On the wall, opposite Jidé's bed, is an enormous map of the world criss-crossed with green and red silk thread, leading to drawing pins stuck into different countries.

'What are those for?' I ask.

'The red ones are the countries I've been to and the green ones are the ones I want to go to the most.'

I follow the string-tracks across the world.

'You've been to . . . Wales, Scotland, Ireland, France, Brazil and India . . . you've been to *India*?'

He nods. 'Haven't you?'

I shake my head. 'My Grandad Bimal's from India, but I've never been. I really want to go though.'

230

'You should.'

'What about Africa? You were born there, weren't you?' I follow a red string to a place in Africa. 'Is that Rwanda?'

Jidé nods.

'I don't remember anything about it, but one day I'll go back.'

'I thought you said there was no point . . . going back.'

'I'm frightened to go back, but a bit of me thinks I should . . .' smiles Jidé sadly.

I think of Nana's tiny artichoke charm and of the layers and layers of protection that Jidé has already had to grow around his heart, and I lean towards him and *I* kiss *him*, and this time I don't feel like laughing, not one bit . . . It doesn't feel like any other place I've been to. This kiss with Jidé Jackson is like travelling to another world.

'Pizza,' calls Jidé's mum from the kitchen.

'How was school, Jidé?'

It's amazing that all parents, even teachers, can't think of a better question to ask.

'Boring, we had History.'

'Ha ha! Wait till you get *me*, next year,' laughs Jidé's mum. 'What's your favourite thing at school, Mira?'

Jidé does an enormous yawn, as if to say, 'Could you be more boring?'

And to make it even more uncomfortable for me he keeps nudging my foot under the table, in an attempt to make me laugh.

'Art. I like Art,' I giggle.

Then the phone rings.

'Sorry, Mira,' she sighs, striding off.

'Typical!' Jidé raises his eyes to the ceiling. 'Grace and Jai have always got some massive project on, to save the world.'

I listen in to her conversation for a few minutes. The way she talks, you can tell she's the sort of person who gets things done.

'It's the meeting I told you about transforming the Rec into a community park,' explains Jidé.

'I'm hoping that you and some of your friends will join the youth committee,' Jidé's mum calls over to me as she slings on her jacket and grabs her bag. 'We could do with some girl power!'

I smile politely and Jidé groans. I suppose everyone's parents are just as embarrassing.

'Don't be too late walking Mira home, Jidé. I'm so sorry, Mira. I can't get out of this meeting today. Hope we can chat more next time.' She kisses Jidé on the forehead, tousles his hair and is gone.

'She'll probably bring the whole meeting back here later.'

'Your mum's on a mission,' I say.

'You make her sound like Superwoman.'

'That's what she looks like to me.'

When she's gone, the flat is quiet again. Our house is never quiet.

'Leave me at the corner,' I tell Jidé. 'Mum thinks I'm at Millie's.'

Jidé laughs. 'It can get you into trouble, lying,' he grins, his face moving closer and closer towards mine until we are lost in another kiss. My first thought is to ask Notsurewho Notsurewhat to please not let anyone I know see me kissing Jidé Jackson, but then my mind empties and I am starting to understand why kissing isn't such a weird thing to do after all, because I forget everything in this kiss and everyone, except for Jidé Jackson . . . And it feels, well, it feels . . . like flying. When it's over, I rummage around in my pocket for the keys and with them I pull out the note I had folded away in my pocket. The note that I never thought I would show anyone, especially not Jidé Jackson . . . the note that says:

Horse, Artichoke, Green, Rwanda.

I hand it to him without saying a word. He unwraps it carefully and reads.

'We're both green then,' he grins, and plants

another playful kiss on my lips, and another, and another! It's as if he never wants to leave me.

It's probably my too-strong imagination but I feel as if Jidé's eyes are burning into my back. I stop myself turning round to see if he's still watching me cross the road. As I climb the steps to my front door, I glance sideways and out of the corner of my eye catch him waving to me. I pretend I haven't seen him, but he carries on waving anyway, as if to say, 'I know you know I'm still here!'

I fit my keys in the lock and let myself into our quiet house. I lean against the back of the door until my heart finally stops racing, and I breathe it in, for the first time ever, this sweet silence, because I know it won't last for long.

Saturday 21 May

Krish, Dad and me are in Nana's flat. We're here for Krish to choose something of Nana's. Krish didn't even want to come . . . He only wants to be with Laila since she's come out of hospital. Today, Krish looks more miserable than I have ever seen him. He goes around the flat peering into boxes and eventually finds a silver baby rattle on a blue ribbon for Laila. After that, he seems to lose interest. Dad's busy looking through stacked-up papers and boxes in the cupboard. I can't believe how organized Nana is. He finds some documents in one of the boxes to take back to Nana Josie. I roam around the flat showing Krish things I think he might like, but he just shrugs or shakes his head. I know what he means. It's miserable being in Nana's flat when she's not here. It makes you remember all the fun we had here, in the past.

'Remember that burping competition you had with Nana when we came to tea once?' I ask Krish.

His face starts to brighten up a bit.

'Or the time when you fell into the gloop by the pond, and me and Nana had to hose you down?'

He's warming up a bit now.

'And when we were little, how we used to climb over the wall, and Mum and Sheena from opposite broke down a bit of the fence so that me, you and her three boys could have a double-sized garden.'

'Yeah! But then they moved out and the new family boarded up the fence.'

Cheering Krish up is going to be hard work today.

'Remember May who lived in the flat upstairs? She used to wave to us from her window and throw us sweets in shiny wrappers. You thought it was raining sweets, the first time she did it.'

As soon as I say this, I know it's a mistake.

'Then she died,' Krish sighs.

I have days like this too, since Nana was ill. Dad puts his arm round Krish's shoulders, hugging him close, and, for a change, he doesn't pull away.

'You don't have to take anything, if you don't want to,' Dad tells Krish, but Krish thinks Nana will be upset if he doesn't choose something. Then Dad has an idea. He walks over to the cupboard he's been looking in and takes out a blue cardboard box, covered in fine dust like brown flour, which Dad gently blows off its surface, making us all sneeze. In it, there are all Grandad Kit's letters and photographs.

Grandad Kit died just before Krish was born. Krish often says things like, 'At least *you* met Grandad Kit,' and he seems quite jealous of that, although the fact is I only know things about Grandad Kit that other people have told me . . . it's not the sort of knowing I have with Nana Josie. But I do sort of remember sitting on his knee. Once Mum told me the story of the day Grandad Kit died. She went to the hospital with Dad, saw Grandad's body and held his hand. When my mum told Grandad Bimal that Grandad Kit had died, he asked my mum if she had touched his body.

'Then the spirit of Kit will go into the new baby,' Grandad Bimal told Mum. That baby turned out to be Krish.

Dad opens up the blue box and takes out a navy blue beret covered in medals as Krish fires questions.

'Which war was Grandad Kit in? What did he do in the war? Who's this in the photograph?'

When Krish finds out that Grandad Kit was a gunner in Malta during the Second World War, he is transformed; his arms morph into machine guns shooting planes down from the ceiling of Nana's flat. I don't think that Nana Josie would approve, somehow.

'Can I have that painting of Grandad Kit eating fish and chips?' Krish asks, stopping suddenly with his arm-gun firing in the direction of the painting, which has always been there, but I suppose he's never really noticed it before. Actually, if you look closely, it's the fish eating the chips, not Grandad Kit. This is the painting where Claude the Newfoundland dog has a head bigger than Grandad's. Nana does some very funny paintings where she gets the perspective all wrong on purpose. The style is called 'art naive', but I think Nana really does see things a bit the way children do. I've done a painting of Laila in an art naive style where her head is too big for her shoulders and her arms and hands look really little in comparison to the size of her head. People say it does look a lot like Laila.

'Take the easel, Mira.'

I hear Nana's voice order me, as clearly as if she was standing right next to me in this room. I fold down the legs and drag it towards the car. Dad sees me struggling and takes one end and we carry it to the car together. Nana's easel is surprisingly heavy.

As soon as we arrive at the hospice, Krish runs up to Nana to show her Grandad Kit's things. He's happy again, full of energy, but when he approaches Nana's bed he sees how weak she's become. Dr Clem keeps trying to get the right combination of drugs for her so she won't feel any pain. He has to keep changing her painkillers because the cancer pain is changing too . . . getting stronger.

You can tell when Nana has been in pain because her skin goes grey and her eyes sink into her. If she's had a bad night, she can hardly lift herself up off her pillows, but when she sees Krish, so enthusiastic, she tries really hard to look lively. He shows her the beret and the photos and the box and Nana puts on her glasses to read some of the letters from Grandad Kit.

'I'd forgotten about these love letters from your dad.' She looks up at my dad and smiles. I think of Jidé's secret note to me. I think it probably is my first ever love letter.

For a moment Nana is lost in the photographs of her and Grandad Kit, black and white photographs taken on the Embankment with Toro their bulldog.

'Look how young we were,' Nana whispers.

'You look like models out of a retro photo shoot. Errol Flynn and Audrey Hepburn!' Dad says.

Nana sighs, as if to say, 'Where has the time gone?'

'Can I have Grandad's beret then?' asks Krish.

'Of course you can,' she says, but I can tell she thinks Krish has made a strange choice. I understand him though. It fills a gap in the jigsaw and there's nothing Krish hates more than losing a piece of a jigsaw. He inspects the beret with all the medals on it and touches the textures on each one, as if trying to take hold of Grandad Kit.

'It's because I know you, Nana. I don't really need anything of yours, unless you want to give me

239

something . . . but I never knew Grandad Kit, or anything about you two together, when you were young.'

I think of Jidé . . . all he has of his sister and his mum and dad is a bit of cloth.

Nana holds Krish's hand for a minute and he looks at her with his bright blue eyes.

'Oh, and I forgot.' Krish lifts up Nana's painting for her to see. 'I found something that both of you are in. You painted it and Grandad Kit's in it. Can I have it, Nana?'

'Yes, that one worked out well.' Her laugh trails away into a distant memory that belongs only to her. 'It made Kit laugh too.'

For a while Nana seems to be lost in the past, until her eyes come to focus on Mum feeding Laila, whose little body relaxes as her hand falls, slow motion, through the air. She's still a bit weak after her illness. Nana picks up her thin wrist.

'Shame she's losing her fat bracelets. What did you choose for Laila?' Nana asks us.

Krish shows Nana the silver rattle on a blue ribbon.

'Apparently, that was my first rattle. Good choice, Krish.'

Nana tries to rattle it, but she doesn't even have the energy to make the little bells ring.

Laila has fallen fast asleep. Mum lifts her gently and lays her on the bed next to Nana. Nana's so small now, there is plenty of room. She puts her arm round

Laila and sighs as if she's the happiest person in the world. Mum sits close to the bed in case Laila rolls over, because if she needed to Nana would not be strong enough to pick her up by herself. Somehow Laila looks bigger than Nana; even after her illness she looks plumper . . . more alive.

My dad's Uncle James and Aunty Ella arrive. Krish and me call her 'Aunty Elegant', because she is. Ella delicately picks up Laila's rattle.

'What an exquisite old rattle,' she says, inspecting it.

'That was mine, Ella,' Uncle James tells her. 'Mine had a blue ribbon and Josie's had a pink one, but I won't fight you for it, Josie!'

'I should think not, James,' Aunty Ella laughs.

The phone next to Nana's bed rings. Dad picks it up.

'Dan . . . ?' He doesn't know who it is. 'Ah! Yes, *Dan* . . . from Suffolk . . . Yes, yes, Dan . . . of course, I do.'

Now he knows who it is.

'Can you talk to him?' whispers Dad to Nana, so as not to offend Dan if she doesn't want to speak. She hardly wants to talk to anyone these days.

Nana nods.

'I'm putting Josie on the phone for you. She might not be able to speak for very long, but she's listening.'

Dad holds the phone up to Nana's ear. I'm sitting right next to her so I can hear exactly what Dan's saying.

'Josie, I'm calling you from your cottage. I've been sitting in your garden all morning watching the flycatchers. You've got three chicks. They've come back to the same old pot, mouths open. Mum and Dad are in and out, feeding them all day long. I wish you could see them.'

Nana's eyes have welled up. She can't speak, but she passes the phone back to Dad and makes the shape of 'thank you' with her lips. Aunty Ella and Uncle James look worried, so I tell them the news from Nana's garden.

'The flycatchers have arrived.'

You wouldn't think something like birds nesting could make you feel so happy and heartbroken at the same time, but it does. Dad speaks to Dan for a bit longer, thanks him for calling and hangs up.

Nana closes her eyes. These days, that's the signal for us to leave. We all file past, kissing her. She doesn't open her eyes. I am the last to say goodbye.

'Did you take the easel?' Nana whispers through her tears.

I nod.

As we walk out into the corridor, we pass Question Mark. I stand in the doorway for a moment, watching him walk across the ward to Nana's bed. He pulls up the comfy chair, sits beside her and holds her hand. Question Mark feels me watching him and smiles up at me, a distant smile. Suddenly, I'm the stranger intruding on Nana and Question Mark ... the stranger standing on the outside of their dying world.

When I get home, I run up to my room and call Jidé and we talk and talk and talk ...

Sunday 22 May

The smoke alarm squealing, Mum wafting her tea towel around like a lunatic, Laila spitting out great gobs of baby porridge and Krish dribbling his football around the table . . . Just for a moment it almost feels like everything is back to normal, just an ordinary Sunday.

'How's it all going now at school?' Dad asks, trying to sound like it's just an off-the-cuff sort of question.

'Yeah, all right. I like the writing group we're doing.'

'What are you writing about?'

I'm not going to say Nana, because somehow I think that would worry him.

'Next week we've got to take in an object or something and we have to write about the object as if it's got a personality.'

'Ah, yes . . . personification, I remember it well.'

'Pat Print called it something else. I can't remember what . . . something about fallacy.'

'I know what I'd take in, this *blasted* alarm!' shouts Mum as she stands on a chair and nearly topples off, reaching up for the red button of the smoke alarm, and finally silencing it.

'Language, Uma!' Dad grins.

'I thought I'd take in Nana's charm.'

'Good idea. Go and get it then, and I'll fix it on for you,' says Dad cheerily as I collide with Krish and his football in the doorway.

'Do you have to be so annoying?'

'Where else am I supposed to play?' he huffs.

'I'll take you out later for a kick around,' offers Dad.

'Yes!' shouts Krish, punching the air and shooting me that look as if he's got one over on me.

'As if I care,' I mumble.

I run upstairs to my room, and there's the bracelet still sitting in the orange tissue paper on my old-fashioned school desk that Nana gave me . . . but the charm . . . I'm sure I put it safely in the inkwell. Maybe it's rolled off. So I scramble down underneath, flattening my body against the floor to get a better look, but it's too gloomy to see properly. I feel every inch of the carpet near my desk, but it's not there. I'm starting to get hot and sweaty and I have an empty, sick feeling in my belly. I cast around the room for a glimpse of it, looking in the same places over and over again, but they are always empty.

'Come on, Mira!' shouts Dad from downstairs.

How can I tell Dad that I've lost Nana's charm?

'Let's do it later,' I say, hanging on the banisters.

'Why not now?'

'Because . . . I can't find it,' I whisper.

We search all day, everywhere. Mum even empties the vacuum cleaner bag in case it's been hoovered up.

'Dad! You *promised* you'd have a kick around with me,' moans Krish.

'All right, all right . . . I'd better go.' Dad sighs. 'You just keep looking, Mira. It's bound to be around here somewhere.'

By the time Krish and Dad come back we've given up hope. Dad keeps saying, 'It'll turn up,' but, by the end of the day, it seems like it's not going to.

'Maybe Laila's eaten it,' suggests Krish, which is not as funny as you would think, because in the past she's had to be taken to A&E for eating money, beads and buttons and sticking sweetcorn in her ears and peas up her nose, not all at the same time, of course. Anyway, the thought of anything else happening to Laila is too horrible. When she hears her name, Laila crawls over to Krish and clambers up his leg.

'Have you swallowed the charm, Lai Lai?' Krish sings in his squeaky baby play voice.

'Kish Kish,' Laila chants as Krish picks her up and cuddles her.

'That's all we need! I'll check her nappies,' offers Mum.

'Gross!' groans Krish.

Before I get into bed, I hunt through the whole of my bedroom for Nana's charm, opening every box, bag and drawer. I think it's lost.

Monday 23 May

Nana says, if you think about it, dying is just like a battery running out. Your heart stops beating and then you die. For some reason I can't stop thinking about my furry dog I gave to Laila that used to yap and walk and do a somersault, but we never replaced the batteries, because it was actually quite annoying, so now it just sits there on the shelf. I tell Nana about the dog and she laughs and says, 'Yes, something like that,' but then, when I think about it, it's not at all like that, because we could put batteries in it if we wanted to, and make it bark and do somersaults, and you can't do that with a person; you can't just make them come back to life. I tell Nana that I think she's wrong. Dying is nothing like a battery running out. She laughs and hugs me to her.

'So young and so opinionated, Mira.'

Nana holds my wrist, feeling for the charm.

'Still no charm, Mira. Don't you like it?'

'I love it, Nana. Dad just hasn't had the time to fix

it on,' I lie, praying to Notsurewho Notsurewhat that she doesn't ask him.

'You know, I was thinking about those protective layers I was telling you about. I don't need them any more. I've shed them, all of them . . . All these people I love have come to see me and I've made my peace. Maybe that's the journey . . . getting back to that state of love.'

I flick through a catalogue from the William Blake exhibition we went to together. It's full of paintings and drawings of angels and people dying.

'Can I borrow this for my R.E. lesson?'

She just waves her hand as if to say, 'Take it. It's no use to me any more.'

Then she closes her eyes and drifts. That's what Nana calls it now, not sleeping, 'drifting'. Sometimes, I get the feeling that it's all the same to Nana now . . . the drifting and the talking to whoever's visiting. It's as if she's in a dream, moving further and further away from us. I get up to go, but Nana shocks me by grabbing hold of my wrist with a strength I didn't know she still had.

'Wear the charm, Mira,' she whispers.

When I get home I hunt all over the house for the charm. I even get a torch to shine under the furniture, but it's no good. I slump down on my bed and pick up my mobile to call Jidé but then change my mind,

flipping the lid closed again. What would I tell him –
that I'm so upset because I've lost Nana's charm?

*Question Mark is leaning over Nana's bed, holding her
hand. He takes off his white coat and underneath there is
one huge white feathery wing. He holds it tight and rips it
off his back, hard and quick, like you pull off a plaster, because otherwise it hurts more. There is a loud cracking noise,
like a bone breaking. His whole face is full of pain. Then he
hands his wing to Nana and she smiles at him.*

Tuesday 24 May

School is getting in the way of me and Jidé. We can't find any time just to be alone together, without all the rest of them gawping at us. At the end of school he runs after me, slipping his hand into mine, and we stroll along the walkway together.

'Do you want to come back to mine?'

'I'd love to, but I've got to see Nana.' I smile at him.

'Sorry I haven't called you . . . I just can't seem to think of what to say to you now, on the phone.'

'Nor me!'

'If we could find somewhere on our own, I could *show* you how I feel,' he says, winking at me.

I giggle and elbow him in the side.

'That hurt!' He doubles over in mock pain, looking up at me pleadingly.

'Get up, Jidé!' I laugh.

'All right! I'll walk you back home,' he says as if accepting defeat, taking my hand in his as a consolation prize.

When we get level with my door, he makes his move to kiss me, but just as our lips are about to touch I catch sight of Mum in our front window. She smiles and moves away.

I am crimson red when I get in, so I run straight up to my room.

'Get ready to go and see Nana,' Mum calls up the stairs.

As soon as I see Nana, I show her the sketch I've drawn of my dream of Question Mark Angel.

'Do you believe in angels, Nana?'

'If you believe in angels, then you have to believe in devils. I've never really gone in for all that . . . but I think maybe there *is* something otherworldly about Mark.'

Her voice is so weak and cracked now you can only just make out the words.

She points for me to pin my drawing on the wall right above her bed.

Later, when Question Mark comes to sit with Nana, she points to my sketch of him. He looks up and studies it. When he peers back down at me, I have the strangest feeling that he's looking down from a very high mountain.

'Do you think there are angels?' he asks.

I shrug.

'Do you?'

'I don't have any answers, I'm afraid,' he sighs.

Krish is driving me mad. He has snuck into my bed, and now he's insisting on keeping the light on because he says he's got to finish his Aboriginal drawing tonight.

'Why can't you do it in your own room?'

'I don't want to be on my own,' he shrugs, trying not to make a big deal of it. Sometimes I forget that Krish is younger than me. Suddenly, it feels like there's much more of a gap between us than two years.

I must have fallen asleep at some point during the night, but when I wake up the light is still on and Krish is still working on his picture. Dark rings circle his eyes. I peer over the duvet. It's amazing what he's done. Billions and billions of tiny pinhead-sized dots, starting with dark colours on the outside and getting brighter, spiralling into the middle. The dots in the centre are oranges, yellows and reds like fire, or the sun. When you look at Krish's picture, it feels as if all the energy he's put into it is leaping off the page at you, like swirling sparklers in the dark on bonfire night. It makes you breathless. I tell Krish that I think it's the best thing he's ever done. I ask him if he didn't get bored doing all those millions of dots, but he just shakes his head. I ask him if he was thinking about Nana when he was drawing it, but he says no; he wasn't thinking of anything at all except the colours.

Wednesday 25 May

'No sign of the charm?' asks Dad at breakfast.

I shake my head.

'Best not to bother Nana about it then,' says Dad, wrapping his arms round my shoulders and pulling me towards him. 'It's a bit of a mystery that, but it'll turn up . . . when you're not looking for it any more, probably.'

'I'll always be looking for it,' I say.

'I lost Nana's heart,' I whisper to Millie as Pat Print reads out an example of . . . *that* was it . . . the pathetic fallacy. Millie shoots me her 'What *are* you talking about?' look.

'Millie, tell everyone your Lockhart story,' shouts Ben, who's wearing his baseball cap back to front today.

So Millie reads it out.

'I really wanna read that book,' Ben booms.

'There you are, Millie. You can't get a better endorsement than that,' beams Pat.

'The problem is I still don't know what happens next,' sighs Millie.

'You know that expression "She's lost the plot"? Well, that's just it. In real life most of us haven't got much of a clue what the plot of our life is. We might think we have, then something random comes at you and suddenly you're in another plot line . . . That's one of the joys of writing – you have a bit more control to pull the plot out of your imagination.'

'That's what I did for the beginning,' says Millie.

'Then carry on. In the end the characters will lead you to the plot.'

Millie nods.

'What do you mean, you lost the heart?' Millie whispers to me while Pat Print chats to Jidé and Ben.

'I've looked everywhere. I've lost it. Nana's silver heart charm, the one she gave me for my birthday.'

'Now who's brought in an object to talk about?' asks Pat.

Ben's sitting, ready and waiting, with his skateboard on his knee.

'Let's have it then, Ben.'

Ben adjusts his baseball cap, switches his iPod on loud and starts rocking his skateboard back and forth, building up a rhythm before he entertains us with this one that he has definitely rehearsed. Because he's got his earphones on he has to shout even louder than he usually does, above the heavy rap beat.

I have graffiti on me.
Once a month I need a make
over
because every time he wheels me out
to hit the cold grey concrete,
I get beaten up.

Sometimes
he carries me under his arm
to cross the white line
where the giant tyres queue up,
but if no parent spies are looking out
I'll fly him across.

When we're together, there's no stopping us.
I feel the rhythm from his earphones pulsing through his
feet,
twisting, turning, gliding, bumping, falling through the
air.

I sit and wait all day for the sound of his feet,
the treads of his trainers on my wooden back.
Then we're off . . . flying down the track.

As he finishes, Ben hits his heel against the back of his board, and it seems to jump to order straight into his arms!

'I loved that, Ben. You've gone and seen the world

from the perspective of a skateboard. That description of the road with the giant wheels queuing up, and the parent spies, is inspired,' gushes Pat Print, genuinely impressed.

Ben grins.

'That's one of the things you absolutely have to do when you write, see things from different perspectives. Anyone want to add anything?'

'I liked the way he performed it, he's a real actor,' Millie says, actually looking a bit embarrassed.

'It's all about finding your voice, that sort of confidence . . . Ben, you're a natural but, let's face it, with your vocal cords you've had a head start on the rest of us.'

I laugh, which sets Jidé off too.

'What's so funny?' asks Pat Print.

'Mira's laugh.' Jidé smiles at me and this time I manage to keep my head up. 'It's like it belongs to someone else.'

'Now you're getting there, Jidé, observing human behaviour in action. I'll make a prediction, if you'll allow me, Mira. I have the feeling that one day soon that big laugh and that small speaking voice of yours will meet and that day will be a happy day for Mira Levenson.' Pat Print smiles at me.

'Jidé, how about you? Got anything for me?'

He nods and shows us a photograph of himself sitting between Grace and Jai. They have their arms wrapped round him and all three of them are smiling, the same smile. He looks about six years old, but he's still clinging on to that piece of orange cloth. You can tell so many things about Jidé Jackson from this portrait. I wonder, if I didn't know his story, whether I would be able to spot it, that heart with bodyguard protection . . . Probably not.

My eyes are not like his or hers, not my nose, not my lips, not my chin, but no one looks too closely because I have dark honey-coloured skin and one and one make two. It's amazing the things people say to Grace and Jai . . . about me. A woman on the 124 bus, when I was six years old, looked at Grace with her pale skin and her golden hair and green eyes and she looked at Jai with his dark brown skin and his black eyes and then she turned to Mum and said, 'Look at those eyes. You so make the best-looking ones though, don't you?'

And my mum said, 'What exactly are you talking about? Liquorice allsorts?' She's outspoken like that, Grace.

'That's all I wrote,' shrugs Jidé.

'That's not all you wrote. What you've written is full of what we call subtext. I can read between your words a hundred other thoughts, left unspoken, but if you wrote those words your writing wouldn't be anywhere near as powerful as it is.' Pat pauses. 'Any comments?' she asks.

Nobody says anything, but suddenly I feel the need,

for Jidé's sake, to fill the silence.

'It's like my brother Krish . . . he's practically blonde. Even though Grandad Bimal's Indian and Nana Kath's English, my mum looks really Indian, and my dad has dark hair and dark eyes, like Nana Josie, and I'm like I am . . .' I burble on.

'Your point is?' interrupts Ben.

'My point is that Krish, well, he's blonde and you wouldn't think he would be . . . and he's got these sparkly blue eyes like Nana Kath and people say stuff in front of him that really upsets him like, 'Where did this one come from?' Or, when me and Krish were little, people thought my mum was child-minding Krish. Sometimes they even ask Mum if he's adopted or stupid stuff like, 'What colour eyes does the milk-man have?' The funny thing about Krish is he looks exactly like my mum, but most people can't see that because he's white. Mum says genetics are a bit more complicated than what you learn in GCSE Biology, which is where most people's knowledge stops.'

'And your point?' repeats Ben.

'I know what you mean, Mira,' says Jidé, elbowing Ben hard in the side.

'Man, what was that for?' yelps Ben.

'Millie, would you like to go next?' Pat smiles. Millie shakes her head in that slow determined way she has that lets you know she's made up her mind and she's not changing it.

'Mira. Did you bring me anything?' asks Pat, looking a bit confused and attempting to change the subject before it all gets out of hand.

'I wanted to bring you the charm Nana gave me, but the chain broke and now I've gone and lost it. It was a tiny silver charm in the shape of an artichoke. I'll read you what Nana said about it when she gave it to me, if you like.'

Pat Print nods.

So I flick back in my red leather diary to my birthday, the day Nana gave me the charm, which feels like years, not days ago.

'I've given you this, Mira, because most people, by the time they get old, have grown themselves tough little shells around their hearts . . .'

'Now, that's a true example of the pathetic fallacy,' says Pat Print. 'What powers does Mira's nana think the charm holds?'

'I think it might be a symbol of how delicate love is,' answers Jidé, smiling at me. 'She thinks adults learn how not to feel by protecting themselves from feeling too much.'

Pat Print nods, glancing from Jidé to me. She can tell that something's going on between us.

'What do *you* think?' Jidé whispers to me.

'I don't know. I just feel terrible because she's worn

it nearly all her life and now I've gone and lost it,' I whisper back.

When Jidé talks to me now, I feel like everyone's eyes are on us, especially as he insists on sitting so close to me. It's terrible, but because of Jidé I can't really focus on Pat Print's carefully chosen closing words. It's obvious that she's rehearsed what she's going to say beforehand, but even so Pat Print is no good at saying goodbye. Now she's telling us how proud we should be of the work we've produced and how she hopes to see us all in print one day. 'No pun intended!' she laughs, that blueberry-coloured rash starting to rise up her neck, as it does when she feels emotional about anything.

As we all leave the class, Pat Print calls Millie back, so I wait for her a bit further up the corridor and inspect the trail of mud that Pat Print has left again, like her personal signature. I wonder where she walks to get so much mud on her shoes.

'What did she want?' I ask Millie.

'She asked me why I was so quiet today.'

'I didn't notice.'

'That's because you and Jidé were doing all the talking!'

'So what did you tell her?'

'I told her that I was quiet because I was so amazed to hear you speaking out like that . . . and I don't

261

know . . . I've been trying to work out what's so different about you.'

Now I really do feel guilty . . . because it's not that long ago that Millie knew *everything* about me. I practically couldn't even walk into school without her holding my hand, but since Jidé, well, I haven't needed her so much.

'I've started my periods,' I blurt out.

'Really! When? Are you all right?'

'On my birthday. Great present!'

'That was ages ago. Why didn't you tell me?''

I shrug, feeling even more guilty than before.

'So come on then, what's it like?' prods Millie.

'It's like blood,' I say stupidly.

'Well, I *know* that. I mean how does it feel?'

'I don't know. It's like everything's changed. I can't stop it happening, can I?'

Suddenly Millie looks worried. 'Does it really hurt then?'

'Not hurt. I just sort of felt heavy, and a bit achy . . . oh, and I got spots.'

'Oh, yeah! I remember now,' laughs Millie.

'Thanks!'

'Was your mum surprised?'

'A bit,' I lie.

'I hope *I* start soon.'

'Why would you *want* to start your periods?'

'I dunno, I'm just ready for a change,' grins Millie.

262

Thursday 26 May

Jidé and Ben join Millie and me on our high wall at break, but somehow there is nothing much for us to say to each other, altogether like this.

After a while Ben and Jidé wander off, leaving Millie and me on our own. I wonder what she's not saying to me about Ben, because I know what I'm not saying to her about Jidé, and even though we sit here side by side, like we always do, we might as well be at opposite ends of the courtyard.

I watch Nana sleep. This is the first time I've visited her when she hasn't even known I'm here. Doris, Dr Clem and Question Mark come and go, more often than before. All I can do is watch her sleep and wait. She is waiting now . . . and we are waiting . . . for the end.

Friday 27 May

When I see the empty bed, I am sick all over the floor. I hear someone screaming like a siren. That someone is me. Question Mark appears, sits me down and helps me clean myself up.

'Your nana has been moved to a room of her own,' he says. 'Don't you remember? We told you yesterday.'

I don't remember.

'Is she going to die soon?' I ask.

'She's very weak now, Mira,' he says, walking me to Nana's new room. Question Mark's hand is smooth and cool, like powdered silk. The moment my hand's in his, I start to feel calm.

NO ENTRY reads the sign on Nana's door. Question Mark says that Nana Josie doesn't want any other visitors, only 'immediate family'. I ask what 'immediate family' means. Dad says it means 'only us'.

I open the door, but somehow it still feels like I shouldn't go in, so I stand in the doorway watching Nana. Her Dying Room has a view on to those enormous Hampstead houses that look like the ones in Mary Poppins that rise up and up 'to the highest heights'.

Right outside the Dying Room there are two huge oak trees just coming into flower. The window takes up one whole side of the room. The sun streams in and shines on Nana's face, warming her blankets. Dad asks if he should close the blinds, but Nana smiles 'no' with her mouth. She's enjoying sunbathing.

Nana talks silently now as much as she can. I think she's saving her energy for dying. I sit next to her. I don't dare lie on the bed any more, because she's so thin I might squash her. I gaze out of the window and across the street. I can see straight into what looks like an artist's studio. There are two enormous windows on either side of the room so that, through the far window, I glimpse the green of the Heath stretching out into the distance.

'They must have a great view of London,' I say.

'Perfect,' Nana whispers. Her voice is dry and scratchy. 'I'd like to see that room.'

'Just imagine, Nana, if I open this window, and they open theirs, you could fly out of here across the street, into that room and then straight out the other side.'

Nana is squeezing my hand. 'How's someone some-one?' she whispers, smiling.

There doesn't seem much point denying it now.

'He's fine,' I whisper, smiling back.

Then suddenly Nana starts to cough. I think I've

been making her talk too much. Doris comes in and props her up on her pillows. Nana calls Doris 'the poet' because of the way she sings when she talks, so you almost forget the meaning of the words; you can just taste something sweet in your mouth.

Doris sits in the sunshine on Nana's bed. She takes a little white bag from the trolley. Inside it is a soft stick, like a toothbrush the size of a cotton bud, which she smoothes around Nana's teeth. Afterwards, she takes out a tiny sponge, which she dips into drinking water and squeezes into Nana's mouth. Doris's hands are small and shiny like they've been rubbed in oil. I think it's a shame that she has to slide her beautiful hands into those chalky white gloves. Doris dips the sponge in water again and touches it against Nana's lips, so gently, dab, dab, dab. I do not think I have ever seen anyone do anything with more love than Doris performs Nana's tooth-brushing ceremony.

Nana sighs and closes her eyes. Question Mark walks silently in and asks Nana if she's comfortable. She nods twice with her eyes closed. Everything seems to have slowed down here in the Dying Room. There is nothing on Nana's bedside table. No art books, no paintings, no fruit, no water . . . no water.

I try to hold Nana's hand, but her fingers are all curled up.

Krish brings Nana his Aboriginal picture. My mum

has mounted it on a board, so it looks even better. He doesn't say anything, but he holds it up for her to see. She just stares at it, lost in the millions of colours swirling around and around. Then she looks at Krish and mouths 'thank you' and Krish bows his head on to Nana's knee. After a while he is very still and his breathing is quiet. He has fallen asleep. She lifts her hand and places it on his head; just the effort of that movement makes her breathless. I tell Nana that Krish spent all night finishing this picture. She gestures for me to prop it up on her bedside table. As I leave the room, Nana is lost somewhere among the billions of coloured dots.

On the way out, we drop into the Family Room. Mum's talking to Jay, who's brought a fruit salad for Nana. When Jay opens the fridge door and sees that Nana's shelf is full of little plastic boxes of food that haven't been touched, she puts the fruit salad back in her bag and empties Nana's shelf. Tears roll down her cheeks as she wipes the shelf clean.

In the hospice people talk with their eyes, with a quiet hand on your arm, or a nod. You have to really look to see what's going on. Twice today, I have seen Dr Clem and Doris in silent conversation with my dad and Aunty Abi. They have these conversations where no words escape when they pass each other in the corridor. After one of these silent conversations my dad walks off to the Family Room with his head and eyes lowered.

Saturday 28 May

Question Mark calls from the hospice.

I put on my watch. It's the first time I've worn it since my birthday. I took it off because I thought maybe it was making time speed up . . . maybe the watch had something to do with Nana's coffin arriving and my periods starting, and I thought if I took it off it might make it all slow down, but now I know there's no going back. Some things you can't change, no matter who or what you pray to.

When we arrive, Headscarf Lady quickly buzzes us through the security door. Usually she has a little chat, or makes a joke, but today she just nods and bows her head. As we walk through the doors, I hear her speaking on the intercom.

'The Levenson family are on their way up.'

Doris is waiting for us. She has her head lowered. She holds out her arm for us to follow her into the Family Room, where we sit down on the comfy chairs to hear the news. She folds her hands together on her knees and sits very still for a moment. She has a gentle, sad smile on her face.

'Josie died this morning. Mark and I were here with her, and Abi sat with her all night.' She soothes over these words in her honey voice. 'She passed so peacefully, like a feather on a breeze.'

'What time did she die?' Krish asks.

'A few minutes after ten o'clock this morning.'

These are the things you have to know . . . the date and the time people die and are born. That was the first question people asked when Laila was born.

The moment when Nana died, when her heart stopped beating, we were driving past Hampstead Heath on our way to the hospice. I think I know the exact moment because I checked my watch at exactly 10.05 a.m. At exactly 10.05 a.m., eighteen minutes ago, I looked up at the people: young people, old people, children, walking dogs in the sunshine, great big dogs, tiny yapping dogs, all sorts of dogs. I remember having the thought that all these people could be my Nana Josie in different parts of her life, and then I thought about something that made me feel happy. When Nana is dead and I walk on the Heath or in Suffolk . . . I could always step into the exact same footprints as she did. Even with my maths, I worked out that Nana has done so much walking in these places that the probability of stepping where she once did could be quite high.

That thought made me feel happy at exactly 10.05 a.m. That was the moment my Nana's heartbeat stopped. I suppose that is a number fact.

The NO ENTRY sign is still up in Nana's Dying Room. Aunty Abi sits in the armchair next to her bed. Dad and Aunty Abi give each other a long hug. Dad's back is heaving up and down and he's making a horrible strangled crying noise. Aunty Abi is calm, but her eyes are sore and puffy.

'I was here,' says Abi. 'I sat with her all night and I just popped out into the garden with Piper this morning for a few minutes and when I came back she'd gone.'

Dad says nothing but his back is still shuddering with emotion. Piper is lying on top of Nana's feet as if he's guarding her body.

Someone has put an orange lily on the pillow next to Nana Josie's head. All the windows are open, and the room smells fresh and empty. I look over to the studio. The window facing the hospice is flung open and the window on the far side is open too. Maybe Nana did get to look around that room after all.

Dad sits in the chair next to Nana's bed, hardly moving at all. His body is almost as still as Nana's. I thought I would be afraid to look at her, but with the life gone out of her, it's as if Nana's body is just an empty shell.

This is not like I thought it would be . . . the end . . . so quiet and still and final.

Doris and Question Mark say we can stay in the room with Nana for as long as we need to. Of course, now that Nana has gone, it's all about what *we* need. But we don't know what we need so we start packing Nana's clothes away, because it doesn't feel right to sit and stare at her body when it really does feel that Nana has left it behind. So all of us help to pack away her clothes and everything we've brought to the hospice.

The way we move around the room, folding and packing away, is like a strange silent ceremony. Mum goes to pack up Krish's Aboriginal drawing but I ask her not to, not yet. I tell her to leave it till last. I don't know why. Then we take Nana's clothes out of the wardrobe and pack Nana's belongings neatly away into her soft canvas bag.

There is a knock at the door. It's Doris with Laila. Doris has been doing a tour of the ward, showing Laila off to all the patients . . . to give Mum a rest.

'Here's your darlin',' Doris coos, gently handing Laila back to Mum, who takes her up the corridor to the Family Room, where Krish has been watching football with the man who got married.

Then we all wait for Dad and Aunty Abi. When we get up to leave, it is four o'clock.

'See you later, mate,' the man who got married says, ruffling Krish's hair.

'See you, Jo.'

I didn't even know his name. I didn't realize Krish knew him so well, but I suppose they've watched a few matches together since the wedding. Jo gets up and waves to us from the door, but Krish just stands with his hands in his pockets, looking up at Jo.

'I could come and see you, if you want,' offers Krish.

He's trying to make it sound as if he doesn't care either way.

'No, son, you get out there and get on with it.'

Then suddenly Krish runs at Jo and hugs him round the middle. They are both crying now. We are all crying, because now we understand about real life endings . . . how hard it is to say goodbye forever.

'Come on, you Spurs!' calls Jo as we walk down the corridor.

We pass the Men's Room, where the woman who got married to Jo is arranging flowers in a vase. She comes over to say goodbye to us. Mum hugs her and rests her hand on her tummy, which I think is an odd thing to do, so I look at her, and see, for the first time, that she's going to have a baby.

'Keep in touch, Lyn.'

My mum scribbles our number on a scrap of paper. Dad and Lyn hug, Aunty Abi and Aunty Mel hug her too and even Piper tries to jump up at her.

Everyone's faces are red and puffy and soaking wet with tears. I feel sad for us that Nana has gone. But for Jo, Lyn and the baby, who isn't even born yet, everything's in the wrong order.

We pass the room where Doris and Question Mark and the other nurses sit. My dad says 'thank you'. I have heard those words so many times in my life, but I have never heard anyone say them in the way my dad thanks Doris and Question Mark.

'It was our privilege,' says Question Mark, holding Dad's hands in his.

Dad asks if Dr Clem's on duty. He's not, but Doris says he knows about Nana and he was planning to drop in and see us before we leave. Somehow it doesn't feel right to leave without saying goodbye to Dr Clem.

We stand outside Heath Ward, waiting for the lift. It takes ages to come. Krish doesn't even try to run down the stairs; he just stands very still, patiently waiting. When it finally comes, the lift is empty. At the bottom, the doors open and Dr Clem is standing in front of us. He backs away to let us out, and leans his shopping bags against the wall. Dad sets down Nana's bag and Dr Clem glances towards it, sadly. He says he's glad he managed to catch us. He looks at us with his droopy eyes, each of us, one by one. This noise escapes from my dad's mouth, which is something like a very low cough that shakes his body. Dr Clem holds Dad, as if to steady him. Then Dad grasps on to Dr Clem, their hands patting hard on each other's back. They make me think of gorillas comforting one another. Dr Clem must have seen thousands of people dying, but he still cares for Nana Josie, and for us. When Dad and Dr Clem finally unclasp, he notices me and Krish peering into his shopping bags full of crisps and lemonade.

'They're for my daughter's birthday party . . . so I'll always remember your nana, on this day.'

He has obviously only come here today to see us, because now he turns round and walks back out again.

As we follow him on to the pavement I hear Headscarf Lady calling to us. We have forgotten Krish's artwork.

'Your Nana Josie loved that so much. I think it helped her, in the end. Whenever she opened her eyes, she just seemed to be lost in it,' Dr Clem says, resting a comforting hand on Krish's shoulder.

Krish nods, with his head bowed low. Then he turns to Headscarf Lady. 'Here, you have it.'

She shoots Mum and Dad a look, as if to ask if it's OK, and I see them both smile and nod.

Headscarf Lady gathers Krish into her arms, before he has time to protest, and squeezes him tight.

'You're an angel,' she says. Krish just looks up at her and shrugs.

Dr Clem walks up the road, clanking his party

bags. At the corner, he stops and glances up at a flock of tiny birds wheeling through the sky. I follow their path, arcing upwards, riding the air. Dr Clem smiles, turns the corner and is gone.

The sky is bright blue and there's a real heat in the sun today. It's a holiday atmosphere. It's like the whole of London has decided to walk on the Heath. I like the fact that all these people don't know that Nana has died. We walk past the ponds where people are swimming in the gloopy green water and up Parliament Hill, like we have so many times before with Nana and Piper. Krish doesn't race Piper up the hill, like he usually does. There are kite flyers zigzagging all over, getting their tails tangled . . . Dads, mostly, on a promise to get their children's kites to fly, but the day is too still.

'Where are we going?' asks Krish.

'To Nana's flat,' answers Dad.

'Why?' I ask.

'Because it feels to me like the right thing to do,' he sighs.

It doesn't feel right to me.

'I'm staying here,' I say to no one in particular.

Mum and Dad give each other that look, where they're checking out what the other one thinks. Mum shrugs. Dad shrugs. Everything's changing. No one knows any more what's the right thing to do.

'Be back at Nana's in half an hour,' Mum says, handing Piper's lead to me. 'Are you wearing your watch?'

I tap my wrist to show her.

'That's not fair! Can I stay?' moans Krish.

'No!' Mum wraps her arm round Krish's shoulder and leads him off down the hill with Dad walking beside them, pushing Laila in the pram.

Mum turns back to me when she's halfway down the hill.

'Have you got your mobile?' she shouts.

I wave it in the air for her to see. Then I slump down on the bench where Nana and me always used to sit. I look up at the bright blue sky, but there is no Nana Josie flying through the air on Claude's back, no Jidé either. It's nothing like my dream. Piper jumps on to the bench, nuzzles up to me and whines, as if he's looking for Nana too.

Then he's off, running down the hill, barking, tail wagging frantically, and, as I try to catch sight of him, that's when I see her walk towards me.

'Mira!'

Pat Print sits down next to me and I see Piper bounding back towards us. We watch Moses and Piper frolicking around like a couple of puppies.

'On your own?'

I try to speak but my voice gets choked by the sadness that rises up in me like a surging wave. It's very hard to say the words, especially the first time you say them . . . as if you make it real by saying it . . .

'My nana died this morning.'

It comes out as not much more than a whisper. Pat Print doesn't know what to do or say. What she does is stroke Piper on the head. I think this is her way of comforting me. Piper whines.

'Poor old Piper . . . Shall we walk?'

We trail off down the hill, following Piper and Moses on their windy path of pee trails. Then Piper disappears into a bit of woodland at the bottom of the hill.

'Piiiiiper,' I call, but he doesn't come out. So we go to investigate, Pat Print and me.

He is rooted to the trunk of an oak tree, barking like a lunatic. It's probably a squirrel. I look up into the tree and a flash of red catches my eye. That's when I spot it, Nana's hat . . . her cherry-red crochet hat, caught on a high branch.

'That's Nana's. She lost it on a walk with me last Christmas. She had me searching all over for it.'

'How on earth did it get up there?' says Pat, peering up through the branches.

'Do you think I could get it?' I ask her.

Pat Print shakes her head.

'No, but I can,' she says, and before I can argue with her she is climbing up the tree, branch by branch. She seems to know exactly where to place her

277

feet. Pat Print is an expert tree climber! She is dangerously high up – most people wouldn't even think of
going up that high . . . At the trunk, Moses is barking
wildly. Pat Print reaches out for Nana's hat, but she
can't quite get hold of it so she knocks it loose and it
falls towards me through the branches, just as it fell
from Nana's head in my dream . . . leaving her long
black hair streaming like the dance of a kite behind
her. I catch it and put it on.

'Suits you,' smiles Pat Print, jumping down off the
last branch.

'You're a brilliant climber.'

'I'm never happier than when I'm sitting at the top
of an ancient tree. I've always dreamed of living in a
tree house,' she laughs. 'I've climbed a tree just about
every day of my life since I was four years old.'

We walk off down to the bottom of the hill where
the path divides in two. I am so grateful to her for
not asking me anything about Nana. It's a shame they
never met, because I think Nana Josie and Pat Print
would have really liked each other.

'Did you manage to write the rest of that diary?'
she asks.

'Every day, so far.'

'I had you down as a diary writer,' says Pat. 'I'd
love to read it, if you want me to? You can give it to
Miss Poplar. Well, this is my track.' Pat Print points
towards the nature pond.

'And this is mine,' I say, pointing up dog-poo alley towards the road.

'Well, I'm sure our paths will cross again,' Pat smiles. 'Moooooooses!' she calls . . . and he chases after her.

Sunday 29 May

Question Mark phoned Dad to tell him that tomorrow Nana's going to be on the radio programme called *Start the Week*. Question Mark didn't want us to come across it by chance, in case we had a shock, hearing her voice.

There is nothing to do. On Sundays we always visit Nana. Even though Dr Clem said we are always welcome to drop in and see them at the hospice, it would seem odd without Nana. Anyway, Nana's body's not in her room any more. It's been moved to what they call the Chapel of Rest. We could go and see her there, I suppose, but Dad says he doesn't feel the need.

I lie on my bed reading the same lines of my book over and over again, without taking any of the meaning in. It doesn't feel like I'm alone because of Nana's easel. It's a bit like having another person sitting in the corner of the room, watching me. I couldn't sleep last night. I just kept feeling Nana's hand clasping my wrist and chanting, 'Wear the charm, Mira . . . wear the charm . . . Why aren't you wearing the charm?' This morning my head aches as if someone's tightening a clamp round it, so I could really do without Mum in my room right now. She's brought up a bag of Nana's old clothes for me to look through.

'Some of this is real vintage stuff, Mira. It would be a shame to throw it away. Have a look and see if you want anything.'

I suppose she gets the hint when I don't answer, because she closes the door quietly behind her, leaving me alone with the bag. As soon as I open the zip, Nana's sandalwood smell fills the room, like a genie escaping from a bottle. There's a suede green jacket that looks 1960s, two pairs of jeans and lots of pretty Indian tops, strappy sandals and walking boots. I try on the jeans and they fit me perfectly. I put on Nana's orange beaded top that still smells of her. I love the feel of Nana's clothes against my skin. I am trying to work out if wanting to wear them is weird, but it doesn't feel wrong . . . it's just like a memory of her, and that's what's left when someone you love is dead . . . and their smell.

What else is in this bag? One whole boxful of Nana's carefully folded wrapping paper. There are a few scraps of beautiful colours, and full pieces that Nana must have bought ready to wrap . . . And there's ribbon too, fine and wide, in every colour of the rainbow . . . For each piece of wrapping and each coloured ribbon, she had someone in mind . . . There's some deep blue ribbon and white tissue paper and some stickers with runners on them. It's Krish's birthday in a week's time. I bet that was meant for him.

I am thinking of moving Nana's easel out of my room, because in the darkness, with only the landing light casting shadows around the room, it looks even more like a person standing in the corner, watching me. I am afraid to go to sleep. I don't know what I'm afraid of, except that I hate the thought of Nana's body still lying in the hospice. If only she could be moved to her flat, or even to our house, so that we could look after her ourselves. Dad says her body is just a shell now and that her spirit is free and I think he's right. But the question is where is Nana's spirit? In the gloom, I look over to her easel. I swear it's beckoning to me.

Monday 30 May

I wake up wanting to tell Jidé about Nana dying . . . In a way I wish it wasn't half term. For the first time in my life I wish it wasn't the holidays. Then I remember my mobile. Even though I want to talk to Jidé most, I call Millie first. The phone goes straight to answer machine. I remember now that she's away on holiday. It's not the sort of message you can leave on someone's answerphone, is it? 'My nana's dead, but you can listen to her on the radio this morning.'

So I just hang up and hover over Jidé's name before pressing the call button.

'Yep!'

'Jidé!'

'Mira!'

He sounds happy and surprised to hear my voice.

'It's about my nana.'

'She died?'

He says it for me.

'Yes,' I whisper.

'Are you all right?'

'Not really,' I mumble. 'She's on the radio this morning; they recorded her in the hospice . . . I thought you might want to listen.'

I don't know why I want Jidé and Millie to hear Nana talking, but if I had her number I would call Pat Print too.

'What time?'

I give him the details and after that I can't think of anything else to say.

'I'll listen,' he says. 'When's the funeral?'

'Saturday.'

'Do you want to meet? I mean . . .'

'I don't think I can . . . with all this going on.'

'OK, just call me if you need me.'

Before I spoke to him, I felt all right, but now the tears are streaming down my face and my voice is all choked up.

'I hope it's . . . well . . . I'll be thinking of you.'

'Me too,' I squeak in my high-pitched teary voice.

Just as I hang up I hear him say my name . . .

'Mira?'

I wait, to see if he calls me back, but he doesn't.

If someone is dead and they come on the radio, it's like they're not dead at all. It's just as if they're really talking to you . . . ghost-talking. If someone you love dies and you keep hearing their voice on the radio,

284

or see them in films or on the television, you could pretend that they're still alive by listening to them or watching them over and over.

I was there when the woman interviewed Nana for the radio. But when I hear her voice, everything sounds different. For a start, they've added music, the kind they would play at the Pope's funeral. I want to tell Jidé that it's nothing like my nana would choose. There are other people that I haven't heard before, talking about what they believe in and how what they believe in affects the way they feel about dying. I wonder which of the people talking are still alive.

We sit around the radio, like I've seen loads of times in old films, when they show that moment when Neville Chamberlain announces that Britain is at war with Germany. We huddle around, waiting to hear Nana speak to us, and somehow it helps to feel that Jidé is listening in with me. It takes me a while to realize that Nana has already started speaking, because Laila's making such a racket talking to baby Su Su, her doll. Mum says, 'Shhhhh,' to Laila, who is alive, so that we can listen to Nana Josie, who is dead.

Nana's voice sounds different, sort of velvety. Dad says the radio technicians can put your voice through a warmer to make it sound richer. I don't think they should change people's voices like that. Even the things she says, which I have heard before, somehow seem different . . . more important. First of all you hear someone talking about the Pope. Then you hear Jo and Lyn talking about their wedding day and the baby and about how they have 'faith in each other'. After that there's a short bit with the supposed-to-be-famous person who turns out to be *Crystal*! Dad says she's an actress, but none of us have even heard of her. Then you hear Nana talking. I know why the radio woman made Nana such a big piece of her story, because out of all of the people talking, my nana is the one who sounds the most alive.

Tuesday 31 May

Mum and Dad are on the phone all day, letting people know the news. I can't believe how much there is to do when someone dies. Dad has to arrange to register Nana's death. It's the same town hall he went to for Krish's, Laila's and my birth certificates. It must feel really strange, to have a piece of paper in your hands that tells you the exact end date and time of your mother's life.

Nana's left loads of instructions about the funeral and who she wants Mum and Dad to contact and who she wants Aunty Abi and Aunty Mel to call. It's like she's planned a great big party and our house has been turned into the planning office, only there's nothing fun about it.

The letterbox clanks and I run downstairs wishing it could be Millie with an escape plan. I would like more than anything else to get out of this house. If I had the courage, I would call Jidé back and ask if I could go over to his place. Instead of Millie or Jidé, a tall lady, as solid as a door, wearing square glasses, stands on our step. The way she nods towards me reminds me a bit of Moses – the coffin man, not the dog.

'Is this the Levenson household?' she asks.

I nod, but don't let her in. There's something about her I don't like – maybe it's her smile, which is dead behind the eyes.

'Who's that?' Dad calls from the kitchen.

'Tell your father that I'm the celebrant.'

'She's the celebrant,' I call back.

Dad appears in the hallway and shakes hands with the woman, as if she's someone quite important. I sit and listen to them talking for a while. This woman is going to be the person who keeps the funeral service together, like a priest but without the God bit. She calls herself a celebrant, because she says we will be celebrating the life of Nana Josie. That's OK for her, because she never really knew my nana. How am I supposed to celebrate?

I don't see why we need her to do it anyway. I can't understand why Nana chose this woman. She never liked people who spoke too slowly or too quietly. 'Controlling behaviour,' Nana used to call it. Celebrant Lady does both as she sits with Mum and Dad, filling in forms and making notes, planning the schedule for Nana's funeral.

'And Mira here, she wants to read a poem, or say

something.' Dad smiles at me, probably trying to make me feel involved.

'Ah,' sighs Celebrant Lady, without looking my way. 'When it comes down to it, it can be very difficult for children to deal with these big emotions. I can always read it out for you,' she says, half smiling in my direction. 'What's the name of your poem?'

'I don't know yet,' I lie. Just because I feel like being as unhelpful as possible towards her. 'I know the music Nana wanted though,' I tell Dad.

'Do you? That's great. Tell me later,' whispers Dad, looking sideways at an impatient-looking Celebrant Lady.

'Well, let me have the title and author of your poem as soon as you can, and a copy, just in case,' she says, packing away her sensible black notebook.

I can't believe that this is actually her job. What she wants to do with her life. Plan other people's funerals.

When she's gone, Mum and Dad are back on the phone. It's as if Krish and me and Laila don't exist any more. Laila's been plonked in front of the television in a little nest of cushions and Krish is sprawled out on the sofa, still in his pyjamas. He hasn't moved all day.

I wander up to my room to find something to do. But there it is waiting for me . . . Nana's easel. Every time I look at it, I can't help but feel as if it's calling me over. It's something about the way it leans.

Today, it's bending even further to the right than ever. I take out my charcoals. It's as if I'm walking towards another human being, but I know it's only an easel, made of wood and spattered with Nana Josie's paint. I fix the canvas in place; it's as if I have no choice . . . As I start to draw, I can feel something of Nana inside her easel. It must be all those hours she's spent standing in front of it. I don't even have to adjust the height. It fits.

It's not like I've really thought about what I'm going to draw. I just pick up my mirror and put it on a shelf behind the easel, so that I can see myself and draw at the same time. This is my first ever attempt at a self-portrait, and as soon as I start, I realize how difficult it's going to be. It was much easier to draw Nana than it is to follow every detail of my own face. I work on it for hours, drawing in lines and smudging them out again. It's not just the shape of the face that makes you look like you – you have to try and catch what's coming to the surface. Like the day I understood that Nana was trapped in her body. No matter how accurate you are with the lines and proportions, if you can't catch that, you can't bring a person to life. Finally a face emerges which has something in it that belongs to me. That's the best I can do, for now.

I am lying in bed staring at my first attempt at a self-portrait, on Nana's easel.

Mum knocks on the door. She never used to knock.

'Everything all right, Mira? You've been very quiet today.'

Mum walks over to the easel, looking from me to the canvas.

'That's a very sad and sombre you,' says Mum, wrapping her arms around me.

I nod.

For a while we just lie there together, looking at the girl in the picture, who is me.

'She looks like I imagine you'll look, when you're older . . . maybe sixteen, but this terrible sadness will pass,' says Mum, moving the mirror back to the dressing table.

'I just looked in the mirror, and tried to draw what I saw,' I tell Mum.

Now that I've finished, the easel's straightened up. It's not calling me over any more.

When I turn the light off, there is nothing sitting in the corner of the room watching me. It's just Nana's easel with my first attempt at a self-portrait sitting on it. It's as if it's peaceful, now that I've done what it wanted. Can there be such a thing as a peaceful easel? Pat Print would say there could.

Wednesday 1 June

I wake with an acid taste in my mouth and a dull ache in my belly . . . I know what's coming and I actually want it to come right now. That way, by the time it's Nana's funeral, it will all be over. Today I feel like lying in bed, doing nothing, seeing no one.

'I've got a job for you today,' says Mum, opening a box full of programmes for Nana's funeral. There are hundreds of them.

'Are there that many people coming?'

'It's hard to know, Mira, but Josie wanted glitter, so glitter she must have.'

For the cover of the programme Nana chose a photo of her by the sea in Suffolk. She's throwing a piece of wood into the waves for Claude, her Newfoundland. She wanted us – me, Krish and Laila – to sprinkle glitter on the waves in the photo. So that's what we try to do, but it's impossible with Laila 'helping', because she either keeps trying to eat the glitter or just splodges it on to the cards. Mum says it doesn't matter, but I think it does. Nana would have liked the idea of Laila joining in, but not if she made a mess of the cards. After ruining about five of them, Mum finally realizes that it's just not going to work, so she takes her off to the swings.

Krish sits in silence, carefully sprinkling just the right amount of glitter on to each wave. I have mixed the glitter to be the colour of the Suffolk sea on a warm summer's evening . . . silvery-blue.

You know that there's something wrong when Krish is this still and quiet.

'I've done twenty – how about you, Krish?'

That should wind him up enough to get a reaction. But Krish just counts his pile, without looking up.

'Fifteen,' he shrugs, as if he doesn't care.

'Are you all right?'

He doesn't answer, but just carries on gluing and glittering.

Glitter is sprinkled all over this house, but there is nothing here to celebrate.

Thursday 2 June

Aunty Abi, Aunty Mel and Piper arrive to take Krish off to buy a suit. His first ever suit. I see that Mum's already decided that I'm going to wear what Nana bought me for my birthday, because she's washed and ironed it and hung it on the back of my bedroom door. I wonder if she saw the blood. I suppose I *have* to wear it now because if she didn't see it there's no excuse not to wear it.

When Piper sees Krish and me, he barks and jumps all over us, licking our faces like he's really missed us.

'Can we take him for a walk?' Krish pleads, jumping up and down in excitement. It's the first time I've seen him anything like his usual lively self since Nana died.

'*After* we've got your suit,' says Abi.

'Boring!' sighs Krish.

Krish hardly ever wears anything except sports clothes or, if he's being really smart, jeans. So going shopping for a suit is not exactly his idea of heaven. I would love to go out and choose something to wear, something I really like, but I wouldn't go today, not to try things on . . . just in case. One thing that does make Krish happy is the fact that Aunty Mel has taken the roof off her beaten-up old sports car. As they drive off, Krish waves like the queen, probably to make me jealous. Irritating though he is, I'm actually pleased he's more his old self again.

I lie on my bed for most of the day, flicking through Nana's giant art books . . . her art books *and* her collection of catalogues from all the exhibitions she ever went to in her life . . . she left them all to me.

The phone rings. Mum's voice is shrieking at the same unbearable pitch as the smoke alarm. Suddenly the atmosphere in the house is charged. To make matters worse, Laila sets up her wailing. I jump off my bed and listen from the landing.

'What do you mean, run off? How long ago?'

Mum fires question after question down the phone. I run downstairs to see that Mum's face has turned Payne's Grey. Dad's rocking Laila, too fast, backwards and forwards, straining to hear what's going on over Laila's wailing. Mum's holding her hand over her mouth, trying to calm herself down. She looks as if she can't believe what she's hearing.

'OK! Sam and Mira will come over to look with you. If we don't find him in an hour, we'll call the police.'

Dad hands Laila to Mum.

'Abi's on her mobile,' says Mum. 'They're looking over the Heath for him.'

'Get your shoes on, Mira,' orders Dad.

Suddenly we are speeding towards the Heath. This is the second time in a month I've been in a car with my dad in a total panic. Pat Print was right: a lot can happen in a month. We're taking the same route that we always took to the hospice and that's what gives me the idea.

'Maybe he's gone to the hospice.'

'Why would he do that, Mira?'

'I don't know. He's been very quiet since Nana died.'

'It's worth a try, I suppose,' Dad says, picking up his mobile to call them, but right at that moment his phone rings.

'Uma . . . where? Mira thought he might . . . Ran all that way . . . Have you called Abi? Good. I'll pick him up.'

Dad smiles his 'you know best' smile at me and we drive, a bit less dangerously than before, to the hospice. When we arrive in reception, Headscarf Lady gives Dad and me a huge hug . . . It feels like we're coming home.

'He's upstairs, with Jo. He ran all the way from the other side of the Heath. Can you believe it?' Headscarf Lady says, buzzing us up.

I can. That's no further than one of his competition runs.

When we get to the Family Room, Krish is playing table football with Jo. He looks worried when he sees Dad, as if he's going to get told off, but Dad just scoops him up and holds him in his arms, as if he's Laila's size. It would look ridiculous now, if Dad tried to carry me like that.

'We would have brought you, if you'd asked us, Krish.'

'I wanted to see Jo,' sobs Krish.

'That's all right, mate,' says Jo, patting Krish on the back. 'We just had a few things we needed to sort out.'

Dad sits on one side of Krish and Jo on the other, each with an arm around him. He looks tiny sandwiched between them, almost disappearing into the folds of the sofa. As Dad and Jo talk, Krish's eyes grow heavy and he falls fast asleep. I don't think he's slept since the day he gave Nana his painting.

'Looks like he's out for the count,' smiles Jo.

Dad shakes Jo's hand, pats him on the back, hoists Krish up over his shoulder and carries him along the corridor, down in the lift and out past Headscarf Lady.

'Bless him!' she says. 'He must have tired himself out with all that running.'

Dad settles Krish into the back seat and he stirs for a moment, opens his eyes and nestles his head into the curve of my shoulder. Normally, this would really irritate me, but not today.

Just as we're about to set off, Dad adjusts the rear-view mirror and, as he does, he catches sight of his own face and stares at himself, smoothing his fingers over the map of lines fanning from the corners of his eyes.

'I've aged more this month than any other time in my life. There are whole years where I've aged less than this, Mira,' sighs Dad.

Me too, I think to myself.

Friday 3 June

Krish has been bugging me all day. I want to tell him to get out of my room, but after yesterday I can't risk upsetting him.

'Why did you run off like that anyway?' I ask him.

'I didn't think about it. I just ran.' Krish shrugs.

'What did you want to talk to Jo about?'

'Will you two get into bed,' Dad yells up the stairs. 'It's a big day tomorrow.'

When Krish finally leaves me in peace, I turn the light off, close my eyes and try to think of nothing. I am beginning to drift off when I hear the door open and somebody creeping on tiptoe around my room. In the half-light from the hallway I see Krish heading over to the easel. I don't move an inch, but I clearly see him place Nana's charm on the little ridge where the canvas sits.

I whisper his name. 'Krish.' He jumps and stumbles, crumpling himself and the easel into a great clattering mess on the floor. It's strange that Krish is such a good runner, because he often falls over; like Laila's spinning top, he's only got his balance when he's moving fast.

'Why did you take it?' I whisper.

'She never actually *gave* me something, like she *gave* things to you,' I hear Krish's tiny hurt voice cutting through the darkness.

The light switch snaps on and I shield my eyes from the blinding brightness.

'What on earth is going on in here?' shouts Dad, staring at Krish as he tries to untangle himself from the easel.

'Nothing.'

I jump in quickly, before Krish has a chance to answer. 'He just fell.'

'Please go to bed,' Dad pleads, picking up my portrait and having a good look at it.

'Is this you?'

I nod.

'It's good . . . makes you look older than you are though,' says Dad as he bends down to pick up the easel. Then he drops down on to his knees and starts rummaging around on the floor.

'You'll never guess what I've found . . .' Dad stands up triumphantly and hands me Nana Josie's charm. 'Shall I take it and fix it on to your bracelet so you can wear it tomorrow? It must have been there all the time,' he says as I hand him the bracelet to fix the charm on to.

'It must have been,' I say, looking over to Krish, who's refusing to meet my eye.

Dad kisses me and Krish goodnight, and practically skips down the stairs.

The sound of waves fills every sense in my body, as if the sea is flowing in and out of me. I hear a little girl humming . . . in and out flow the waves in even patterns . . . a sweet lullaby . . . in and out softly sighing shhhhhhh. The girl floats towards me. She's holding her fingers to her lips. Shhhhhh sound the waves in and out, somewhere inside me, but still she floats on, the waves appearing and disappearing from my sight, a little girl of about four years old.

'Who are you?' I call to her, but I know who she is. She has Jidé's face, his eyes, his expression.

'Shhhhhh,' answer the waves. She holds her finger to her lips and hums.

'What's your name?' I whisper.

'Shhhhhhhh,' echoes the sea.

The girl's lips are sealed.

Then I catch sight of it under the waves, Jidé's bright orange cloth shining through the grey water, floating towards me. I follow it through the wave, grabbing at it, until it's safely in my hands. Shhhhhh, sighs the sea. Then the little girl takes her finger from her mouth, smiles at me and sings.

Saturday 4 June

The first thing I do when I wake up is look for Jidé's piece of orange cloth. It was the kind of dream that follows you from night into day. Of course when the sleep wears off, I realize it's not real . . . but I discover something that is.

It *had* to be today of all days. I take the charcoal and draw a pair of moon-shaped earrings on my self-portrait. Something good has got to come out of having periods.

At breakfast Dad takes hold of my hand and attaches the charm bracelet to my wrist. He struggles with the catch for a few moments before he finally closes the clasp. I look up at him and see that his eyes are full of tears.

'Your nana was very proud of you, Mira.'

Krish keeps glancing my way with a worried look on his face. He thinks I'm going to tell. I shake my head to reassure him. I won't tell because I think I understand how he felt.

'Oh, for God's sake,' shouts Dad, dusting off his suit, 'there's glitter everywhere.'

I laugh. By the time we've had breakfast we're all covered in glitter . . . it feels like Nana's joke. She wrote a note in the hospice to say that nobody is allowed to wear black for her funeral so I suppose it is right that I'm wearing my butterfly skirt, all pinks and greens and sequins . . . Nana's birthday present to me. I'm beginning to think of this as my period skirt. After today, I will never wear it again.

Krish is wearing his new blue linen suit with an Indian collar, the one Aunty Abi and Aunty Mel bought him, before he ran away. If my brother wears blue, his eyes sparkle. He keeps fiddling with his tie, like it's strangling him. I think he feels about as comfortable in his suit as I do in my skirt.

Me and Krish have been given 'roles' for the funeral. I'm going to read a poem from a book Nana gave me, and Krish is handing out our glittery programmes with a biography of Nana's life in it.

Nana's body is being cremated at Golders Hill Crematorium. Dad says it's the same place where Grandad Kit was cremated. Grandad Bimal says he wouldn't mind ending up there too, when his time comes, because he would like to follow in the footsteps of the maharajas whose names line the walls.

'If it's good enough for them, it will be good enough for me!'

Getting cremated means your body gets burned and what's left is just ashes, but you get the ashes back. I remember Nana laughing when she told us that she wanted her ashes sprinkled in her garden in Suffolk because they would 'improve the soil'. I think the ashes are just for the living people because it's so hard to think that there is nothing left of the actual person's body, and so people just want something to hold on to . . . and ashes are better than nothing.

We are all standing outside the chapel. Quite a lot of people I have never seen before are meeting each other and hugging.

Dad can't speak to anyone. He's trying to 'hold it together'. He keeps looking at his watch . . . waiting for the funeral car to arrive.

The car is white. Just an ordinary car, one of those long estates. In the back is the coffin which my dad, a friend of my dad's, Uncle James and Dunwich Dan are going to carry. Dan volunteered; he said it would be 'an honour' to carry Nana's coffin. It slides on wheels out of the boot, and then they have to lift it up on to their shoulders. I think of Dad and Moses struggling to carry the plain white box out of the rusty blue Volvo. Today, these four men lift it up smoothly, counting one, two, three, and all lifting at exactly the same time. It matters that it's done gracefully.

Even though the coffin is light and Nana was so tiny when she died, it's quite hard for them to lift it up on to their shoulders. A blue silky cloth covers the coffin, but it slides off as it's lifted. I hear a gasp. That's when the painting is unveiled. Everyone stands in a circle, huddled close to get a better look, voices hush to silence and the circle starts to turn as people wheel round the coffin.

I feel so sorry for my dad, because he's carrying his mum's body in a coffin on his shoulders.

A noise comes out of me. It comes up through the earth, into my body and out through my mouth. It's a very old noise that somehow you recognize, even though you've never heard it before. It's the same noise that came out of my dad, the day Nana died. Then I finally realize what it is, that noise. It's the sound of a heart breaking.

The coffin bearers walk slowly into the chapel and everyone else follows behind. When the coffin is placed on the table, Jay, my nana's friend, the cook and the artist, settles a white dove she has made out of pottery on the top of a nest of wild flowers. Nana's coffin looks like a Matisse painting. On its corner I spot my tiny dog peeing into the sea. It's as if Nana's winking at me.

Aunty Abi walks behind the coffin, holding Nana's *Funeral Pyre* painting, which she places on a table at the front of the chapel that's something like a church altar. In front of the painting is Nana's sandalwood Buddha candle. Abi lights it. For a moment I feel like rushing up to her and blowing the candle out to stop it from melting away.

'I'm not having my coffin disappearing on a cruddy old conveyor belt . . . that's always such an indignity . . . let people file past me, but light my Buddha candle, and let it melt to nothing.' Those were Nana's instructions.

The smell of sandalwood fills the air. Its perfume changes everything. Now the chapel feels more like a temple sealed off from the outside world.

I look at the *Funeral Pyre* painting Nana did when she went off to Thailand, after she found out that the cancer had come back. Two girls stand in the foreground with their backs to us, their long black plaits snaking down their backs. They have their arms wrapped around each other, standing close to the bright red and orange flames where someone they loved is being cremated. A little bit further away is a crowd: old people, children and babies sitting on the floor. They are also looking towards the fire. The people facing us do not look sad, they look more, well, interested really. This is the brightest painting of clashing colours I have ever seen Nana paint. You can feel the heat of the flames. There is nothing private about this way of dying. Not like it is here in this chapel.

The Celebrant Lady speaks too slowly, even though, when we met her, she kept saying that 'on the day' we've got to make sure *we* don't take too long when we speak!

She says some things about Nana, I don't remember what. I think Humanist people believe in humans and not God but I don't think they believe in the spirit like Nana did. Piper's yapping is putting her off a bit, because she keeps shooting Aunty Abi and Aunty Mel not very kind looks, as if to say, 'Can't somebody shut that dog up!'

Then all the family stand up together and say something about Nana. It's all the things we worked out beforehand so we know exactly what we're going to say, and which order to say it in. I only hear a few things that other people say, because my mind empties. The sun comes streaming through the window at the back of the chapel, casting everyone in a pool of bright colours and lighting up the modern stained-glass angel. All I can see is the glitter sparkling off people's clothes, hair and faces, and casting the chapel in a silver glow.

Uncle James says, even as a child, Nana was a rebel . . . she used to sneak out of her bedroom window to go dancing when she was only fourteen years old. Mum talks about what a wonderful grandmother Nana was to me and Krish, and how happy she was to be around for long enough to meet baby Laila. Dad tells everyone that Nana was a fierce campaigner, always writing letters . . . he says, at her height, she was writing a letter a week to Margaret Thatcher. Dad thinks somebody should probably write to Margaret Thatcher and tell her that she has lost an old foe.

It's my turn. I look at all the faces in front of me. I see Grandad Bimal and Nana Kath and that makes me feel better. Mum wraps her arms round me and gives me a little squeeze, but I can't speak. I shake my head. Celebrant Lady was right . . . I can't do it; the words are all swallowed up by my tears. My head is spinning. Celebrant Lady is shuffling her papers, getting ready to read out my poem. There are so many people at Nana's funeral that there are two or three rows of people standing up at the back. Then I see them, Jidé Jackson and, standing right next to him, holding his hand, is the little girl I saw in my dream . . . Jidé's sister, and next to her is Pat Print. They smile at me, the same encouraging smile . . . and suddenly the words are in my mouth and I don't even recognize the way I sound. That high-pitched squeak, like a violin grating on the wrong note, has gone. My voice is soft and strong . . .

I am about to start the poem I picked to read out, but somehow that's not what I want to say any more. Suddenly I hear Nana's voice in my head . . . 'Tell them some of my anecdotes,' she orders me.

'Nana used to tell me funny things . . . that I loved. If I got too serious, she would tell me to stand on my head because the world looks funnier upside down . . . She said it's better to have a caravan than a mansion, because you can always change the view with a caravan . . .'

I hear Pat Print's hearty laugh coming from the back of the chapel and I look up at her and smile.

The Celebrant Lady is staring at me as if I've gone mad. This is not in her plan, but Pat Print has sent a ripple of laughter through the chapel.

Nana's silver charm glints on my wrist, willing me on.

'She gave me this tiny charm for my birthday. It's in the shape of an artichoke. Most of you have probably seen her wearing it. When she gave it to me, she told me all about it. I didn't really understand then, but now I think I do. She told me that when we are children our hearts are tender, like the heart of the artichoke, and that's the precious bit. But then the things that happen to us, the difficult things, they make us grow tougher and tougher layers to protect ourselves from getting hurt. But those layers also stop us from feeling so much. A few days before she died, she told me that she had shed all the layers she'd built up in her life, she had no fear and she just felt love for everyone around her . . . all her friends and family . . . everyone here.'

Jidé Jackson nods at me solemnly.

There is a lot of crying going on now. I suppose it must be the point of funerals really, to cry and laugh together. When Nana was dying, I learned more about her life than I ever knew before, but when I look around this room at all these strangers . . . I know that

I will never piece it all together, her life, because only the pieces I have belong to me. Now Nana's Italian song starts to play, the one we listened to together when we painted her coffin.

On their way out of the chapel, people walk past the coffin, Nana's *Funeral Pyre* painting and the melting Buddha. Aunty Abi has placed a bowl of ruby-red rose petals at the end of the coffin so that people can scatter them as they pass.

'She was a wonderful woman,' the man standing next to me says as he walks around the coffin, inspecting it from all sides, and smiling as he catches sight of Piper peeing into the sea. 'Such a sense of fun.' It takes me a while to recognize him in his smart grey suit. It's Dusty Bird from the art shop. Then he sees the little blue handprints on the side of the coffin. 'I suppose that's her signature.'

'One's hers and one's mine,' I tell him.

He peers closer at the two identical-sized handprints with different lines, and nods.

'What's the colour?' he asks, smiling at me.

'Ultramarine Blue Light,' I answer.

'I'll be seeing *you* in the shop,' he laughs, taking a handful of rose petals and scattering them over Nana's coffin.

When I walk out of the chapel, the first person I see is Pat Print.

'I warned you about that voice!' she smiles, resting her hand on my shoulder.

I look up at her questioningly. Is she really here?

'I heard your nana on the radio . . . as soon as I heard her, I knew it must be her. I popped into the hospice and they told me the funeral was today.'

'Thank you . . . I mean . . . for everything.'

Sometimes words are just not enough, are they? To say the things you want to say . . .

'Now, I must get on, there's someone else here, keen to talk to you.'

And before I can think of what else to say to her she's disappeared through the crowd. I look down at the ground; there is not a trace of mud in sight.

Jidé Jackson is walking towards me with his arms outstretched, just as he did in my dream. We hold each other, in the middle of all these people . . . and I don't even care who sees, because I can feel his heart beating against mine and that is all that matters.

Jidé takes my hand and we walk into the sunshine to look at the flowers that are placed by Nana's name.

'A lot of people loved your nana,' Jidé says.

I don't say anything, but he can obviously read the question on my face . . . 'Why are you here?'

Jidé points to Grace and Jai, who are sitting away from everyone else in the rose garden, as if they don't want to intrude.

'I told them about your nana dying . . . that you

311

called me. We listened to her on the radio, like you said . . . and I was upset for you when I heard her voice, and I told Grace I didn't know what to say to you or how to help. I couldn't even phone you. Then I think she called your mum and she asked me if I wanted to come . . . and . . . I've never been to a funeral before . . . I hope you don't mind?'

How can I tell him how much I love him for being here?

Jidé's mum and dad sit with their arms round each other, looking towards us. They both seem so quiet and sad.

'So many people in Rwanda with no funeral at all,' sighs Jidé.

Now I know why she came here . . . Jidé's sister. To say goodbye. I think about telling him that I saw her standing right next to him . . . how she sang to me in my dream . . . but then I hear her softly sighing shh-hhhh . . .

Dad's standing next to us. I can tell he's waiting to be introduced. Mum looks over too and smiles. I think Dad's trying to listen in on our conversation. It's so annoying, because I can feel myself blushing for the first time today.

'This is Jidé, my friend from school, Dad.'

Dad shakes Jidé's hand, looking him squarely in the eyes.

'It's kind of you to come along.' Dad smiles . . . a

sparkly smile . . . he's got glitter on his teeth!

Jidé shifts from one foot to the other. I've never seen him looking nervous before.

'I'm sorry about your mum,' mumbles Jidé, wrinkling a deep frown into his forehead.

Dad just peers from Jidé to me with a question in his eyes, but before he can say anything else someone is leading him away.

People stand around and talk. Actually people don't talk a lot, they just sort of huddle together like cows in the rain. Jidé is humming to himself . . . a nervous hum. I'm not sure he even realizes he's doing it.

'Is that your sister's song?' I whisper.

Jidé nods at me. He looks as if I've jolted him out of another world.

I watch Jidé, Grace and Jai walk off towards the tube. Jai has his arm round Jidé's shoulders. Now I know why he said he was lucky . . . to have a family like that. Pat Print's right, Jidé Jackson has courage, so do Grace and Jai . . . and Jidé's sister.

All the people from Nana's funeral start to get into their cars, all except Protest Simon, who is busy refusing lifts. People don't seem to understand that Simon not only doesn't have a car, but refuses ever to get into one.

'I'm walking,' says Simon. 'I'll be there in half an hour . . . If the traffic's bad, I'll probably get there before you!'

As he predicted, Simon is one of the first back, but eventually Nana's flat does start to fill up with people. The table is covered in salads, bread and cheese. Nana's friends have all brought a dish. A lady with long grey plaits and sparkly eyes wraps her huge arms around me and my brother. Krish squirms out of her grasp as she tries to gather us into the folds of her flowery purple dress that brushes the floor. It's called a kaftan. Nana had a few of those, but when she wore them she looked like a little girl in a nightie. This lady looks as if she's wearing curtains.

At first, people's voices are quiet, almost whispers, but then they start to get louder and some people smile and laugh. I go out to the pond to look for frogs. Simon is sitting there like a garden elf with Piper lying quietly by his side. Simon points to a frog's eyes peeping out of the water. We watch it, all three of us, and it watches us. We do not move an inch. Then suddenly it leaps and splashes gloop at us, sending Piper into a frenzy of yapping.

After everybody has gone there is a lot of clearing up to do. I curl up on the garden bench next to the pond, where I used to sit with Nana. Out of the corner of my eye I see the frog make a dash back into the water. I get the feeling that it's been watching us all this time. I think of all the fairy stories Nana loved to tell me, about frogs turning into princes, about princesses sleeping the sleep of the dead but, right at the last moment, being magically woken by a prince's kiss . . . all those happy endings.

I watch Dad's sad shoulders as he locks the wooden gate on to our secret garden . . . and a time when I still believed in fairy stories.

Sunday 5 June

Today, I don't feel like me any more. It's like my whole life, up to now, I was someone else. I look at this me in the mirror, trying to see who she is. I brush her hair and wash her face where a rash of spots coats her once smooth forehead. I choose some clothes for her to wear. Everyone will just have to get used to the idea . . . this girl in the mirror is me.

Mum comes in and puts her arm around me and we sit together looking at our reflections. I try to fix this in my mind, the way my mum's head leans in close to mine, the place where her hand rests on my arm, the slight curl up to, nearly a smile, on the corner of her lips. The way that she is like me, skin colour, same hair, same little nose, same round face, same look in her eyes . . . and the ways that she is not.

She walks over to the easel and picks up my painting and studies it for a long time.

'That one's for you, Mum,' I tell her.

'You've had your ears pierced, already,' smiles Mum, looking back at me.

'Can I?' I ask, getting ready to explain the whole period thing to her.

'Yes, I promised, didn't I?'

No questions, nothing.

'What a mess!'

Mum scurries around my bedroom, tidying, folding and picking up the clothes I have scattered all over the floor. Usually she'd tut and tell me off, but today she just starts sorting through, occasionally asking me if I've worn this or that.

She opens my wardrobe and sighs as the pile of clothes I have flung in there, in one of my tidying-up sessions, avalanches towards her. I pass her the clothes and she places them on hangers in my wardrobe. I wonder how it is that Mum doing something so normal, like picking up clothes and folding them and just not saying anything at all about my periods starting, or Jidé Jackson, can make me love her so much.

Now I am twelve . . .

I thread a piece of navy blue ribbon through the holey stone, measuring its length against mine, threading it through, looping it around and pulling it tight. Then I start to wrap layer upon layer of tissue, just enough so that she won't make out the shape. I choose silvery grey paper . . . the colour of the sky on the day I found this holey stone.

I glue a love-heart shape on to the top layer of tissue and sprinkle it with the leftover glitter from Nana's funeral. Now I get it, why Nana spent so much time and care and love wrapping . . . presents are the giver's secret, just for a moment, until they pass from one hand to another.

The letterbox clanks. I take the stairs in threes, hurling myself down, flinging open the front door. Standing there, with a worried look on her face, is Millie, but before she can say anything I order her to close her eyes and hold out her hand, pressing my secret parcel into her palm. She opens her wise owl eyes and giggles as she slowly unwraps my present . . . it's the moment before you actually know what's inside that's the most exciting. Millie traces the stone with her fingers through the thin layers of tissue paper.

'A holey stone! You found me one!' Millie throws her arms round me and clamps me in the tightest hug, as if I've given her the most precious jewel in the whole world. When we unclasp each other, she tips her head forward, letting her hair ripple towards the ground in a golden wave so that I can tie the ribbon in a tiny knot at the nape of her neck.

'I'm sorry I wasn't here for the funeral,' she says.

'It's OK!'

I check my watch. It's still so early, not even eight o'clock, but we walk to school anyway. The first person we see is Orla, waiting on a bench outside the school gates. When we're halfway down the path, she turns, and for a minute I think she looks pleased to see us.

'Sorry about your nana, Mira.'

'Thank you.'

'I heard her on the radio. My mum and me . . . on the programme about the Pope. Why didn't you tell us she was famous?'

'She wasn't, really,' I shrug. I don't know what to say. Orla has never ever been this nice to me.

'What's *that*?' she asks, pointing at Millie's holey-stone necklace.

Here goes, I think. Now she'll go in for the kill.

'It's a present from Mira.'

Then Orla notices my holey stone, which I've forgotten to tuck inside my blouse.

'My nana and me, we used to collect them on the beach.'

Orla nods.

'Could you get me one?' she asks, smiling shyly at me.

I can't believe that Orla Banks wants *me*, Mira Levenson, to find her a holey stone!

'Looks like your nana's started a new craze,' laughs Millie.

At break we sit on our wall, Millie and me, as if nothing's changed . . .

'You found your charm then?' Millie picks up my wrist to get a closer look.

'Turns out I never lost it,' I say.

She tells me about her holiday and I tell her about Nana Josie's funeral. I want to tell her about pretending to go to hers for tea but going to Jidé's instead, and about Jidé and his sister and Pat Print turning up at Nana's funeral . . . and about my dreams . . . but somehow I can't think of a way to tell her any of these things. Suddenly I remember my deal with Notsurewho Notsurewhat the day I saw Pat Print on the beach; the day I found Millie's holey stone.

'Do you believe in ghosts?' I ask Millie.

She shoots me one of her 'Do you have to be so random?' looks.

'No, Mira, definitely not.'

That's what I love about Millie. She's always so sure about everything.

'How about spirits or angels then?'

'I spy with my little eye . . .' Millie stares through her new holey stone, scanning the sky for signs of spirits or angels.

'None that I can see,' she laughs, focusing her gaze closer to home until it comes to rest on Ben Gbemi.

And through the eye of *my* holey stone I spy Jidé Jackson striding towards me, closer and closer . . . Nana Josie's voice fills my head . . .

'People who need charms, you'll know them when you meet them.'

Acknowledgements

Writing a first novel is quite a journey. Although the author's name is on the front cover of a book, there are so many other people behind that name who have also made huge contributions to making a dream become a reality. Firstly I wish to thank my husband, Leo, who has given me the love, time, encouragement and support needed to write a novel in the midst of bringing up a young family; my children, Maya, Keshin and Esha-Lily, who are a constant inspiration to me. I would especially like to thank my daughter, Maya Harrison, whose extraordinary relationship with her grandmother is at the heart of this book.

I have been blessed with the most beautiful (in every sense) agent and editor in publishing! I wish to thank my agent, Sophie Gorell Barnes at MBA Literary Agency, for championing *Artichoke Hearts*, and my editor, Samantha Swinnerton at Macmillan Children's Books, for being so passionate about this book, and for crying when she first read it (apparently Sam doesn't cry easily, so her tears made her fellow editorial team sit up and take notice!).

Thanks also to authors Maria Beaumont and Louise

Millar, playwright Noël Greig and poet Wendy Jones, for their encouragement and insightful reading of early drafts; to Maria Levenson, for lending me her surname and sunny support; Sophie Lockhart, for her excellent criticism and permission to use a little of her character; Gabrielle Bikhazi, who looked after Esha-Lily while I wrote; the unique Simon Gould; Mira Basak, my greatly missed aunt and namesake for my heroine, and I wish to thank my mum, Freda Brahmachari, for her love, courage and spirit.

Final thanks are for Bill Tyler, Diana Tyler, Leo Harrison and Trilby Harrison, for giving me permission to write a story inspired by an extraordinary woman loved and remembered by so many family and friends. On behalf of our whole family I would like to express our gratitude for the work of the Marie Curie Hospice. Sadly, part of growing up is having to say goodbye to treasured loved ones – perhaps those who have passed away deserve our greatest acknowledgement for the gifts that they have bestowed on us. So it is that I send my most heartfelt thanks to my father-in-law, Bernie 'The Book' Harrison; the beautiful, bohemian inspiration of this book, Rosie Harrison, and my beloved father, Dr Amal Krishna Brahmachari.

Jasmine Skies

Sita Brahmachari

Fourteen-year-old Mira Levenson is about to begin the adventure of her life. She travels alone to India to meet her family and is quickly swept into a sweltering, chaotic world – full of new sights, smells and deeply buried secrets. Nothing is as she imagined it. Mira faithfully writes, as promised, to her boyfriend, Jidé, but there's one person she doesn't mention. From the moment Mira meets Janu she feels a potent connection and he becomes her guide through the vibrant and often dangerous streets of Kolkata. As her time in India draws to an end, Mira is determined to uncover the truth about her family, whatever the consequences, and she must also make a decision that will break someone's heart . . .

Coming in April 2012

Jaclyn Moriarty

Feeling sorry for Celia

Dear Ms Clarry,
It has come to our attention that you are incredibly bad at being a teenager.

Yours sincerely, The Association of Teenagers

When Elizabeth Clarry's best friend, Celia, runs away to join the circus, Elizabeth has to hurry to the rescue – not easy when she's generally incompetent at being a teenager. Then gorgeous Saxon Walker decides to lend a hand and things get even more complicated. It's a good thing Elizabeth has a new pen pal to talk to – because feeling sorry for Celia is turning out to be a full-time job.

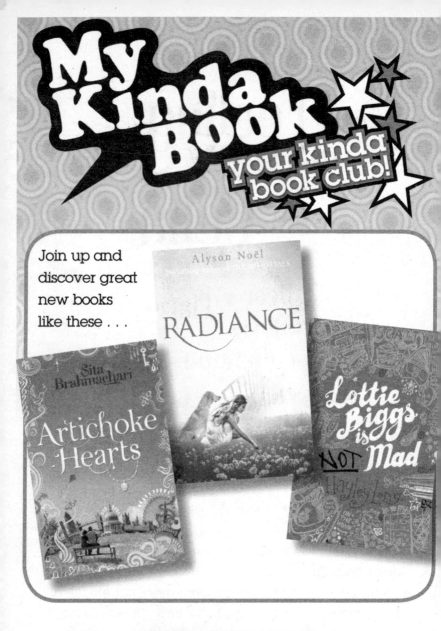